Deep Strike

A Novel

By
Barry Lando

KCM PUBLISHING
A DIVISION OF KCM DIGITAL MEDIA, LLC

CREDITS

Deep Strike by Barry Lando

ISBN-13: 978-1-939961-67-9
ISBN-10: 1-939961-67-X

First Edition

Publisher: Michael Fabiano
KCM Publishing
www.kcmpublishing.com

Praise for Deep Strike

"With his latest novel, Deep Strike, former CBS "60 Minutes" producer Barry Lando once again demonstrates his mastery of intrigue and spy-craft. What's more--Lando's electric story of a nation at risk, crackles off the page with the energy and currency of the morning headlines. His fiction clearly demonstrates the very real challenges to Western democracy and the very fragile nature of the thread by which it hangs.
— Jim Bittermann,
CNN Senior Correspondent Paris

"I couldn't put it down. Barry Lando has transformed today's startling headlines into a thrilling fictional read. Loved it!"
— Ali Velshi
Anchor MSNBC

"*Deep Strike* is a sinister, suspense-filled tale of sex and love, violence and vengeance, which nonetheless manages to be optimistic. Anyone who was appalled by Donald Trump's election should read this novel."
— Lara Marlowe
The Irish Times

"Deep Strike pulls the reader into a world of audacious conspiracies, vivid personalities, egregious venality, and gripping intrique...."

— Lee W. Huebner
Airlie Professor of Media and Public Affairsm,
The George Washington University

"Barry Lando's assassins, informants and CIA agents inhabit a dark landscape. This is a story etched in the brutality of their world—and our's. Don't miss it."

— Dave Turecamo,
Producer, CBS News Sunday Morning

"The White House, Russia, CIA, Twitter, Secret Bank Accounts. If you thought fiction could not compete with political reality--think again."

— Timothy Ryback
Journalist, Historian "Hitler's First Victims"

To my wife, Elisabeth, whose
encouragement, support and love, once again,
brought it all about.

Contents

Foreword

Like most works of fiction, this is one that began with a "what if."

What if, I wondered after the last presidential race, what if a small handful of CIA agents who investigated Russian hacking, were outraged by the blatant interference in America's democratic process?

What if those agents were infuriated by the unwillingness of congressional leaders to react to their findings, and further inflamed by the refusal of the new president to acknowledge that the hacking had even taken place?

What if they were scandalized by the fact that America's intelligence agencies and colossal military force would now be under the command of that same new feckless leader?

What if, pushed to the breaking point by the death of a colleague, three of those agents go rogue to take on the President and all his vast powers, and attempt to drive him from office?

To write this fiction, I made use of voluminous news reports about the U.S. and Russia, accounts of America's vast intelligence apparatus that the president controls. I received valuable input from a plastic surgeon, from an expert on Moscow, from hackers and cyber professionals.

But the characters in this novel – their backgrounds, their thoughts and words and interactions – are all invented. The crimes and corruption my agents uncover, the climactic ending to their struggle, are all spun from my own imagination.

It's all fiction. It never happened.

But could it?

Deep Strike

A NOVEL

By
Barry Lando

CHAPTER ONE

Fountainhead Regional Park

Brian Hunt was fired up, an explosion of energy, as he tore up the Bear Claw Run, the most grueling mountain bike course in northern Virginia. The young CIA officer powered through it every Saturday morning. Pumping and slithering around the switchbacks and boulders, he pounded away with sinewy legs and core muscles of iron. The image of a pouncing tiger leapt across the front of his crimson crash helmet.

He skidded through a corrugated patch of mud and leaves; shifted his weight to handle the most treacherous switchback of the run. He could manage it easily, knowing it was there. He slithered around a sharp turn to the left; then rattled along a narrow rock ledge. There was a clearing in the woods on one side on the other an ancient wooden barrier, the only thing that stood between him and the cliff that dropped precipitously to the ravine far below.

Suddenly, two masked figures dressed in khaki and wielding rifles rose from the clearing on the left and lunged towards him. "What the fuck?" screamed Brian, instinctively swerving around his assailants. He felt a huge blow on the front of his head and heard his helmet crack as he went sprawling in the deep grass of the clearing. He was on his back, trying to gather his senses, when another masked face loomed into his vision. All he could see were the emerald green eyes. He felt a cloth cover his nose and just managed to recognize the faint, ether-like smell before he passed out.

When he regained consciousness, his head was pounding and a blindfold was covering his eyes. "Where am I?" he groaned. He tried to move, but couldn't. His arms and legs were bound. He could hear the gurgle of water filling some kind of basin, and murmuring voices. One of them seemed to be a woman's. The emerald green eyes?

"Okay, let's go," he heard her say.

"What the fuck is going on?" he rasped, fighting the pain in his skull.

"We want to know what you are up to." She seemed to be standing over him. "What you and your friends are planning."

"Up to… about what? Who the hell are you?"

She spoke with a southern drawl, but her voice had a metallic edge to it – military.

"We know you're trying to organize something."

"Organize—to do what?"

"Overthrow the president."

"Stokes? You're crazy!" he yelled.

"We heard you plotting."

"Heard me what?" What seemed like a nightmare was actually happening.

"Trying to get your agency friends to commit treason."

What the hell was she talking about? That night in the bar two days ago with a few of the other CIA officers when he was drunk...over the top, venting the fury and frustration he'd been accumulating over the past few months? Who wouldn't be outraged? After half a year of investigation, the team led by the CIA had nailed it. And he'd been a key player. They'd uncovered chapter and verse on Russian hacking of the U.S. elections. They'd briefed the Oval Office, the top people in the administration, the heads of the intelligence community, and the leaders in congress. As the story leaked—as it was bound to—they'd generated headlines across the country and around the world.

And what had happened? Nothing. Their findings were ignored by congressional leaders; played down by the wimp in the White House; derided during the campaign by the Republican candidate, Walter Stokes, who, incredibly, was now the new president. It was scandalous. Who knew what Stokes owed to the Russians? Who knew what deals had been made by those around him?

Yet no one was willing to act; not Congress of course, controlled by the Republicans; not even the members of his own CIA team, yellow-bellied chicken-shits. It was nauseating. Instead of reacting with outrage, they'd crawled into their offices to lick their wounds. Plotting to overthrow Stokes? What a joke. No way.

"That's bullshit." Brian said to the green-eyed woman. "We were arguing over drinks. I was upset, angry. But no one's doing anything. Nothing! Who the hell are you, anyway?" he repeated

"All right, let's do it," she said.

Whatever he was tied to was picked up, carried towards the sound of flowing water.

"You've seen water boarding," she said. "You know what to expect."

Of course, he'd seen water boarding—at Bagram prison in Afghanistan. He'd never done it himself, but he'd watched on several occasions when he was stationed there. It was a technique used by other groups, very rarely by the CIA itself. He knew some Special Forces guys who underwent water boarding as part of their training. They lasted an average of fourteen seconds before they panicked. To a man, they testified to its horrors.

He was in the air now, above a basin of water or bathtub he supposed. His body was tilted, his feet a few inches higher than his head. Terror filled his being. "This is crazy!" he screamed.

One part of him knew they wouldn't want to completely fill his lungs with water, to asphyxiate him. He knew their purpose was to trigger an instinctive reflex in the body—a terror of drowning, of death, so that he would plea for the torture to end and tell his captors anything they wanted. But there was nothing to tell them. His heart pounded wildly.

A rag stinking of grease was placed over his face. His mouth was forced open, and water poured in and over the rag into his nose. It would keep the water clinging to his face, filling his throat, mouth, and sinuses. His inclined head kept his throat open; made it easier to pour water into his nostrils.

"No! Don't!" his scream was smothered by the putrid rag. It would act as a one-way valve, opening to let more air out then closing again to prevent inhalation. He gasped then gasped again as water poured through the cloth.

He knew that trained CIA officers tried to outlast the torment by exhaling slowly through the upturned nose. That would keep water out, but only for a few seconds. He felt the water surging through his sinuses and larynx and fought desperately for breath. He could feel his lungs collapsing. There was no breath left in his body. No way to get the water out. He was drowning. No one could hear his screams. He could feel himself defecating.

Then suddenly they lifted him up and removed the cloth over his face. He fought for air and vomited. Water spewed from his throat and sinuses. He couldn't stop retching and gasping.

"Horrible, isn't it?" said the woman. "You know you can't fight it. So why keep trying? Why not talk?"

"About what?" Brian wheezed. He was shivering uncontrollably. Still filled with panic.

"Don't play stupid. You've nothing to gain. What are you up to – you and your friends in the agency?"

"What friends?" Brian rasped.

"The ones who worked with you on the hacking investigation?"

"We're doing nothing! Nothing!" He was still trembling, on the point of tears. "You have to stop. I've got nothing to tell you."

"But you will." she said. "Everyone does."

Again, the filthy rag was placed over his face, his mouth forced open, the water cascaded into his throat and nostrils; again the frantic gasping for breath, the panic, and terror.

He lost track of how many times they repeated the hellish procedure. He was hallucinating now, delirious, in and out of consciousness. Between each session, he could feel her hand on his throat, checking the pulse, ensuring he had enough oxygen in his blood to remain conscious.

"The prick's not going to talk," he heard her say when they removed the rags again.

"End it," she ordered. If he could talk, he would have blessed her.

The board was lowered into the water until he was completely covered. This time there was no rag on his face. This time the water flooded into his lungs. For the last time, the terrifying reflex of drowning kicked in. He alone heard his scream.

They pulled him up again after five minutes. The woman leaned forward and again put her thumb on his neck. No pulse. She took off her mask. She was wearing khaki dungarees and black boots. The left side of her face was very attractive: sensuous mouth, up-tipped nose, lustrous green eyes.

It was the right side that was straight out of horror film: from her eyes to her chin the skin was fiery red latticed with white scars and scales almost like the skin of a snake, her scabrous right ear looked as if it had been torn off and partly replaced.

Her name was Captain Jean Swanson. She'd served three tours of duty in Special Forces in Afghanistan and one in Iraq, as an intelligence officer. She'd been severely injured and burned in an attack on a firebase near Kabul. The medics at first thought she'd never recover. After two years and eighteen different surgical procedures, she returned to active duty.

CHAPTER TWO:

Arlington

Brian Hunt's funeral was held four days later on a damp, gray morning at the First Presbyterian Church in Arlington, Virginia. It was a red brick, neoclassical building, with a graceful white steeple, at the top of a grassy hill.

Most of the three hundred or so people filling the high-pitched nave didn't know Brian had worked at the CIA. They thought he'd been a statistician with the Department of Transportation. In fact, among his colleagues at the agency, he was considered one of the sharpest analysts of cyber intelligence. They knew he'd spent most of the past year in a special unit investigating possible Russian hacking of the American elections. The subject was incredibly sensitive, the work highly classified.

Brian's body was found a day after he disappeared while biking in the Fountainhead River Park. He had died in what appeared to be a freak accident. The coroner ruled the cause of death was drowning. Now the body lay in a closed, polished oak casket beside the pulpit. There was a slight sandalwood fragrance emanating from the four tall candles flanking the casket; a single red rose lay on top. Joanne, his wife, had asked that there be no flowers; she also requested the choir sing one of Brian's favorite songs, "Candle in the Wind," before the minister began the service. Joanne sat in the first pew, her arms around each of her twin six-year-old sons.

Steve Penn sat two rows behind Joanne, wearing a dark, single-breasted suit. He was fifty-three years old with broad shoulders, graying sideburns, and a deep furrow between his hazel eyes. He was the man who ran the Russian hacking investigation for the CIA. He had an aura about him of almost permanent worry. Some women judged him handsome; many didn't. His nose was too prominent; chin too pointed. His right eye often drooped when he was tired or bored.

Today he was neither. His mind was seething. Steve and Brian had been very close—almost like family. They'd first met when Brian and Joanne moved to Virginia from Boise, Idaho, six years ago and Brian went to work for the agency. Impressed by his analytical abilities, Steve picked Brian to be a key member of the CIA team investigating Russian hacking.

On Steve's left sat a stunning woman, Sarah Levin, with high cheekbones, olive skin, almond eyes, and full lips. A combination only dreamed up by God, Steve thought; the daughter of a Vietnamese refugee who married a Jewish dermatologist. Who would have pegged Sarah as a former child musical prodigy turned

CIA expert in artificial intelligence? This morning in the church, her eyes were brimming. "It's horrible, just horrible," she whispered to Steve.

The funeral service lasted forty-five minutes and was moving without being maudlin. The pastor spoke about the many friends Brian and Joanne had made since they moved to the community, Brian's dedicated service to the church and the community. There were a few other speakers, friends of the family, the captain of the Lincoln High baseball team that Brian coached when he was not travelling. Of course, no one spoke from the CIA since, officially, Brian, worked at the Department of Transportation. It was the president of the local mountain biking club, who spoke last about Brian's passion for the sport and his love of the wilderness. "How tragic," he said, "that such passion could lead to his death."

As he left the church, Steve's attention wandered to an attractive brunette in the back row. At least, she seemed alluring when their eyes met briefly—hers were a luminous emerald green, but when she turned to exit, he noticed the terrible red scar disfiguring the other side of her face. Probably ex-military, he thought. He'd seen so many burn victims like that in Iraq and Afghanistan.

After the service, he walked with Sarah on the way to the cemetery, "Very nice words about Brian and his biking," she said.

"Yeah," said Steve, "But I can't help wondering if his death is more than just tragic." Steve was an inveterate biker himself. Fifteen years older than Brian, he frequently joined the younger officer on his regular weekend outings.

"What do you mean—more than tragic?" said Sarah.

"I spoke to a buddy with the park police. He said it looks like Brian skidded on some rough washboard just after the crest and went over the side. Forty feet to the bottom. The railing there's old and rotted. Like most of the so-called guardrails on that trail." Steve raised both hands. "We've been complaining about it for years to the park board."

So, why the suspicion?" said Sarah, "Couldn't he have just skidded off like they say?"

"Not an experienced rider," said Steve. "Everyone who does the run knows about that bad turn. Like the back of our hand."

"Then how do you explain it?" insisted Sarah.

"I don't," said Steve. "That's just the point."

"Didn't the coroner rule that Brian drowned?" said Sarah.

"Right," Steve, scowled. "Brian supposedly tumbled down the hill, landed on the rocks, head lying in the river. Yet it took them more than a day to find him—even with their hound dogs."

Sarah shivered, "Awful,"

"More than awful," said Steve.

"Morning guys," a tall black man wearing a dark suit joined Steve and Sarah at the graveside. He kissed Sarah on the cheek then shook Steve's hand. Another very unlikely CIA officer, thought Steve; at six foot four Charlie Doyle once dreamed of playing basketball for the NBA, but wound up joining the agency instead. "Can't believe this is happening," he whispered to Steve as the pastor read a short prayer.

Steve stared over the heads of the other mourners into the gray willows as the coffin was lowered into the ground. Then he looked across the grave to where Joanna was sobbing quietly, with her arms around the two boys. How many times Brian had talked to Steve about his family and his guilt about not spending more time with them or his fear that President Stokes's crazed politics could endanger their very future?

"It's all so terribly ironic," Steve whispered to Charlie. "A freak biking accident ends Brian's life at precisely the time his professional career is also headed down the tubes."

"Yeah, thinking the same thing myself," said Charlie.

"You believe it might have been suicide?" said Sarah.

"No way." Steve shook his head vigorously. "Brian wasn't that kind of guy. He had a great family, friends."

"But professionally he was dead meat," said Charlie.

"Hell, if you want to look at it that way," said Steve, "my career is also washed up.

"Brian was the top analyst on the hacking report but I was the lead author. That puts the bulls-eye right on me. I can forget about any career as long as Stokes and his people are running the country. Brian and I helped brief the joint congressional committee prior to the election. I can't believe we actually exchanged high-fives after that session."

"We all thought the report would be a bombshell," said Charlie. "I still can't get over the Republicans refusing to act. Hell, even the White House wussed out."

"But not Brian," said Steve.

He remembered how they'd last come together a couple of days before Brian's death. It was early evening in O'Shaughnessy's Pub on King Street in Falls Church. Brian was already there. The young officer raised his Guinness before relaying the latest news.

"Guess what," said Brian, "Stokes not only claims our investigation was bullshit, he's also threatening to veto any plans to punish the Russians. What a crock!"

Though seething within, Steve kept his resentment bridled. Passion and outrage were not his thing. After twenty-eight years with the agency, his cynicism was baked in. "Of, course, there's another way of looking at all this," he said. "From year one at the agency we've been doing exactly what we're now accusing Russia and Kozlov of doing."

"What do you mean?" said Sarah.

"I mean meddling in the most sensitive affairs of other countries. We did it in Italy, in Guatemala, in Iran, in Chile. We did it all over. Admit it!"

"I was up to some pretty wild stuff in the Congo and Venezuela," said Charlie.

"No! This is different," said Brian. "When we did it to other countries we were fighting Communism or radical Islam or whatever."

"Not much of an excuse if you're from the Congo or Venezuela," Steve persisted.

"Goddamn it," said Brian. "You'd be willing to give the Russians a pass for anything. This is our own country! It's in our face. We're supposed to be the most powerful nation in the world and we're sitting here like a bunch of assholes. We handed Kozlov a victory he could never have won by force!"

Steve's mind returned to the present as he was handed a shovel by the gravesite. Brian was right, Steve thought, tossing a clod of earth onto the casket. Now he's gone, and Stokes and his slimy, bootlicking crew are there, in the White House, all triumphant. We've been played for fools.

Afterwards, they went to the nearby home of the dead agent's brother in the Aurora Highlands. Brian's brother had obviously done well. It was a large two-story Cape Cod-style house with a lush lawn and meticulously trimmed hedges. A Mercedes and BMW were parked in the open garage. More than a hundred people were already there, filling the large living room, spilling over into the library, hallways, and kitchen. There were several pictures of Brian – with Joanne on their honeymoon in Hawaii, coaching the Lincoln High School baseball team, skiing in Aspen with the family, and in biking gear next to Steve, each one astride his mountain bike.

Joanne was seated on a sofa, wearing a black dress, drinking coffee, and surrounded by friends. Steve bent to take her hand. "I'm going to miss him," he said. "He was like a brother to me." He was startled when Joanne looked at him blankly, then turned her back to speak to the woman beside her. What's all that about? he thought. Brian's two sons, each with a black ribbon pinned to his white shirt, passed cookies and cakes. Steve accepted a brownie and patted each on the head.

Many of the mourners were in couples. As often happened in such situations, Steve felt very much alone. No wife. No children – at least none alive. No parents – they'd taken off when he was just a young kid. And woman friends – not much in that department either. The few affairs he'd begun had ended quickly. The woman usually accused him of being self-centered, selfish, and closed-off. It was hard for him to deny the charge. There was just Maya and she was thousands of miles away, and that was the past.

He poured himself a scotch and moved into the den where Charlie and Sarah were standing.

Gesticulating with a bottle of beer, Charlie was skewering the latest presidential executive decrees. "That asshole has just declared the U.S. will continue using black sites in other countries to interrogate suspected terrorists. And, last but not least, Gitmo will remain open and ready for business.

"For show. It's all for show," said Sarah. "For the crazies in Wisconsin and Michigan."

"Dead wrong," said Charlie. "Stokes really believes in the stuff he's doing. He's nuts."

Steve's mind, however, was elsewhere, still probing the details of Brian's death. He poured himself another scotch. "It's all too pat," he muttered. "Too fucking pat," he said louder. The others turned to stare.

"What's too fucking pat?" asked Charlie.

"Just too goddamned much coincidence," said Steve.

"Coincidence?" asked Sarah.

"Look," said Steve. "Brian bitches about Stokes killing our hacking report. He keeps insisting we have to do something about it. Gets louder and louder. Practically calls for an insurrection in the agency and then conveniently dies in a biking accident. He took another sip of his drink. "Death by drowning? No way."

Charlie looked at Sarah, her eyebrows skeptically raised. Steve was notorious for his dogged investigations. But he also had the reputation of inventing conspiracies. And they knew how close he was to Brian – like an older brother, he was always saying.

"Steve, this is the real world. Stuff happens," said Sarah, placing a hand on his arm.

"But when it happens like this," said Steve "you can't just shrug and walk away. I'm not imagining it. There's something there."

"So what are you going to do?" asked Charlie, still with that mocking gaze.

Steve looked at him squarely. "I'm going to find out what happened."

"I thought we knew,' said Charlie.

"No bloody way," said Steve.

CHAPTER THREE:

Fountainhead Regional Park

Steve got little sleep that night. Questions about Brian's death continued to roil his mind. He wandered about his apartment in Falls Church, tried to read a book, peed a couple of times, downloaded the latest episode of *Homeland*, paused it after the first five minutes, turned off the TV, and stared out the living room window at a few distant street lamps. The silence in his apartment was total. What would it be like, he wondered, to no longer be alone?

At the first pearl-gray light, he brewed coffee and had breakfast reading the morning's *Washington Post*. At eight, he called the agency and told the assistant of the deputy director that he was ill: headache, vomiting, diarrhea, probably the flu. He'd probably be out for several days. He'd check back tomorrow. First time he'd ever taken sick leave; must be age creeping up.

He slapped together a couple of ham and cheese sandwiches, grabbed an apple, an orange, and four bottles of water and put them in his black backpack along with a thermos of coffee. Then he donned his biking gear and loaded his mountain bike on the back of the Jeep Wrangler.

It took less than an hour to drive to Fountainhead Regional Park. He'd come here several times over the past few years with Brian to go biking, fishing, and kayaking. The last couple of times Brian's sons came as well, protesting because they weren't yet allowed to tackle the Bear Claw.

Steve turned in the park's entrance, past the ranger station, then continued through the thick woods for twenty minutes until he reached the gravel parking lot at the bottom of the Bear Claw. There were no other cars around. It was still damp and gray with a morning chill in the air. He unloaded his bike, put on his light red parka and the backpack. He checked his tires and brakes and gears, clipped on his thermos and started up the trail. It was rutted and muddy in places. A huge storm had swept through the area the night of Brian's death. Three inches of rain fell in less than an hour.

It had been more than a month since Steve had last biked. It felt great to ride again; the resentment and anger that consumed him over the past few weeks drained away. The trail wound through the hemlock and birch forest for a few minutes before it began to challenge the steep mountainside.

He had started mountain biking near Seattle when he was seven years old. His brother, Benjy – three years younger – often tagged along, at first peddling madly, often screaming his frustration at not being able to keep up with Steve. But Steve now was fifty-three; he'd tackled the Bear Claw a few times with Brian, but only on condition that the younger man curb his wicked pace.

Perhaps it was time, thought Steve, to follow his doctor's advice: back off that bone-jarring excuse for a sport before you wind up a cripple. Today, in fact, he found himself particularly out of shape and stopping every twenty minutes or so to take deep breaths and drink some water. After an hour, his leg muscles were cramping; his shirt was drenched in perspiration.

To distract himself from the pain, he thought back again to the last time he saw Brian in O'Shaughnessy's. It was a particularly raucous evening, the bar packed with young government apparatchiks on the make, intent on impressing each other, bewailing the latest follies of their idiot bosses. For some reason no one could remember, the bar had also long been a hangout for folks from Langley who lived in the area, like Steve and Brian.

That evening, as often happened, they were joined by the two other officers who'd been a key part of the Russian hacking team. It was the same duo, Steve thought sadly, who'd also gathered at Brian's funeral, Charlie Doyle and Sarah Levin. Their attention was riveted that evening on the news program on the large screen above the bar. In the boisterous barroom there was no chance of deciphering the sound, but they were following the subtitles. Correspondent Ed Diamond was interviewing a former head of the CIA, who denounced the Russian hacking as "equivalent to the attacks of 9/11."

"That's going a bit far," said Sarah.

"Agreed," nodded Charlie.   "It just…"

"You're full of shit," Brian interjected. "It's not just the Kremlin playing games with the U.S. government. Stokes and his buddies are also going to make billions from their secret deals with Moscow. You can fucking well bet on it!" He thumped his glass on the table, knocking over a half-empty bottle.

"For Christ sakes, Brian!" Steve jumped up to avoid getting his slacks drenched. The younger agent's public outbursts were becoming ever more frequent. He was losing his grip and turning into a sloppy, noisy drunk. At first, Brian only ranted about going to the media over the way the hacking investigation had been squelched. Now he upped the ante.

"Whining to the press is going to achieve fuck-all," he raged as the waitress wiped up the table. "It's not going to stop the bastards. We've got to do something."

"Like what," said Sarah.

"Take action ourselves. We can't let Stokes get away with it."

"Easy to say," said Sarah. "But how?"

"Develop a real plan and make the pricks pay!" said Brian.

"Like how?" Charlie scoffed.

"I don't know," Brian shot back. "There's got to be something." He looked at the other agents his eyes wild. "Do we just sit here like a bunch of dumb fucks and watch it happen?"

Steve realized that the others were just as riled up as Brian, but also had no idea what to do. They're waiting for someone more seasoned to lead, he thought. They're waiting for me to come up with some wild plan, to give the signal. But I'm having none of it.

"Look, I'm as pissed off as anyone," he finally said, looking slowly around the table. "But there's no way I'm joining any suicidal crusade. It would be crazy, futile. A rear-guard action and naïve at best, fatal at worst. Stokes is the president. Get used to it!"

Brian glared at him, red-faced. "So you're bailing out!"

"Exactly." Steve said, refilling his glass. "There's a small island near Vancouver, Canada. You pick up oysters off the beach. Dig for clams. I've got a cabin there and a good pension. I can make money on the side as a consultant. So don't count on me."

He raised his glass in a mock toast. His gaze took in not just his fellow agents but everyone watching from the bar. "If Americans want to commit national suicide, turn over their government to a president who's probably linked in some way to Russia, ruled by a Russian leader who worked for the KGB, so be it. I'm outta here." There was some laughter and spotty applause from a few other people in the room, not sure what to make of the boozy dispute between Steve and his fellow agents.

Brian was now standing over Steve, his face livid. "You know what, Penn, you're chickenshit!" He took a wild swing at Steve, missed, and crumpled to the floor. He lay there for a few seconds then tried to get up. There was more applause and laughter from the bar.

"Someone should take him home," said Steve. He downed the rest of his drink and left.

* * *

That was the last time he had seen Brian alive, thought Steve as brought his attention back to the biking trail. It was far more rugged than he'd remembered. He could hear the blood roaring in his ears, his heart thumping. He was gasping for breath. He stopped, dismounted, and continued pushing his bike around boulders and up the muddy mountain track. He was no longer sure what the precise point of this morning's exercise was. He just knew he had to see where Brian died.

He reached the peak and paused for breath, took a drink from his thermos, and remounted. The slope now pitched downward; his bike jounced and slithered between the trees, picked up speed, ever faster, the wind whipping by his face as he careened around the notorious switchback he'd been expecting. He jammed on his brakes and found himself staring out over the edge of the trail. The precipice dropped away sharply to the gray granite boulders of the canyon some forty feet below, where the Fountainhead River ran through.

The state police had placed yellow tapes marking where Brian had skidded off the trail and tumbled to his death. The tapes were still there, but were already falling away. Soon there'd be nothing to mark the place. The wooden guardrail had been knocked away, its supports black and rotted.

So that's it, thought Steve – all that sweating and cramps for this. He took the sandwiches and fruit from his backpack along with the thermos of water, and sat in the deep grass on the side of the track away from the precipice. A gnarled pine bough lay on the ground, probably blown there by the storm a few days ago. Steve removed his parka, sat with his back against the bough. He smelled the fragrance of the pine and damp grass.

As he ate, he listened to the birdsong, watched an eagle circling lazily overhead, and then traded stares with a dewy-eyed deer, which paused for a moment, trembling in the glade. If he could only share this moment with someone. This is what life should be all about – not the tormented, lonely world of spies and intercepts, treachery and deceit, that he'd known over the past thirty years.

He looked once more at the crumbled remains of the wooden guardrail. And again could not understand how Brian could have plunged through it. It was a hazard they all knew about, even joked about. In fact, it was Brian who wrote the formal letter to the park board demanding that it be fixed.

The police had already checked the scene, but if Steve had learned anything during all his years with the agency, it was that investigators – even the best – regularly fuck up, miss the obvious. He walked fifty yards back up the trail and carefully followed the different routes Brian might have taken through the mud and rocks and boulders. Not a hint of anything suspect. Hard to distinguish any particular bike tracks. Then he began searching along the tall grass by the side of the trail. Some of the grass was covered by the large, gnarled pine bough that he'd earlier rested against. The limb had probably been blown there by the storm the night of Brian's disappearance.

Steve hoisted the bough with both hands. It was heavier than he'd expected, and he shifted it to the edge of the clearing. It was then that he saw the bright crimson object that had been hidden by the bough. He bent to retrieve it. It was the front of Brian's biking helmet, with the image of a leaping tiger. There was no mistaking it. There were matted hair and bloodstains on the webbing inside. Steve turned it over and over in his hands, studying it for almost a minute before he slid it into his backpack.

Then he left his bike propped against a hemlock and took a steep winding path to the bottom of the ravine, navigating fallen moss-covered boughs, and large gray boulders, and treacherous patches of thick reddish-brown muck. To control his descent, he grabbed birch trunks as he slithered down the slope. At the bottom, he found the yellow tape the police had put to mark where Brian's body had been found crumpled on the rocks by the river.

Why had it taken the searchers more than a day to find the body? The vegetation was not thick. There were puddles of water covering some of the smaller boulders, but the burbling river was certainly not deep. It would never have covered the corpse.

He sat on one of the boulders and looked back up the mountain to the spot from where Brian apparently plummeted. He took a few photos and started back up the trail, then paused, and returned to the river. He emptied his thermos and filled it with water from the Fountainhead.

CHAPTER FOUR:

Alexandria

The next morning, he phoned the State Medical Examiner's office.

"I'd like to know who signed the death certificate last week for Mr. Brian Hunt," Steve said.

""Who wants to know?" the woman sounded like a wannabe Oprah Winfrey.

"Steve Penn. I'm a colleague of Mr. Hunt."

"Hold on."

He heard her talk with someone else in the office; then she was back, "We don't normally give out that information," she said.

"Yes, you do," said Steve. "It's public. If I were to come to your office you'd be obliged to show it to me."

Again, she conferred with someone else.

"It was Dr. Stone," she said. "Dr. Roger Stone. Goodb…"

"Hold it," said Steve. "I'd like to talk with Dr. Stone."

"About?"

"Brian Hunt's death."

Again, a pause and the doctor came on the line.

"This is Dr. Stone, Mr.….".

"Penn, Steve Penn. I worked with Brian Hunt. You signed his death certificate last Monday, I believe."

"And?"

"I'd like to talk briefly with you about the cause of death."

"I've already said what the cause was."

"I've got new information that might change your mind."

"You are with the CIA?"

"Yes. I can come to your office this morning."

"I can only give you a couple of minutes. I don't usually do this."

"I'm nearby. I'll be there by 10:00," said Steve.

The Medical Examiner's office was on the ground floor at 400 East Jackson Street in Richmond, Virginia. It was 9:50 when Steve arrived wearing a backpack. He asked the receptionist for Doctor Stone. The heavyset woman put down the latest edition of Hollywood Stars and eyed him warily.

"Just a minute," she said. She pushed a button and spoke cautiously into her intercom. He could hear her add, "He's got a backpack."

"Here – you want to see what's inside?" said Steve, opening the backpack for her inspection.

She glanced into it, then muttered, "You'll have to sign in first." She pointed to a register on the counter in front of him. After he'd filled it in, she glared one more time and nodded towards the corridor, "Second door on the left."

Steve walked down the hallway past a portrait of the state governor, and next to it the state seal depicting a triumphant young warrior holding a spear, his boot atop the chest of some fallen despot. Underneath was the state's motto: *Sic Semper Tyrannis.* Thus always to tyrants, Steve thought. Couldn't be more appropriate for the occasion. He knocked on the door.

"Come in." The tight-lipped doctor glanced up from his computer and motioned Steve to take the brown vinyl seat in front of him.

"You're ten minutes early," he said.

"Traffic was lighter than I expected."

The doctor continued staring at his computer screen. His gunmetal desk was crowded with stacks of reports and files. Three rows of bookshelves on the wall behind him were filled with weighty tomes on human pathologies and the requisite framed degrees from the University of Virginia Medical School.

Steve placed his backpack on the floor and sat silently as Stone continued with his digital notes. He was in his early sixties, bald, and beak-nosed, with thin bloodless lips. Like some bird of prey, thought Steve. The stark shadows cast by the reading light give his face an even more sinister look.

At precisely 10:00, the doctor swiveled to inspect Steve with piercing gray eyes. "Go ahead. It's your nickel."

"I'll get right to the point," said Steve.

"Good."

"You said the cause of Brian Hunt's death was drowning?"

The doctor turned back to his computer. "That's H-U-N-T?" he asked.

"Correct"

"And the date?"

"Last Monday."

The doctor brought up the file and read the conclusion: "The cause of death was drowning."

"A couple of questions about that," Steve said.

The doctor scowled.

"First," said Steve. "Hunt fell more than forty feet, before he crashed onto the boulders at the bottom of the precipice. Here let me show you." He took his iPad and flicked through several pictures he had taken at Fountainhead Park the day before.

The doctor glanced at them briefly, then returned his gaze to Steve. His fingers drummed the desk.

"You'd think a fall like that would kill anyone outright, wouldn't you?" said Steve.

Stone shrugged. "You might."

"But if he were dead when he hit, he wouldn't be breathing," said Steve. "So how could he drown?"

The doctor glared. "Are you questioning my professional judgment?"

Steve continued, "I checked with the weather bureau. You remember the storm that hit Virginia the night of his accident? Dumped more than three inches of water in twenty-four hours?"

"Your point?" said Stone, glancing at his watch.

"At the time Brian Hunt had his so-called accident, the level of water in the river was four feet lower than it was a day later when his body was discovered. Which means Brian's head was well above the water when he lay on those rocks. In fact, it must have taken a while for the water to reach him. You're saying he just lay there alive all that time until he drowned?"

"He was probably paralyzed," snapped Stone. "As you noted, it was a long fall." He looked again at his watch. "You said you needed two minutes."

"And all the while," Steve persisted, "Hunt was unable to make enough noise to attract the attention of any of the searchers. Not even the sniffer dogs were able to find him."

"Is that it?" The doctor's eyes narrowed.

"There's also this," said Steve. He reached down and extracted the crimson fragment of Brian's biking helmet from his backpack. "This belonged to Hunt. I just found it."

"And?"

"You can see he obviously took a major blow. There're bloodstains as well."

The doctor shrugged. "He took a big fall."

"Right, except I found this piece by the side of the trail at the top of the cliff. In other words, Hunt was hit on the head *before* he fell."

Stone's lips tightened. "Look, Mr. Penn, I agreed to meet you because I thought you were on some kind of official business. If that's not the case, this meeting is over. If there's anything to change in my report, I can handle it myself."

CHAPTER FIVE:

Arlington

It was raining now; the rhythmic beating of his windshield wipers sounding a soothing, hypnotic note. But the vague doubts Steve had before his visit to Doctor Stone were now shrill questions demanding answers. He called Brian's widow from his mobile.

"Joanne, it's Steve. I'm sorry to intrude at this time, but I've really got to talk with you."

"About what?"

"Rather tell you in person."

"When?"

"Now."

"You're scaring me."

"Nothing to be scared of. I can be there in ten minutes."

"O.K. But I've got to get the kids at five."

Picking up kids from school, thought Steve. What's it like? He'd never done it. Never had a kid who'd lived long enough to go to school.

A few minutes later, he pulled to a stop before the Hunts' shingle-roofed bungalow on North Rockingham Street. It was a quiet, bucolic neighborhood, perfect for raising kids. There was a maple tree in the front yard with an old inner tube hanging from a limb. There were neat flowerbeds under the windows: the crocuses – mauve and orange – were already coming up; the rows of daffodils preparing their own show for spring. Joanna's black Prius was in the driveway. Steve wondered if he was making a mistake, stirring things up like this, going off half-cocked on some wild conspiracy theory without any real evidence. But no, this had to be done. It was still drizzling as he walked to the porch and rang the bell.

Joanne opened the door with one hand, talking on her mobile with the other. She motioned him in. Still on the phone, she led him to the living room. He sat on a leather sofa; she settled into a beige armchair facing him. She was wearing a pale blue jogging outfit, her hair disheveled, and the laces of her sneakers were undone. A large picture of Brian, Joanne, and their two boys was on the coffee table, draped in black.

There were three Afghan kilims on the floor. Brian and Steve had been assured by a bearded doctor in Kabul they were "top quality" "museum pieces." Desperate to get himself and his family out of Afghanistan, the doctor was selling anything he still had of value. Steve had picked up a spectacular crystal vase and a string of amber beads that supposedly dated back to the 16th century.

Joanne frowned as she attempted to end the phone call. "Yes, yes, okay thanks, Denise. Goodbye. Yes, I will. No, don't worry. Okay. Goodbye." She put down the mobile and let out a deep sigh. "That was Brian's mother," she said. "Seems like she's calling me every hour. Wants to come over. Take care of the kids. Do my shopping. I know she just wants to help…but…but sometimes it just gets too much."

She took a Kleenex from a box on the table and dabbed her eyes. "Can't seem to stop crying," she said. "I think it's under control, then it just starts up again."

"It's okay. You're entitled," said Steve. He was trying to figure out how to begin.

"The kids still can't understand what happened," she said. "They were at the funeral. You saw them there. Yet this morning they came into the bedroom and asked when Daddy was coming home. I'll get you some coffee."

"Don't bother, I…."

"It's alright, really." She got up and walked to the kitchen in the next room. "It's already made," she called out behind her.

She returned with her tears dried and a tray bearing a pot of coffee, two cups, and some sponge cake. "You can't believe how many people brought cake. They're still coming."

As she took a seat, Steve poured himself a cup. "Joanne, look…"

She interrupted, chattering on. "It's strange to see you here without Brian. I can't believe how many times we had you over for a barbecue or to watch football, or *Homeland* or whatever. Always trying to fix you up with someone. Never seemed to work, though, did it?"

"Guess not." There was an awkward pause. He put down his cup. "Joanne, it's a strange thing I'm going to ask, not at all easy."

"You're frightening me again." She stared at him, alert to the change of tone.

"You have to request a new autopsy of Brian." There, he finally got it out.

"What?" Her brow furrowed as if she hadn't heard him correctly.

"You have to ask for another examination of Brian's body," he repeated slowly as if talking to a child. "To find out how he died."

Her fingers dug into the arms of her chair. "Are you serious? Dig Brian up? Are you crazy?"

"I'm pretty certain his death was not an accident."

"You're out of your mind," she finally burst out. "Brian said you were always inventing conspiracies. You want to cut him open again? Make us go through it all over again?"

"No, Joanne, listen, I've got proof, just...."

She cut him off, shaking with rage. "Brian told me what a jerk you were," she yelled. "He was almost out of his mind when he came back from the bar the last time he went drinking with you. He said you were a coward. You refused to back him up. He was simply asking for help." She leapt to her feet "But he was wrong. You're not a coward. You're just nuts!"

"Joanne, wait." He reached for his backpack.

"No. Get the fuck out of here!" She shouted before grabbing the coffee tray from the table and brandishing it menacingly.

"Joanne, goddammit! I've got evidence. Look!" He pulled the fragment of Brian's crimson biking helmet from his backpack and held it out, the image of the pouncing leopard towards her.

She stared at the jagged object, then slowly lowered the tray and took the shard into her hands. She turned it over and saw the traces of blood inside, then hugged it to her breast. When she looked up at Steve again, her eyes were brimming. "Where did you get this?"

"At Fountainhead River Park at the *top* of the ridge Brian supposedly fell from. I was there this morning. Joanne," he said. "Brian was murdered."

CHAPTER SIX:

Arlington

Steve promised Joanne he would follow Brian's new autopsy every step of the way. He arrived at the stone gates of the Columbia Gardens Cemetery at 9:00 a.m. on what promised to be another damp, miserable day. His shoes swished in the soggy grass as he walked toward Brian's grave. There was no tombstone yet; a simple black granite memorial would be ready next week. Wearing yellow rain slickers and rubber boots, the same two cemetery workers who had buried Brian now labored to retrieve the oak casket.

Their efforts could be the opening scene of a macabre film, thought Steve, a grisly tale of a life in reverse. First, the dirt comes flying out of the hole in the cemetery; then the coffin is raised; the mud and dirt are brushed off. Then it's carried back to the waiting hearse; driven back to the medical examiner's office. The horror continues: a naked Brian, his body stiff, his skin gray, rises from the coroner's bright steel examining table, stretches, dons his biking gear, puts on his crimson helmet, and rides off to once again challenge the Bear Claw Trail.

Such were the scenes churning through Steve's mind as he drove behind the hearse to the medical examiner's office on Southampton Avenue in Norfolk. Joanne stipulated that it be a different office and a different medical examiner than Dr. Stone, who'd issued the first verdict of death by drowning. Though traffic was light, it took more than three hours before they pulled into the arrival bay of the Norfolk office.

The coffin was unloaded from the hearse and placed on a gantry that ran down to the mortuary in the basement. The residue of filth and muck on the coffin was blasted away by a high-pressure hose, along with a quivering swarm of worms and maggots. An attendant in an orange rubber jumpsuit wearing a pale green mask sprayed an industrial deodorant, but there was still the sweet, cloying smell of purification as the coffin was open and the body lifted out. Despite the mask that had been given him, Steve almost gagged.

Brian's corpse was wheeled into the examining room, placed on a flat steel table, his clothes carefully removed and folded. The walls and ceiling were white. The only discordant note was a United Airlines calendar featuring scenes from Hawaii hanging beside the door. Under the harsh overhead light, the corpse lay there greenish-purple and swollen, like a slab of rotted beef thought Steve. He couldn't recognize any of the features of his friend.

A medical assistant wearing a pale green operating robe and a mask stood by the array of tools carefully laid out by the table: shears, scalpels, pliers, tongs, electric drill, and saw. There was also a row of porcelain dishes ready to receive any body parts the examiner, Dr. Bill Snyder, might want to send to the lab for further study.

Steve introduced himself to the doctor and explained his suspicions about Brian's death. Then he handed him a small carefully labeled glass bottle. "That's the water sample," he said.

The doctor, a large florid man, with a thick neck, graying eyebrows, and steel-rimmed glasses, seemed uninterested in instructions from a layman. He took the bottle impatiently and handed it to his assistant. "Get this to the lab," he barked.

He picked up the large scalpel and nodded coolly at Steve. "Sure you want to stay?"

"I promised I would."

"Your first autopsy?"

"I've seen lots of dead bodies in Iraq and Afghanistan, but yeah, this is the first time for this."

"I'll give you a guided tour," said Snyder. "I also teach pathology at UVA Med School."

"Thanks," said Steve not very convincingly.

The doctor adjusted his facemask. "Frankly, no one likes to do this kind of autopsy – so long after the fact, you might say. It's the smell that really gets to you – no matter how many of these you do – like sulphur, an intestinal gas." He gestured toward the corpse's stomach. "Then there's also the bacteria from the colon that help us digest our food during life." He took a large scalpel and made a bloodless incision down the center of the bloated chest. "But as soon as we're gone, those bacteria go to work on us. A cocktail fact for you: two of the chemicals produced during purification are named putrescine and cadaverine. Interesting, right?"

"Look," he said, pushing his finger into the flaccid skin of the belly and upper arms. "That's the bacteria also. It bloats the body. "You see what's already happening there?" He pointed to the large blood-tinged blisters on the legs and arms, "That's also normal; collapse of the red blood cells. If I wanted to I could peel the skin away like a banana."

Steve made it as far as the green plastic wastebasket by the wall before he vomited.

"Sorry," he said between retches.

"It's okay," said the doctor continuing his work. "Happened to me too the first time around. Happens to most medical students. Not much fun to see and smell what's ahead for us. Sure you want to stay in the room?"

"I told his wife I would," said Steve, wiping his mouth with Kleenex as he returned to the table.

"Understood," said Snyder as he continued his work.

Suddenly the silence was shattered by the wail of an electric circular saw slicing the breastbone. Then the doctor thrust a large vice into the cavity to pry apart the chest wall as if opening a giant clam. The heart and lungs were now on display. Snyder deftly cut through the bronchus and pulmonary vessels on each side removing the lungs.

"Let's see what's doing here," said the doctor as he tipped the lung up and poured out some darkly stained mixture into a specimen pot. He sliced into the spongy purplish tissue of the lungs, and examined the porous mass taking other samples to look at under the microscope.

"Much water?" asked Steve.

"A fair amount," said the doctor. "No question, he drowned. Certainly enough liquid still here for what you're supposedly interested in. It's a mixture of water and guck from the body, but the lab should be able to figure things out." He continued probing the corpse, examining the spine and each swollen organ, dictating his findings into a microphone attached to his gown. He was just about to start on the skull to fully understand the extent of the head injury when the receptionist announced over a wall speaker that there was a call.

"I'll get back in half an hour," said the doctor.

"They say it's urgent."

He grunted, put down the scalpel. "Finish up," he told the assistant, as he walked off. "It's good practice, and the patients never complain."

For a few minutes, Steve observed as the assistant continued. Then, impatient for the report on the water sample, he asked directions to the lab.

"Second floor," the assistant muttered, wielding the shears. "You can't miss it."

Steve mounted the stairs, removing the mask as he went. God, it was good to get away, but the bilious stink of death stuck to him. It pervaded everything.

The lab was small and brightly lit, the technician an enormous blond woman, encased in pale green gown and pants. Her hair, tightly fastened, was also covered with an elastic bonnet. "Janet Ramage," she said, giving Steve a friendly smile with thick fleshy lips. She glanced at her white plastic gloves. "Can't shake your hand, but welcome. Don't get too many visitors back here."

"I'm interested in the case they're working on right now, the Hunt case," said Steve. "The fluid in the lungs."

"Right, just finished that. Kind of special, is it? Don't normally get other samples to look at. You the one who provided it?"

"It's from the Fountainhead River where Hunt's body was found. I want to know if it has the same chemical makeup as the water that was in Hunt's lungs."

'I wasn't sure we'd get enough of a sample from the lungs to test, but we did," she said bringing up the results on her desk PC. She pointed to a glowing chart on the screen with two squiggly lines: one red, one green. "The red line is the water you brought. The green one is what came from the lungs. You can see the chemical content of the two samples is totally different."

"How can you tell?" asked Steve.

"The water in his lungs has fluorides." She indicated a peak on the green line. "It's obviously drinking water from somewhere." She moved her finger to the red line. "No resemblance at all to this sample of river water you brought."

"You're sure of that?"

"Positive."

At that moment, Dr. Snyder stalked in, glaring at Steve. "What the hell are you doing in our lab?"

"Looking at the results of the test," said Steve. "Your technician here very kindly gave me the answer. Is there some prob…"

The doctor cut in, "Get the hell out of here." Then he turned on the startled technician. "You never give results to the public. Never!" he snarled, and wheeled back to Steve. "Out. Now."

Steve didn't flinch. "What about the results of the autopsy?"

"I've no longer got the case," Snyder barked. "Hunt was with the CIA. His file has been classified. It's out of my hands. Out of yours too."

CHAPTER SEVEN:

Falls Church

One of the few advantages of Steve's ground floor apartment in Falls Church was that it gave him direct access to the large garden at the back and the barbecue. Without a family, he wasn't much interested in the garden, but he used the barbecue a lot, even in the off-season, when he cooked over the open flame and served the meal inside. This was one of those nights. He'd bought thick rib-eyes from O'Rourke's, considered the best butcher in Arlington. He'd seared them and was now letting them cook along the edge of the grill. He was justifiably proud of his barbecue sauce. The secret he'd picked up from the American ambassador ten years ago in Moscow was the muscovado sugar and the superb wine vinegar he made himself. He'd just cracked a raw egg and was tossing it into the Caesar salad, another specialty for which he considered himself renowned. Aside from the quality of the romaine, the parmesan, and the garlic, the secret was the croutons, which took several hours to prepare.

He'd invited Charlie Doyle and Sarah Levin. They'd both been in O'Shaughnessy's Bar the night Brian took a swing at him. It was the last time any of them had seen Brian alive. They'd worked intensely together for more than a year on the Russian hacking investigation – becoming part of an incredibly close-knit team, something unique, Steve thought as he poured glasses of Brunello for his guests.

"To Brian," he said.

"To Brian!" they replied, each of them curious about Steve's motives for the backyard gathering.

Steve's throat was tight. He hadn't planned the words that spilled out: "You know, to me Brian's death was like the passing of a close relative – a brother, a son. He can never be replaced." He paused, "I guess I've come to think of us all as family."

For a few seconds, no one said anything. Seeing Steve this emotional was almost embarrassing.

Charlie took a sip of wine and broke the silence. "Family. Yeah, well, if you ask Brenda, she'd agree," he said in his lazy South Carolina drawl. "She's always saying I spend more time with you guys than I do with her and the kids. Says I prefer you creeps – even to basketball. " He laughed. "Sometimes, maybe she's right."

It had been Charlie who found the suspicious digital fingerprints in the servers of the Democratic National Committee and tracked the hackers to a cyber-warfare unit of the Russian army.

"You did a great job with the Russian hack, Charlie. You both did," Steve said as he served the steaks and the salad. "The bastards in the White House may try to ignore our report. They may say it's bullshit. But we've put it all on the record. They can't erase that. One day they'll pay for what they've done."

He grated a bit more parmesan on to the salad before he asked about their future plans.

Charlie stroked his goatee. "Don't know yet. Might go to England. I've already been approached by some big-time operators from the Gulf. They say I could commute from London. There's a pile of money to be made there." He shrugged. "Those guys at least realize I'm the best hacker around."

"Hey, Charlie" said Sarah, putting down her fork, "You're good, but let's not exaggerate; remember you told me that the only reason you wound up with the agency was to keep out of jail."

"It's a bit more complicated than that," said Charlie.

"OK, so what really happened?" asked Sarah.

Steve, who'd recruited Charlie for the CIA, knew the story; Sarah obviously did not.

Charlie shrugged, took a sip of the wine, and turned towards Sarah. "Ok, I'll give you the short version. I was a great basketball player. I mean, really great. By the time I was a sophomore in high school in Detroit, scouts from the NBA were already after me. But I never got the chance to turn pro. I was expelled from school. Hacked into a Pentagon war game from the school's library. Just fooling around, but they didn't see it that way. University was out. Parents couldn't afford it. So I set myself up as an independent contractor.

Me – an independent contractor!" He pronounced the last two words slowly, with a proud grin. "I went to work for anyone willing to pay the tab. Amazing how many customers there were! Along the way I figured it would be a good idea to learn some Russian too."

"But you couldn't keep out of trouble," said Steve, pointing his fork at Charlie.

"Made a bet with a couple of guys. It took me two weeks, but I managed to hack into the NSA. Too bad WikiLeaks wasn't around then. I would have beat Snowden by ten years. Anyway, the cyber sleuths at the NSA finally caught up with me. Bottom line: I was offered a choice of three years in prison or going to work for the CIA's new cyber unit. They were looking of the best coders.'

"Of course that was you," said Steve, grinning.

"Absolutely. I was it," said Charlie. "That's why you wanted me too. Right, Steve? And I did a great job. But we've been royally fucked. Guess I made the wrong move."

"I hope not," said Steve.

They helped him clear the table and waited with anticipation as he portioned out a French apple pie he'd just baked, adding a scoop of vanilla ice cream on top of each piece.

"Steve, you are truly amazing," said Sarah, lifting her glass of wine in appreciation. Charlie joined her.

"Thanks," said Steve. "Living alone forces you to develop certain survival skills." The pie was warm from the oven. Steve let them finish eating it before asking, "And what about you, Sarah? Any idea what you want to do?" They both shifted to look at her – looking at her was always a pleasure.

"Think you might go back to teaching at MIT?" asked Charlie, already reaching for another piece of pie.

"Possibly," she said. "Or maybe NYU. There's also an opening for first cello at the New York Philharmonic."

"Hey," said Charlie. "Don't forget 'Victoria's Secret.'"

At twenty-one, to promote her career, she outraged classical music purists but delighted millions of fans by posing for a lingerie ad wearing only a black lace bra and a thong, her long legs wrapped around a cello. She used one of those pictures as a cover for her first album. Later, the number of heartbroken male staff at the agency was legion when Sarah announced she was gay and took as her partner a leading LGBT rights activist.

* * *

"It's a nice, clear night," said Steve after they'd finished washing up. "Why don't we walk to Lincoln Park?"

There was an uncomfortable silence. Charlie looked at Steve inquisitively. Nighttime walks in the park this time of year were not a normal pastime.

"Let's just do it," said Steve, already heading towards the door. I'll bring along a few beers in my backpack.

It was a crisp evening, the sky filled with stars, the smell of approaching spring in the air. But it was evident from the start that this was no ordinary stroll. "Take the batteries out of your phones," ordered Steve as the group turned up Maitland Avenue toward the park.

Lincoln Park, Steve always thought, was right out of a Norman Rockwell painting – America as it would like to be. During the day, it was filled with mothers strolling past the daffodils or azaleas or roses with their toddlers or gossiping among themselves as the kids played in the sandboxes and on the slides. After school and on the weekends, came the older children, playing baseball or football or basketball, depending on the season. Retired people ambled by slowly, arm in arm or alone, or sat on benches in the sun, nodding over a book or just snoozing.

This particular evening, however, except for a twosome locked in an embrace on a wooden bench at the entrance and another two or three couples walking the paths, the park was empty. "Put your mobiles over there under that maple," said Steve. After they reluctantly complied, he led them to a secluded picnic table with tree trunk stools, shielded from the public by a grove of birches. The two others sat down and Steve handed each one a bottle of beer.

"So, what's up?" said Charlie. "You'd think we were in Moscow or something."

"It's about Brian's death," said Steve.

"What about it?" asked Sarah.

"Brian didn't have a biking accident," said Steve quietly. "He was murdered."

The two other officers glanced at each other. Was this another of Steve's imagined conspiracies?

"He didn't just skid over a cliff," Steve continued. "He was first bashed on the head." Pulling Brian's crimson helmet from his backpack, he used a penlight to show the others. "He wasn't wearing this when he went over the side. I found this in the grass beside the bike trail. Someone smashed him on the side of the head first. That's his blood inside."

"Sweet Jesus," said Charlie.

"I figure he was probably taken somewhere else and tortured and most likely water boarded and killed."

"How can you be so sure?" said Sarah.

Steve told them about the results of the new autopsy and the lab test. "Brian drowned in water that came from a drinking faucet, not the river."

"Water boarded?' said Charlie. "By who and what for?"

"To find out what he was doing," said Steve. "To find out what *we* were doing."

"Doing about *what*?" said Charlie.

"About Stokes. About the Russian hacking."

"But Brian wasn't doing anything," said Sarah taking a sip of her beer. "And we aren't doing anything. He couldn't get anyone to act."

"You know that," said Steve. "I know that. But the people around Stokes don't know that. And the way Brian was mouthing off during his last few days, he was practically calling for a CIA insurrection."

"So Stokes had him tortured and killed?" asked Sarah. "Pretty hard to believe."

"Probably Stokes himself didn't give the order, but someone close to him did," said Steve. "They'd want deniability. Look, we know that Stokes's paranoia has no limits. He sees enemies everywhere. He offered to pay the legal fees of anyone who beat up hecklers at his rallies. He even threatened to jail his opponent. Now he's president, he's boss of the largest army and intelligence organization the world has ever known. He's surrounded by yes-men and women, people who encourage his darkest instincts. Compared to Stokes, Richard Nixon was a model of sanity."

Sarah put her finger to her lips and gestured to the nearby path. The couple from the bench was approaching. The three looked silently at each other until the couple passed under a streetlight and left the park.

"You can be sure that Stokes has already got an enemies list a mile long," Steve said. "I've also heard rumors he's set up his own secret security operation – answerable only to him."

"I've heard the same thing," said Charlie. "Something like Nixon did, but much, much larger."

"They're probably the ones who offed Brian," said Steve. "Stokes will use any means whatsoever to destroy his opponents. Water boarding's just for starters. He's always been a big fan of torture, of secret black sites. Who knows what other Guantanamos are being set up?"

"I still can't believe it," said Sarah.

"How else do you explain Brian's death?" asked Steve.

No one replied.

Steve continued. "After I created a ruckus about a new autopsy, the same guys who were suspicious of Brian are likely now very interested in me. I've not been publicly screaming about the hacking investigation like Brian was, but to test my theory, I did a thorough sweep of my own apartment earlier today. Spent six hours on it; tore everything apart, looked under and behind everything I could get at. You know what I found? Listening devices in every room, including the bathrooms. All very professional, all government issue. I left everything in place."

"They could be doing the same with us," said Charlie, looking at the others. "I've got nothing to hide, but you guys…"

Steve ignored the joke. "They'll keep tabs on everyone they suspect – everywhere and always. And it's only going to get worse. You should do the same kind of check I did. If you need help, let me know. Meanwhile, don't say anything to anyone about all this unless you're goddamned sure there's no way you can be overheard. Remember they can hijack your laptop, your mobile, even your Amazon Echo."

"So what do you suggest we do?" asked Sarah. "Sneak around like this forever? Always looking over our shoulder? Accept Brian's murder as an accident?"

"No way," said Charlie, "we're going to get the bastards."

"Steve, there's only one thing I don't get," said Sarah.

"What's that?"

"Why the abrupt change? I mean, when Brian tried to wind us up in the bar a week ago, you put a damper on it. It was useless, you said, hopelessly naïve. Now all of a sudden you're itching for the fight. What's up?"

"I'm pissed about our investigation being totally ignored. I'm pissed to find Stokes in my face. I'm pissed because I'm convinced that people working for Stokes killed my closest friend."

"Still doesn't explain it all," said Sarah. "I'm not convinced"

Steve hesitated. This was not the conversation he came for. "Brian was also like a younger brother to me."

"Yeah, you've said that before," said Charlie. "Did you actually have a younger brother?"

"Two years younger than me."

"What happened?" asked Sarah.

Steve felt his throat tighten. "What do you mean?"

"To your brother, obviously."

"It's a long story," Steve said, averting Sarah's gaze. "I'm going to need another beer,".

"Here," said Charlie, handing him one.

Steve took a long drink. "Okay. My father was a wannabe poet, took off when I was three. Never returned. A year later, my mother ran off with a dentist to Texas. Left me and my one-year-old brother with her parents, my grandparents."

Sarah leaned forward with a sympathetic look on his face. "Your brother's name?"

"Benjamin—Benjy."

"So you and Benjy were dumped with your mother's parents."

"Yeah, then the year I turned eighteen," Steve continued, "was also the year my grandparents were killed. Head-on crash with a truck. It was Grandpa's fault. They found an empty bottle of vodka beside him. My brother and I went to live with my grandparents' neighbors. They didn't really want us, but I guess they felt bad about the situation. I kind of took care of Benjy. That's when I started cooking. I tried to protect him. Helped him with his homework, stuff like that. He didn't do as well as I did. Got into drugs in high school."

"Consuming?" asked Charlie.

"And dealing; I knew what was happening, and I tried to prevent it. He listened to me. Stopped hanging out with the druggies, agreed to join a group to help him stay clean. His marks got better. Things were really looking up, or so I thought," Steve paused.

"Then?" asked Sarah.

"I lucked out. Got a scholarship to Stanford."

"So where did that leave Benjy?" said Sarah.

"You a mind-reader?" asked Steve. "Benjy insisted I take the scholarship. He'd learned his lesson. He would be fine. So I left. At first, it seemed okay. We talked every day, but then, less and less. There was always something getting in the way. But he insisted everything was fine, school going great, etcetera, etcetera, bullshit."

Steve paused and took another drink, wondering how the others had gotten him to disclose so much about himself. He'd never revealed this to anyone.

"One night in my second semester, the neighbor, who was supposedly keeping an eye on Benjy, called. They'd found him dead in his bed, he'd OD'd from heroin. When I went back for the funeral, I spoke with his so-called friends. Within the first month after I'd left for Stanford, he'd begun shooting up, then dealing himself. He'd stopped going to classes. All the stuff he'd been telling me over the phone was bullshit. If I'd stayed of course, it would never have happened."

"You did what you had to," said Charlie. "He did what he had to. It's karma."

"That's also bullshit." Steve took another long sip of his beer and looked squarely at Charlie. "It's an excuse to make people feel good for stuff they should have done but didn't. For me, guilt doesn't wash off that easy."

"That's crazy," said Sarah. "Besides, Brian wasn't your brother. He didn't die because of you."

"He had the guts to demand action when Stokes was elected," said Steve. "I kept silent, yet I was the one who led the hacking investigation."

"So now you're making up for it?" said Charlie.

"Also I can take the lead in this. I don't have any family. I've got less at risk than you guys. And I'm determined we're going to deal with Stokes," said Steve. "We just have to figure out how."

CHAPTER EIGHT:

Arlington

The Hampton Motel in Arlington had only two stars in the guidebooks. The neon sign in front proclaimed, "ICE and TV in every room." Paint was flaking around the main door. Despite the occasional cleaning, the odor of stale cigars pervaded the lobby and corridors. The tattered carpets looked like they hadn't been replaced since the hotel was built in the Reagan era. The rooms, however, were clean, the linen changed every day or after every guest, whichever was more frequent. The receptionist dealt mainly in cash and never asked to verify I.D., which made it easy to register under an assumed name, as Steve Penn did two days after his evening meeting with his fellow agents in Lincoln Park.

Steve booked a deluxe room, with a queen-size bed, a couple of beige armchairs and a matching convertible sofa. For a one dollar fee, one of the armchairs provided a five-minute full-body massage. There were framed lithographs on the walls, scenes of 19th century London.

Steve took a bottle of bourbon from his attaché case and set it on the coffee table next to the bucket of ice and two glasses the bellboy brought up.

Ten minutes later, Senator Bill Gurd knocked on the door.

When Steve ushered him in, the senator's eyes immediately darted into the shadows.

"No one else," said Steve. "Just us."

"This meeting never happened," said the senator, tossing his coat and an old-fashioned broad-brimmed hat on the bed.

"You've got my word," said Steve. "You have your mobile with you?"

"Jane told me not to bring it," Gurd said.

Jane Nagler was the senator's legislative assistant. She'd been working for Gurd for the last ten years. Prior to that, she'd been at the CIA, where she became a coffee-time buddy of Steve's.

"Jack Daniels," said Steve, handing a glass of bourbon to the senator. "Jane says it's your only vice."

"Don't believe her." The senator took a sip, lowered himself onto an armchair, and undid his double-breasted jacket. White goatee, gray vest, gold watch chain: he looked like Colonel Sanders – a throwback to another era, which he was. The senior senator from Arkansas was a respected constitutional lawyer who had served on the Judiciary Committee for thirty years and headed it for the last ten. He was a vanishing breed of Republican – one with principles.

"Thanks for coming," said Steve.

"Pleasure," the senator said dubiously.

"I wanted to talk with you about your president," said Steve.

"Not mine alone," said Gurd with a soft drawl. "The American people elected him."

"A minority," said Steve. "If the leaders of your party had more guts, Stokes would never have made it."

The senator leaned forward. "Look, Mr. Penn, I agreed to meet as a favor to Jane. She says you're serious and for real. I was impressed by the brief you gave us before the election. Damn fine job. But if you want to talk just to break my balls, I'll leave right now."

Steve held up his hand. "Apologies. I don't mean to rake you over the coals. But I want you to understand where I'm coming from. Our team spent a long time investigating Russian hacking. Some of us put our lives on the line. We got chapter and verse. We showed how the Russians and Kozlov intervened to help get Stokes elected. We provided solid information about meetings between some of his key people and Russian leaders. Even before the elections, Stokes refused to criticize Kozlov, no matter what kind of stuff the Russians were up to. And what did the congressional leaders do about it?" Steve snapped his fingers. "Zip."

"Wasn't just the Republicans," said Gurd. "The democratic president also played it down. Not to mention the FBI."

"Senator, almost none of the Republicans stood up to him. Even today, after all the crazy stuff he's been doing, you're still pretending he's sane. At least to the public."

"Not true. I've criticized him several times," said Gurd. "I said he went too far on the Mexicans and the illegal aliens, spoke out when he insulted the Canadians."

"And then two days later you were at the Republican retreat patting him on the back along with all the others."

"I warned you once," said Gurd, shaking a finger at Steve.

"Senator, let's not play games," said Steve, pausing to refill Gurd's empty glass. "I know for a fact that privately you're disgusted with the man. You were dead set against him before the election. You'd like nothing better than to see him tossed out."

"Jane talks too much," said Gurd. He took another large sip, and then looked squarely at Steve. "Okay. We made mistakes, serious mistakes. But that's the past. Fact is, Stokes won; he's president. I was told you wanted to talk about the future…not history."

"Senator, Jane also said I can trust you, that you're a real patriot."

"Son, we're both trusting each other right now."

"Understood. There's a small group of us who worked on the hacking report. We're very good at our job. We think Stokes is a great threat. Not just to America but the world."

"Agreed," said Gurd.

"Agreed also," said Steve, "that at least for now, there's no likelihood of a military coup."

"Not yet," said Gurd. "But who knows what crazy orders Stokes might try to give the generals down the road?"

"We can't count on that," said Steve. "Which means that the Congress and the Senate are the only ones who can protect this country. But what are you doing? You've already seen how unhinged he is: the visa disaster, the fiasco in Iraq, Yemen, the threat of a naval blockade of China. The constant lying and insults. Announcing policy by Tweets. What more do you need?"

"It's too soon," said Gurd.

"Too soon? Do we wait until he launches a real war to distract attention from the huge mess he's created at home? What do you think he would do if there were another terrorist attack in this country? It would be like the Reichstag Fire."

"Some of us are worried about just the same possibility," said Gurd.

"*Only some?* Why isn't there a mutiny?"

"Mutiny?"

"The 25th Amendment – you know it by heart, Senator."

Gurd took another a long sip. "If the vice president can convince the majority of the cabinet that the president is incapacitated in some way, then they inform the speaker of the house and president of the Senate and the Vice President then takes over."

"A kind of mutiny," said Steve.

"Except," said Gurd, "there's no way this vice president is going to do that – not yet anyway."

"Isn't he ambitious?" said Steve.

"Of course," said Gurd, "but not suicidal. Like I said, it's premature. Don't forget, also according to the 25th Amendment, if the president wants to resist, he can. Then Congress has three weeks to vote on the question. And you can be damn sure Stokes would lash back with a vengeance. Two thirds of each house would have to agree that Stokes is incapacitated. My fellow Republicans control both houses. You think they're going to toss out their own president? Not even if there were pictures of him on YouTube buggering the pope!"

Gurd put his hand on Steve's arm. "Let me give you a bit of American history, son, something most people haven't heard. When Ronald Reagan totally lost it in his second term, when his attention span was nil – *nil*, the folks around him finally become alarmed enough to consider using the 25th Amendment. But even then, they never did. Instead, they covered up for him, left him in office until the very end, with his quivering finger on the nuclear button."

"What about impeachment?" asked Steve. "If Congress was willing to impeach Bill Clinton for lying about an Oval Office blow job... Look what you've already got on Stokes."

"Same problem," said Gurd, stroking his goatee. "You still need a majority in the House and two thirds in the Senate. Bottom line, son, to date, not a single U.S. president has been removed from office by impeachment in the House and conviction in the Senate. God knows more than a handful merited it."

"So you're willing to let a lunatic control the nuclear codes."

"Lunatic? Let us not exaggerate."

Steve leaned forward, "Senator, Stokes is seriously unbalanced—probably psychotic."

"I take it you are an expert in this matter?"

"Ask any good psychiatrist," said Steve. "I have. Plenty have written about it. He's a pathological liar, an extreme narcissist--out of control."

Gurd raised both hands. "All right. Let's suppose he's not completely sane. He's also a viper. Most of my colleagues are cowards to the core. They're scared shitless of Stokes and his Tweets. They were spineless even before he took office. Now that he's president with all the power in the world, don't expect any rush to oppose him. Not until they think he's been defanged."

Steve leaned forward again to refill Gurd's empty glass. "There's something else you haven't mentioned, Senator, he said. "We found that the Russians also hacked into the Republican National Committee's files. You can bet they dug up plenty of outrageous stuff: corruption, hypocrisy, sexual habits that would make a Moscow whore blush."

The senator's lips tightened, "Yes, I must say I have heard something along those lines."

"None of what they found ever got out to the media," said Steve. "We're pretty sure the Russians fed some of the wildest tidbits to Stokes so he can keep uncooperative Republicans in line."

"The Russians must also have plenty of stuff on Stokes himself," said Gurd.

"Do they have stuff on you too, Senator?"

Gurd avoided Steve's gaze. "They may have."

"May have?"

"They do."

"Jesus," said Steve, raising both arms. "Does that mean it's all over? You've already surrendered? How outrageous do things have to get for you people to act?"

The senator put down his glass. "Look, Steve, I can get the Republicans to crawl out from under wherever they're hiding – and I include myself there – but only if you've got overwhelming evidence to nail the bastard. It's got to be stuff that will make even the white workers in Milwaukee scream for his scalp. Give us that, maybe we can do something."

"Maybe?"

"That's all I promise. But I'll give it everything I've got."

"What about the stuff the Russians have on you?"

"I'll cross that bridge when I come to it."

CHAPTER NINE

Falls Church

The following day, Steve called into his office again to say he was still sick. "It's the flu, the doctor says. I'll be out for another few days. Boring as hell staying at home, but I've got no choice." What he didn't add is that there was nothing for him to do in the office, either.

Then he contacted Charlie and Sarah, gave them a rendezvous for the next evening at Big Chimney Park in Falls Church. "No cell phones; leave them somewhere, don't just turn them off as you come close. Make damn sure you're not tailed and Moscow rules."

Moscow rules was shorthand for precautions drilled into all field agents during their training: Assume nothing. Never go against your gut. Everyone is potentially under opposition control. Do not look back, you are never completely alone. Go with the flow, blend in. Vary your pattern and stay within your cover. Lull them into a sense of complacency. Do not harass the opposition. Pick the time and place for action. Keep your options open. And Steve's favorite: Technology will always let you down.

Difficult to believe, thought Steve, that he would ever feel obliged to use such rules in America. But already his country was no longer America. On the way to the park, he changed taxis three times, always alert to the patterns of traffic and faces. He walked the last mile on foot, wearing his backpack. Twice along the park paths, he reversed his route. He finally met the three other agents at a wooden picnic table in a grove of hemlocks, shielded from anyone casually passing by.

"If this is going to become a habit," said Charlie, "we should at least bring hot dogs so it looks for real."

"Thought you'd never ask," said Steve. He undid his backpack and brought out four pizza boxes, French fries, napkins, plastic utensils, and beers. He popped open a Bud. The agents passed around the food and began to eat.

"First order of business," said Steve, "from what you've each told me, whoever placed bugs in my home, did the same with all of you."

"One in each room," said Charlie, "even the bathroom."

"Same with me. My partner's also damn mad," said Sarah, sipping her beer. "And I can't even tell her why it's happened. Thank goodness I found it first and I told her when we were out of range."

"The bastards," said Charlie, turning to Steve. "Okay, we're riled, but what can we do?"

"That's what I'm trying to figure out," said Steve. As they continued eating, he told them about the conversation the day before with Senator Gurd. "Bottom line: The senator might be able to get his honorable colleagues to move against Stokes, but only if we come up with something that will blow Stokes right out of the water. Even then, he said it's not a sure thing." He looked at the two others, "So, that's the challenge."

"Not enough," said Sarah cutting the last pizza. "You called us here for some reason, for more than just that."

They were both now staring at Steve just as they had after Brian Hunt's tirade at the bar in Alexandria. I refused to step forward back then, thought Steve. I failed them, failed Brian.

He rose and looked at the two officers , "You know the other night when you were pushing me on why I felt so strongly about taking on Stokes? I've been thinking a lot more about it,

"And?" said Charlie,

"Well I don't know how it was for you, but when I joined the agency, it was the end of the cold war. But there was still a sense of evil and good in the world, and no question which side was the good. It was us. At least in my mind."

"Not in mine," said Charlie. "Not any longer."

"Right. Things have changed. The differences are no longer clear-cut. Who's the evil? These days we're told its Isis? Radical Islam? What about our invasion of Iraq? Our endless war with Afghanistan? Our drones? Everything is hazy now, muddy.

"But as far as I'm concerned there's nothing hazy about Stokes. The guy is evil incarnate; a danger to the U.S. and a danger to the world.

"I was looking at Brian's two kids the other day, while we were burying him, thinking what could happen to them with Stokes as president. Brian must have thought about that too. Their entire future's at risk. Forget about irreversible climate change. Stokes doesn't give a shit about that! He's turning this into the planet of the apes!

"The son of a bitch also has the power to start a nuclear war on his own. What would have happened if it had not been JFK but Stokes calling the shots during the Cuban missile crisis?"

"The end of our so-called civilized world," said Sarah.

Steve continued, "That's apart from the murder of Brian and all the other horrors that Stokes and his people are capable of. So, I say, enough. I'm asking you to join me. We go for it; take on Stokes and defeat the bastard. I'm willing to lead."

"I'm in," said Charlie.

"Me too," said Sarah.

She paused. "What do we call ourselves?"

"How about 'True Grit?'" Charlie replied.

"That was a lousy film," said Steve.

"How about 'Deep Strike?'" asked Sarah.

"Sounds like a Tom Cruise movie," said Charlie.

"So what?" said Sarah. "It's very dramatic—and it's true. Everyone's talking about the Deep State. Well, this is like the Deep State strikes back."

"I'll buy it," said Steve.

Deep Strike it was.

CHAPTER TEN:

Palm Desert

There was no way Deep Strike could take on President Walter Stokes without an ample, independent bankroll. It was that quest that brought Steve to the gated community in Palm Desert known as Big Horn. It was the penultimate reserve of the rich with 600 magnificent homes, several of which had already been featured in *Architectural Digest*. Sprawled across the foothills of the San Jacinto Mountains east of Los Angeles, the development boasted two undulating championship golf courses, restaurants, spas, swimming pools, and gyms. Armed guards restricted entry to members or friends of members. Only residents could play the golf courses, and only in exchange for an "initiation fee" of $100,000 and $18,000 a year after that. The five- star restaurants with their European and Japanese chefs were also restricted to owners and guests.

The houses were vast, rambling affairs of steel and titanium, concrete and glass, the only limit being the creativity of the architects and the panache of the landscapers.

Steve Penn had been invited to the most lavish mansion of them all: an $80 million, twenty-five-room spread, which had just won an award from the American Institute of Architects. It was just one of several residences around the globe belonging to Jake Pearlstein, ranked number eight on *Forbes's* list of American billionaires. He'd made his fortune first in real estate, and then multiplied it a hundred times over via angel investments in PayPal, Facebook, Uber, and Snapchat. En route, he earned the enmity of most of his wealthy neighbors by his ostentatious backing of liberal causes. Ironically, it was Republican Senator Dave Gurd who put Steve in touch with the billionaire. "Don't breathe a word of this to anyone," said the senator. "It would destroy both me and Jake if it got out that we've anything to do with each other."

A massive butler with close-cropped blond hair, black t-shirt, white chinos and sneakers answered the front door. His t-shirt was monogrammed with a discreet "P." There was no attempt to hide the bulge of a machine pistol under his left arm.

"Sir," he said, "If you have a weapon, mobile phone, recorder, or camera, would you please leave them here with me?" He spoke with a slight Balkan accent, probably Serbian.

"Here's all I've got." Steve handed over his iPhone.

"Is it all right if I pat you down?"

"Be my guest," Steve raised his arms while the butler's hands moved expertly over his torso and slid down and up his legs to his crotch.

"Now, please follow me, sir." They walked down a marble hallway to a vast, softly lit living room hung with American masterpieces that could have graced the Museum of Modern Art in New York. The sliding windows of the living room opened to a flagstone terrace equipped with wet bar, barbecue pit, a row of lounge chairs, and a fifty-meter pool in which Jake Pearlstein was stroking through his morning swim. Beyond the pool and across the rambling cactus gardens were the cavernous sand traps and meticulously groomed fairways of one of the Big Horn golf courses.

Pearlstein emerged from the pool. At seventy-five, the billionaire had the tight-ribbed body and sinewy arms of a fit and robust forty-five year old. He toweled himself, donned a dark-blue terrycloth robe and leather sandals, and crossed the flagstones to shake hands with Steve.

"Fifty laps a day," he said, "Only way to keep young. Already worked out with my trainer. You're welcome to use the gym or pool. We've got shorts, shoes, whatever you need."

"Thanks," said Steve. "Maybe another time."

The windows to the den were also open. A woman reclined in a scooped leather Eames lounge chair, drinking coffee, and reading a book. "Steve, meet Veronica," Pearlstein shouted. "Veronica, Steve." She sat up to wave, her blond hair spilling over bronzed shoulders. Steve waved back. She was wearing a tiny red bikini: Thirty at most--the vacuous trophy wife, Steve speculated, until he saw she was reading the book *Dark Money*, a brilliant expose of the role of the billionaire Koch Brothers in American politics.

"Veronica graduated Phi Beta from Wellesley," said Pearlstein. "I met her when she went to work for The Rand Corporation. I'm helping her set up her own think tank."

Another attendant in monogrammed t-shirt appeared. "What can we offer you," said Pearlstein, "coffee, eggs, smoked salmon, caviar?"

"Coffee would be great," said Steve. "And maybe some toast. Rye?"

"I'll have coffee, granola, and yogurt," said Pearlstein. "Serve us downstairs." He turned back to Steve. "Just give me a minute to change," he said.

Steve strolled around the living room to admire the Rauschenberg and a Rodin he had spotted by the fireplace.

"A plaster model for "Le Baiser." There's only two in the world," said Pearlstein, now wearing a black jogging outfit. "We'll go downstairs to talk." He led Steve along a white Carrara hallway to an elevator. "People like us can never be too security-conscious," he said as the door slid open. "It's a jungle out there. A crazed world of hackers and the NSA vacuuming up every bit of data on the planet. Everyone's into it: Japanese, Chinese, Russians, Israelis, even the goddamned North Koreans. Not to mention my business rivals. You're never really safe."

They exited the elevator, facing what looked a large bank vault. Pearlstein placed his right eye to a sensor and a massive steel door gaped open. "This bunker could take just about anything," he said, "but a direct nuclear hit." Inside was a large, white-walled room with floor to ceiling cabinets on two sides, like a suburban supermarket. "Enough food and water for a couple of months," said the billionaire. "Bedrooms, bathrooms, kitchen, and study down that hall."

Before them was the closed entry to another room. There was a digital readout of two persons and their respective weight. Pearlstein used the retina scan on his left eye to open the door. "Not there yet." He led Steve along another short passageway. After the door closed behind them, a panel on the wall ahead swung open, revealing a windowless room about the size of a squash court. Inside were five plush leather chairs and a mahogany desk.

"It's as good as anything you folks at the CIA have," said Pearlstein. "This room actually floats on springs inside the other room. Not even the slightest vibration from in here gets out. One of my companies in Israel built it. I've got a room like this in each of my homes: here, San Francisco, New York, and London. They're regularly swept every day. Got a bodyguard and security specialist who travels everywhere with me."

He gestured at a nearby table set with the breakfast they had earlier ordered. "Pull up a chair and let's talk."

Over the next hour, Steve briefed the billionaire about the Russian hacking investigation, the murder of Brian Hunt, and the decision to set up Deep Strike.

"What's your goal?" said Pearlstein, finishing his cereal.

"To get rid of Stokes by coming up with material shocking enough that the Republican Congress will have no choice but to impeach."

"You're how many?"

"Three, including myself."

Pearlstein poured them each another cup of coffee. "Not exactly an army."

"We don't need an army. We're good, among the best in the business. The material to nail Stokes surely exists. It's somewhere. We still have an excellent source in place in Moscow. It may take a few months, but we'll find it."

Pearlstein raised his eyes to the ceiling. "A few *months*?"

"A major problem for us of course is security," said Steve. "If we could operate from rooms like this all the time, it would be one thing. But we can't. We're going be moving around, constantly exposed on a planet where every single communication is monitored."

"And where drones and satellites can identify individual faces from hundreds of miles away," said Pearlstein.

"And our operation is not going to be cheap."

"Which is why you're here," said Pearlstein. "How much are you talking about?"

"No way of knowing yet," said Steve. "But it will certainly be many, many millions."

"Also dangerous; if Brian Hunt's death is any indication," said Pearlstein, wiping his mouth with a napkin.

"It's also dangerous for anyone who supports us. Stokes takes no prisoners. To be frank, I was surprised you agreed to see me."

"And why is that?"

"It could be risky for your various interests. You've got a lot on the line. If Stokes turned against you, he could do a lot of damage."

"Probably," said Pearlstein. He stood and placed his hands on the back of his chair, bent over, and stretched. "I've been pissing off my right-wing friends for a long time, though. With the Koch brothers and Adelson pouring billions into the fascist right, that leaves a few like Soros and myself trying to help the good guys."

"You never had dealings with Stokes?" asked Steve.

"I got into a real estate venture with him a few years back—a housing development near Houston. He screwed me royally, and all the other investors. But that's not the reason I'm doing this."

He sat down again and looked squarely at Steve. "My parents were Holocaust survivors. Their stories were horrific. I became a student of German history. How Hitler rose to power. How the German political leaders and businessmen who might have stopped him, didn't.

"You guys are putting your lives on the line. I might as well chip in. I'm not saying Stokes is Hitler." He raised both hands. "But he isn't George Washington, either."

They talked for another hour about potential operations, what their needs might be. At the end, Pearlstein jotted down details of a special bank account. "It'll be set up by tomorrow. You'll get the password. Also, if you need a secure place to operate in London or

New York, I'll give you access to a room like this in my home in either city."

Steve began to stand. It seemed like they were wrapping it up, but then Pearlstein asked, "What about you?"

"What do you mean?"

"You're basically painting a bull's eye on your back. Why?"

Steve sat down again. It was like the discussion he'd had the other night in the park with the other two CIA officers. "I'm furious because Stokes is now running this country despite everything we found about him and the Russians. I'm furious because I think he's unhinged – borderline psychotic – a danger to this country and to the world. I'm also convinced that people working for Stokes killed my closest friend. Finally, I can take the lead in this battle because I don't have any family. I've got less at risk."

"No wife, girlfriend?" asked Pearlstein.

This was turning again into True Confessions, thought Steve. "Women have always said I wall myself off, that I'm self-centered, selfish, afraid of any real attachment. Maybe. But the year after I joined the agency, I married a woman I'd met in college – Marilyn. It was rocky from the start. Anyway, a few years ago she got pregnant. We thought it would help the marriage. Something fouled up during the delivery, she went into prolonged labor and—" Steve felt the lump again in his throat. "And she died. So I'm alone. No family anywhere to mourn if anything happens to me."

The two men were silent for a few moments. "That's it?" said Pearlstein finally, a strange look on his face, as if he was still waiting for the rest of the story. "No one else?"

"No one else," said Steve. "That's it," he gave a tight grin. "You could say leading Deep Strike is my karma."

CHAPTER ELEVEN:

Maya

A shrewd bastard, that Pearlstein, Steve thought as he boarded the red-eye back to Washington. It was almost uncanny how the old billionaire picked him apart. How he almost sensed the presence of Maya – Major Maya Chertkova – Dancing Bear. But there was no way Steve was going to talk about that part of his life. No, he was not going to go there.

He had first met Maya in 2012 when he was working undercover with the CIA in Moscow. It was his second posting there. He'd gone for a week to Saint Petersburg to attend a conference on SIFT and Metasploit, the newest forensic tools developed for the Internet. Maya was a thirty-one-year-old captain in the Russian army, with an advanced degree in computer engineering. The conference was packed, but he'd managed to talk with her during a few breaks between sessions. He chatted her up as he regularly would any well-placed Russian he met who might be a potential source for the agency. That was his job, after all. It helped that she was also very attractive with auburn hair, broad Slavic cheeks, and the palest blue eyes. She seemed warm, friendly, not at all doctrinaire; concerned that the new freedoms that had bubbled up in Russia under Yeltsin, were in danger of being squelched by Putin. It was their third or fourth meeting when, eyes brimming, she finally told him about her own plight. She had been abandoned two months earlier by her husband – a famous Russian nuclear physicist.

"You would recognize his name if I told you," she said. "He left after our daughter Sonya was diagnosed with severe childhood epilepsy. She is two years old. Here, let me show you." The picture on her mobile showed a small, broadly smiling face with the same hair and eyes as her mother. "The doctor said that Sonya needs weekly injections of a Swiss drug that is very expensive and very hard to get in Russia. It would cost me more each year than my whole annual salary." She gave Steve the figure in rubles. "When I asked him what would happen if we cannot get the drug, he shrugged his shoulders and said Sonya will be dead within a year." She took a tissue from her purse to wipe her eyes.

On one level, Steve was very moved by her tale. He made a quick calculation; she was talking about at least $100,000 per year. But the agent in him couldn't help suspecting that this might be a sob story fabricated for Maya's own personal gain or some kind of scheme cooked up by Russian counterintelligence to entrap him. On the other hand, her plight was just the kind of opening he was looking for. He'd play the next move.

"Maybe I can help you and your daughter," he said.

She looked at him wide-eyed. "It would be a miracle," she said.

When he returned to Moscow, he spoke with the embassy doctor and the CIA station chief. Yes, the medicine was extremely expensive, but $100,000 a year was a worthwhile gamble if they could turn Maya into an asset. Her military position could make her a remarkable resource. At first, Maya stared in disbelief at Steve a week later when he told her he would provide the medicine to save her child; then she broke into tears. "Thank you. You have saved my daughter. What can I say?"

"Don't say anything," said Steve. "Just keep meeting with me whenever you can. From time to time, I may have some questions for you. How many people know about your daughter's medical problems?

"Only the doctor and my former husband. I haven't even told my mother."

"I suggest that you change doctors and don't tell anyone else about the medicines."

"Of course. In any case, I'm sure my former husband doesn't care what happens to our child."

It was necessary for them to meet once a month for him to give her the medicine. They would have to arrange encounters that would not attract undue attention. After a few months, he finally admitted what she already had come to understand – that he was with the CIA. They were in a coffee shop on Stanka Street.

"I'm not going to lie to you," he said. "I am against this system, not against your country. You can also be a patriotic Russian and still work against the people who are ruining your homeland."

"And get the medicines for my daughter?"

Steve gazed directly at her and nodded. The questions began at a very low level, almost like shoptalk: the number of engineers in her cyber unit, the languages they worked with, their morale. As the months passed, his questions became more probing; the information she provided increasingly valuable. Steve's new source was attracting attention at the very top levels of the agency. Many of Steve and Maya's communications were via dead drops, but others required riskier face-to-face meetings, in parks, or cafes, or crowded subway stations.

It was at those meetings that they began slowly to reveal more of their inner selves to each other.

It was a very troubling time in Steve's own life. His wife, Marilyn, was building a career as a graphic artist, and needed to spend an increasing amount of time working with her publisher and gallery in New York. She finally rented an apartment in the East Village. She and Steve now met only every few months, when he returned on leave to the U.S. or she flew to Moscow. The absences were longer, the intimacy drained from their relationship. On two very different tracks, their lives were diverging. Steve realized he was looking forward more to his occasional meetings with Maya, than he was to his encounters with his wife.

It was about eighteen months after they first met that they became lovers. Maya had arranged to use the dacha of an old school friend for a meeting with Steve. She said it was to meet her lover. What was supposed to be a cover story turned out to be true. It was a cold winter day; they were sitting on a worn leather couch in the living room, staring at the glowing embers in the fireplace. She spoke about hopes for her young daughter; the world was changing so rapidly, who knew what was the course to follow? Steve told her how much he regretted not having such concerns, since he never had a child.

"Didn't your wife want one?" she asked.

"She wanted her own career. And I guess I was not that particularly interested. I also felt it would get in the way. So, somehow, we never got around to it. And now I'm over fifty. She's forty-two. It's too late."

"I've known many men over fifty to have children," she said. "And a woman can still have a child at forty-two." She fixed him with her pale blue eyes. "Do you love Marilyn?" She had never asked him that before, never called his wife by name.

"I did once, when we first met, and for many years after."

"Do you love her now?" she insisted, the flames from the fire played across her face.

He shrugged. "Now? I don't think so." He didn't add that he had fallen in love with Maya.

She asked if he would like a vodka. They had one glass and kept on talking, then they had another.

He placed his hand over hers and an electric current shot between them.

They made love that afternoon with a passion Steve hadn't known for years. In retrospect, he realized he had always known this would happen. He'd been drawn to Maya from the first moment he met her.

"This is crazy," she said, as she lay next to him. "There is absolutely no way this can work." She turned towards him, her lips just inches away. "You and me together. It can never last. It is insane."

"Insane?" Steve moved to kiss her.

She pulled away. "Insane. I'm setting myself to be abandoned. All my life has been like this. My father was killed in Afghanistan when I was five; he was beheaded by the Mujahidin. When I got married, I chose a skirt chaser. I man I *knew* would also leave me. We had a daughter with an incurable disease, and..."

Ed put his finger on her lips. "But your daughter, that's just fate. It's nothing to do..."

No," she interrupted him. "No, it's the same thing. I'm terrified she will also leave me." Her eyes bore into his, "And now... Now I'm with you, in a relationship that can never..."

"No. No. We will work something out." He pulled her down to him again, "We will work something out." They made love again. What was binding them together was far more powerful than any rational argument keeping them apart.

Yet Maya was right, Steve realized. What they were doing was totally insane. It was also completely contrary to CIA regulations. They would have to hide their affair now from Marilyn, the CIA, and Russian intelligence.

He had more success deceiving the professionals than his wife. Marilyn had flown in for a surprise visit from New York that morning. Steve, however, decided to keep the meeting he had set up with Maya the week before. Once again, Steve and Maya made love. Only this time, as fate would have it, the plumbing in her friend's dacha broke down. There was no way he could wash. Still he headed home planning to quickly take a shower at the apartment before Marilyn arrived. She had planned to see some friends for lunch; instead, when he walked through the door, she was there waiting for him. Lunch had been cancelled. There was no way he could avoid putting his arms around her.

Her reaction was instantaneous. "Who the hell have you been fucking," she said. "Her spoor is all over you! It's disgusting. How could you?"

Her outrage ended in a flurry of tears. Suddenly filled with remorse, Steve attempted to defend himself by offering an abbreviated version of the truth: this was a very brief liaison with a Russian woman he just recently met. It was an almost forgivable product of his frustration and loneliness at being apart from Marilyn. This one brutish act of his should not be allowed to destroy their marriage.

"You mean after screwing that woman you say you still love me?" She looked directly at him, her eyes red rimmed.

"Of course I do." He didn't really lie, he told himself as he took a long, hot shower. He tried to analyze his feelings towards Maya. Was it love or just infatuation? In any case, there was no real hope that their relationship could flourish into something permanent. His assignment in Moscow was up in another month. He would be transferred back to the United States before being sent to another posting abroad. In fact, he'd made no attempt to hide that fact from Maya. And though they never spoken about it, she also seemed to realize there was no way they could continue together.

Even if Steve left Marilyn, he could not return to live permanently in Russia, nor was there any realistic way he could bring Maya and her daughter to live in the U.S. In any case, Maya was adamant that she would never leave her sixty-five-year-old mother alone in Moscow.

Which left Marilyn. She was bright, charming, intelligent. Perhaps they really could start something new. That night he invited her to one of Moscow's top restaurants, The White Rabbit. He ordered champagne. "We've had a lot of problems," he said raising his glass to her. "We've grown apart. I'd like another try at creating a life together. I'm sure we can make it work."

Afterwards they returned to the apartment and made love.

A week later Marilyn flew back to the U.S. and began arrangements to move from New York to Falls Church and prepare for Steve's return from Moscow. Over the next few weeks Steve turned over the agents he was running, including Maya, to his replacement. He made sure that Maya's daughter would continue to get her medicine.

And Maya promised she would continue cooperating with the agency.

* * *

Steve was surprised to see Marilyn waiting for him at Dulles when he flew back to the United States. She was beaming and threw her arms around him. "Wow! Great welcome!" he said, pausing to catch his breath after a long, sensuous kiss. On the drive in, she talked excitedly about the house she'd rented, "But we may need something bigger," she grinned. He took his eyes off the road to stare at her. "What do you mean?" he said.

"Darling, I'm pregnant!"

Steve almost veered off the road. "Are you sure?"

"Positive."

"Wow, that's great!" he said, trying to collect his thoughts.

"This is exactly what we need to give us a new start," she said. "A real family."

Over the following months, Steve watched Marilyn's belly swell with new life, and felt he was falling in love with her again, but in a very different way. It was a wonderful time. The fetus she was carrying cleansed her of any lasting bitterness about Steve's fling with "that Russian woman." He also tried to forget about Maya, but it was difficult. From the Russian Desk in the agency, he continued to monitor from afar the valuable information she continued passing on. He couldn't help feel a spark of jealousy toward the replacement in Moscow who was now running Maya.

At the same time, he was also increasingly concerned about Marilyn. She was now forty-three, well past normal childbearing age. Her doctors advised her to slow down, and pull back from her professional life, but her career as an artist had taken off. She was determined to maintain her output, as well as attend hectic gallery openings in Washington, New York, and Miami. Still, all the scans indicated that the fetus was completely normal.

Her water broke three weeks early while she was painting in her studio at home. She phoned Steve and told him she'd already called a taxi to take her to the hospital. When Steve arrived, the doctors assured him everything would be fine. Then something went wrong. The experienced obstetrician who had been following Marilyn was on another case and couldn't get free. A much younger doctor was called in.

"Don't worry," Steve and Marilyn were told, "You're still in excellent hands."

Except the young doctor screwed up. Steve could never find out exactly what happened but Marilyn agonized in excruciating labor for more than thirteen hours. Her screams spewed out of the delivery room and down the corridors of the hospital. Steve desperately tried to help, wiping away the perspiration streaming down her face, telling her everything was going to be all right as her nails dug into his hand and her face turned gray. He was telling her he loved her more than anyone on earth when her heart gave out.

The cardiac arrest unit tried desperately to resuscitate her. As if in a trance, Steve watched the heart monitor. He didn't even realize that the nails of his right hand dug into the skin of the left hand until the blood flowed.

But the line stayed flat. They baby was born dead. It was a boy.

CHAPTER TWELVE:

Kabul and Falls Church

Immediately after the funeral, Steve requested to be posted to Afghanistan. He wanted to get as far as possible from the maternity ward in Falls Church, the horrific memories of Marilyn's agonized screams, and the pitiful corpse of the tiny child, which was buried next to his wife.

He spent more than two years in the turmoil that was Afghanistan, facing the daily menace of ambushes, suicide bombers, and improvised explosive devices. It might have been argued that the ongoing casualties the U.S. was suffering and the tens of billions of dollars that America continued to pour into the shattered country were worthwhile, if there were a glimmer of progress. But the truth was just the opposite. In one report after another, Steve documented the rampant corruption of the Afghan government--generals pocketing the salaries of thousands of phantom soldiers. He wrote of the hopeless internecine tribal conflicts, the soaring production of opium, the hundreds of billions of American aid supposed to be rebuilding highways and schools and power stations, going down the drain. But his reports were read, circulated, and filed away along with hundreds of other similar field reports that had been filed over the past few years. And the generals and politicians continued pouring American troops and tens of billions of dollars more aid into the country. Frustrated, his reports became increasingly shrill. It was all so futile.

Early in 2016, he was summoned urgently to pack up in Kabul and return to Langley. He was given no indication of the reason, whether it was to be dispatched to another assignment or relegated to opening mail in the basement. Within three days, he was back on the 7th floor at Langley, wearing a dark gray suit and red tie. He'd been ordered to report to Jim Page, head of the new Directorate for Cyber Security.

In the past few years, Steve's and Page's paths had crossed on several occasions within the agency. Page, in fact had many months ago sent a congratulatory message to Steve for having recruited Maya Chertkova. She'd turned out to be one of the best sources the CIA had inside Russia. Her code name was Dancing Bear. This morning, however, Steve was still concerned that his future with the agency was on the line.

The knot in his stomach loosened, however, when Jim came around his desk to shake hands warmly and offered a wide, friendly grin. "Thanks for getting back so quickly," Page said. "Must be pretty jet-lagged."

"Never get used to it," said Steve. He took a seat across from the Page and gazed at him warily. Always the natty dresser, he was wearing a blue Armani blazer, a club tie, and gray flannels.

"Any idea why we brought you back?" Jim smiled tightly.

"I figured someone upstairs finally got pissed off with my reports from Afghanistan, and I'm being pulled."

"Yeah, well actually, your comments did get under the skin of a few people around here. The stuff about record poppy production and battalions of phantom soldiers were not particularly appreciated at the White House and the Pentagon. They hit just as the appropriations committee was meeting. Or perhaps you didn't know that?" Again, the same thin smile. "But of course, there are a lot of people around here who support you." Steve wondered what Jim's own views were on Afghanistan, but Jim had always been reluctant to stake out a position until he knew what his bosses were thinking.

"So then why did I get yanked?" asked Steve.

Page rested his chin on his hands and gazed directly at Steve. "We want you to go back to Moscow on special assignment."

"Moscow?"

"We've some signs that the Russians under Kozlov are attempting to influence the presidential campaign here."

"That's pretty wild. I know they fooled around in the past during other campaigns."

"But nothing like this," said the director." He tapped a file on his desk. "As a matter of fact, we first got word of it from your Dancing Bear. But most of us didn't really take it too seriously. Never thought Kozlov would dare. But the evidence keeps growing. We'd thought their cyber threat would be, you know, attempting to take down an entire electrical grid, or destroy our ability to respond to a nuclear attack, but now it seems Kozlov may be out to subvert our whole electoral process."

"Everyone knows they experimented with cyber war in the Ukraine and in Georgia," said Steve. "But going after the U.S?"

Page slid a file across his desk to Steve. "For starters, you should read this article by one of their top generals. It was in a Russian army journal. Didn't get much notice, but it should have. He predicts the next world conflict will be largely fought and won on what he calls "the cyber battlefield.""

"I'd say he's right," said Steve, "but where do our presidential elections come in?"

"The general spelled it out. He talked about hacking to create mistrust, to provoke domestic strife, to turn the peoples of one country against each other."

"Hell," said Steve, "We've been doing that kind of stuff for years around the world. So have the Russians. So what else is new?"

Page frowned. "Sounds like a typical Steve Penn comment. Look, Steve, what we're talking about now is much more sophisticated." He was up now pacing back and forth across the office. "It's not just funneling money to opposition parties or playing up to the local generals. The Russians have got entire army units devoted to hacking, to computer espionage, to creating and disseminating fake news stories that look like the real thing. And the point is that – if the early evidence we've got bears out – the Russians have decided they can manipulate us like we're some third-world country."

"To what end?" said Steve. "Is there any evidence they control Stokes?"

"Nothing solid, it may be they're just out to weaken the Democrats. Not that Kozlov likes Stokes, but that he hates the alternative so much."

"Question," said Steve. "What if we do find out they really are trying to make Stokes president. And, despite our knowing that, Stokes actually wins. Then what do you do?"

Page tightened his mouth and raised both hands "That's above my pay grade," he said. "But as the director sees it, there is no way we cannot investigate this. There's going to be a task force set up with us, the FBI, and NSA. Only people that need to know will be informed. Otherwise top-secret." Page pointed his finger at Steve. "And you, lucky man, are our choice to head the CIA team. You know Dancing Bear better than anyone."

"Thanks for the honor," said Steve.

He wondered if they suspected how well he really knew Dancing Bear.

CHAPTER THIRTEEN

Moscow

So in the early spring of 2016, after two days of briefings and reading through classified files, Steve flew to Moscow. It had been only two years since he'd last been there, but despite the new highways and overpasses, traffic congestion seemed much worse. To keep his cover consistent with his previous tour he was assigned once again as an "agricultural attaché" to the U.S. Embassy. He was excited to be back: keyed up by the responsibility he'd been handed, stirred also by the thought of seeing Maya.

Using a dead drop, he left a message for her to confirm an evening meeting at a new CIA safe house; actually a two-room apartment on the fourth floor of an apartment building at 27 Smolensky Pereulok, just up the block from an Orthodox church. Steve arrived half an hour early. He wanted a few minutes to check out the apartment and gather his own thoughts before Maya arrived. There was a bottle of vodka and another of scotch and some packaged snacks on a shelf in the living room. He poured himself a Black Label, opened a bag of potato chips, stared at a watercolor print of birch trees on the wall, and thought of Maya. In his attaché case he carried a silk scarf for her from the duty-free at Dulles Airport, as well as the monthly supply of medicines for her daughter. His feelings about Maya, however, were in turmoil.

So much had happened in the two years since he'd seen her. Before, he'd been a married man cheating on his wife; now he was alone, Marilyn and their newborn child dead and buried. On the other hand, it was insanity to think of renewing his liaison with Maya. She was now one of America's prime agents in Moscow. Any attempt to add a romantic entanglement would only increase the likelihood of the Russians ultimately discovering what she was up to. It would mean the end of Steve's career, but it would mean a bullet in the back of the neck for Maya.

He answered the door when she knocked. His stomach was knotted, his pulse racing. He felt like a high school kid on a first date. She stood for a minute in the doorway looking at him; she was as beautiful as he remembered. But there were dark circles under her eyes and no warmth in her gaze.

"Hello again," was all she said. She brushed past him, walked into the living room, took off her dark brown cloth coat, and tossed it on a chair. She was wearing a white blouse buttoned to the neck and somber blue skirt. She sat on the sofa and looked at him without expression. "You have the medicines?" she asked. We've turned her into a high-priced call girl, Steve thought bitterly, paid to service a John – us.

He opened his attaché case and handed her the packet of medicines. "I brought this also for you," he said, handing her the gift-wrapped silk scarf. She examined the medicines, put them in her purse, but handed him back the gift package without even bothering to unwrap it. "You can give this to someone else," she said coldly.

"Maya, what's wrong?"

"What do you mean, what's wrong?

"You're dealing with me as if I'm the enemy."

"You are," she said quietly.

"Why? How?"

"Your blackmail."

"What blackmail?"

"Don't pretend you don't know."

"Believe me. I don't know what you're talking about."

"You really don't?"

He took both her hands. "Maya, for God's sakes, just tell me what's happened."

She looked at him and paused. "When this began, it was for the medicines for my daughter. I am against what my government is doing, but it was because I had to get those medicines that I started answering your questions – betraying my country."

"It had nothing to do with our feelings about each other?" said Steve.

Her lips tightened. "Yes, maybe, that also. But that only came later. It was the medicines above all. You knew that, you set out the trap for me."

Steve shook his head but said nothing.

She narrowed her eyes. "I am like a fish with a hook in its mouth. I live constantly with the fear of being discovered. Of being taken away and shot. My daughter sent to some orphanage. My mother dying alone in her apartment."

"It won't last," said Steve.

"You're so naïve." She glowered. "Six months ago, I told the man who took your place that I could no longer do this."

"You told George Phelps?"

"Yes, Phelps."

"I told him that my nerves were finished. That this had to end. You know what he said?"

Steve stared at her.

She put her hand over her eyes, "He said I had no choice if I wanted to keep getting those medicines. Then he said not only wouldn't there be no medicines but the agency would let the FSB know I'd been a traitor." Tears were running down her cheeks.

Steve continued looking at her in amazement. "Maya, listen to me. Before returning to Moscow, I read through all the reports about you that had been sent to Langley since the very beginning. There was no mention from Phelps, or anyone else, that you tried to break off. I swear!"

"I don't care what you read," she raised her voice. "That's what happened. Maybe he was too embarrassed to write the truth."

"Maya, I swear again, I never heard a word about this. Believe me, the first thing I'm going to do is talk with Phelps and find out what happened."

"I told you what happened," she was almost screaming.

Steve raised his finger to his lips. "I want to know who authorized him to make such a threat."

She sat staring at him, tears still in her eyes. "You people are the same as the FSB."

He took her hands, "Maya, listen to me. I will deal with this. I will get authorization for your daughter to continue getting medicine for the rest of her life. I promise. And there is absolutely no question of turning you over to Russian intelligence. That would be despicable. I'll see you also get additional payments to take care of your mother as well."

She paused and looked at him. "What do I have to do for that?" Again, he felt ashamed of the situation: dealing with her one would with a call girl.

"Just work with us for a few more months," he said. "Then, I promise it will all be over."

"Why a few more months?" She asked dully.

"Because we have a new, very urgent investigation; it was started by you."

"You mean Kozlov hacking your elections?"

"Yes."

"The strongest evidence we have comes from you,"

"It's all true," she said. "When have I ever given wrong information? It's my unit that's doing a lot of it. It's a stupid move. It will only hurt Russia."

"I believe you," Steve said. "But we need more facts, more hard proof. "

"Like what?" she said.

"We need to know who is responsible for it, does it go right to the top? Are Stokes's people involved in this at all? How are they doing it?"

"You are asking a lot," she said.

"You're the best source we have, Maya. This will be the culmination of everything you've done for us. Once this is completed, you will be completely off the hook. And I guarantee you, the medicines will continue for your daughter and for whatever your mother needs."

"How can I trust you?"

"You know how much I care for you." He said and then immediately regretted it. He wasn't again going to get ensnared by emotion.

"What about Marilyn?" she asked.

"She's dead," he said. "Along with our child."

She stared at him, her eyes wide.

"She died giving birth. We thought a child would save the marriage. It ended it."

"I'm so sorry for you," she said. "It must have been horrible."

"It was."

There was a pause as they both gazed at each other. "So," said Steve, "will you work a few more months with us? And then it will all be over?"

Her lips tightened. "I will, and you will keep your promise?

"I swear."

At 9:10 the next morning, Steve walked into the office of George Phelps on the fourth floor of the U.S. Embassy where the CIA's section was located. Phelps looked up, startled from behind his desk. He had his feet propped up and was reading the morning review of the Russian media. "Ever heard of knocking, Steve?" he said.

He was about forty, red hair, freckles, horn-rimmed glasses, pursed mouth, given to a permanent sneer, a graduate of both Harvard and Yale and never tired of letting people know it. He'd been with the agency for fifteen years, considered bright by many of his colleagues, but also a pompous, ambitious ass.

"Sorry about barging in," said Steve. "But I just met with Dancing Bear last night."

Phelps scowled, "Yeah, I heard after the fact. Thanks. I do the hard work running her for two years, get all kinds of good stuff, and you come waltzing in from Langley like you're king shit and take over."

"Look, Phelps, you've already been told I'm heading a special investigation. Sorry if it put your nose out of joint."

"And us lowly mortals are not even allowed to know what the investigation's about,"

"That's the deal," said Steve. "I didn't chase after this job, I was assigned it, and I intend to carry it out. By now, you should know how this place works. If you've got a problem, I suggest you talk to the chief or go whining to Langley."

Phelps's eyebrows shot up. He took his feet off the desk and faced Steve.

"Is that what you charged in to tell me?"

"No, I want to know if you ever threatened to reveal Dancing Bear's role to the Russians."

Phelps ears reddened. He refused to meet Steve's gaze.

"Answer me," said Steve.

"Who the fuck are you to talk to me like that?" asked Phelps.

"Either you answer me, you prick," Steve said, taking a step forward, "or I'm on the line to Langley,"

"I may have made a vague statement along those lines," said Phelps.

"When she said she had enough and wanted out," said Steve.

"Yeah, she thought she could just walk away after all the money we spent on her and her kid."

"And you told her you'd turn her into the FSB?"

The red flush in Phelps face had spread to his neck. "For Christ's sake, Steve, stop being a Boy Scout. I was just trying to keep her in line, put a little fear of God into her."

"You filthy son of a bitch," said Steve, putting both hands on the desk and leaning toward Phelps. "And you didn't make a mention of any of that, did you, in your reports back to Langley?"

"Because I talked her out of it," said Phelps. "There was no need to rock the boat." He was still defiant.

Steve balled his fists; his breathing quickened. He just managed to restrain the urge to leap across the desk and grab Phelps by his fleshy neck. "Don't you ever go near her again," he seethed.

"Since when do you give the orders around here?" Phelps snarled.

Steve pivoted and left the office, slamming the door behind him.

He went down the corridor to his own office and dispatched an encrypted message to Deputy CIA Director Jim Page. "Jim, just learned that after Dancing

Bear tried to end our arrangement two months ago. Phelps threatened he would blow whistle to the Russians. Dancing Bear still wants out and is clearly upset. I convinced source to stay on promising it would just be for few more months. Also promised that after it's over we would still continue our medical deal for life. This is the only way we can keep our asset on board. The amount involved is nothing compared to the value we get. Need urgent authorization from top." The top was the director of the CIA.

Two hours later, the answer came back. "Authorization granted from top for lifetime commitment. Good hunting."

Two days later in a very brief meeting in the packed corridors of the Belorusskaya metro station, Steve relayed that commitment to Maya. "That promise I made you has now been authorized by our government, at the very highest level," said Steve. "All we ask is a few more months."

"How can I trust you?" she said.

"Because I would never lie to you."

Her eyes narrowed. "We will see."

Over the following months in Moscow, as the U.S. election campaign pursued its frenetic pace, Steve's team uncovered increasingly shocking evidence. The Russian hacking was far greater in scope than even the most virulent Russophobes had previously suspected. As an officer in one of the Russian military units doing the hacking, Maya provided the most solid and devastating information. Almost all of it, however, was coming via dead drops and ciphered messages. Despite the risks involved, Langley was demanding that Steve have another extended face-to-face meeting with Maya to confirm the information she had secretly passed.

He set up another early meeting in the CIA safe house at 27 Smolensky Pereulok. It was a gray evening, pouring rain. Again, Steve arrived early and, despite the gravity of the business at hand, he still felt the same adolescent stirring in his loins, the tingle of desire. He could still smell her skin, feel the silkiness of her hair when she let it down over her shoulders. He remembered the way her nostrils quivered when she was aroused, the soft cry she made when she came. And yet he knew it was not to be. It was all a pipe dream.

He opened the door when she rang.

"Horrible weather," she said as she entered and brushed by him. She put her umbrella in a stand and took off her dripping raincoat "This has to be done in fifteen minutes," she said. Her cheeks were wet from the rain and flushed from the cold. Repressing a crazy desire to take her in his arms, he led her into the living room and motioned her to sit on the sofa; he took a chair across from her. She wore a white wool sweater and blue skirt that came to her knees. There was no sign of emotion on her face: she sat there stiffly, legs primly crossed, waiting for him to begin.

"Would you like something to drink?" he said picking up a bottle of vodka from the bookcase. "To warm you up."

She considered before she replied, "Very well."

He poured a glass for her, then one for himself. He raised his in the air in salute before he drank. Still grim-faced, she raised her glass slightly, then took a large sip herself.

"Maya, the information you've provided has been fantastic," said Steve, feeling the warm jolt from the vodka.

"What do you need to know?" she asked. Once again, he thought darkly, I've turned her into a call girl coming to service her client.

"I need to confirm some key points directly from you," he said, "rather than from coded messages."

"So you would know the messages were really from me?" she smiled bitterly.

"You don't know who could be feeding us information," said Steve. He didn't add that the listening device hidden in the living room would record all their conversation to be later played back to Langley.

"So what do you need to confirm?" asked Maya, taking another sip.

"First, that Russian army units have actually hacked into the files of both American political parties: the Democratic National Committee and the Republicans.

"That is correct," she said. "My own unit was involved. I imagine your bosses back at your headquarters will be listening to all this." Her eyes bored into his. "Next?"

Jolted by her bitterness, he still continued down the checklist. "That President Kozlov himself ordered the hacking."

"I saw the instruction myself. Next?"

"That Kozlov is doing this in order to elect Stokes."

"That I cannot say. I know he is doing it to undermine Stokes's opponent."

"How do you know?"

"I told you: I have seen the instructions."

"Could you get us a copy?"

"Of the secret instructions?"

"Yes."

"Impossible. Each is view-from-application only, access-monitored and watermarked with the name of the person receiving it. There is no way I can do it."

"You also say Russian intelligence has built up its own file on Stokes over the past several years."

"That is what I have heard from people who should know," she said. "I have not seen the files myself. But I have heard they contain very embarrassing pictures; pornography, starring Stokes."

She glanced at her watch.

"Just a few more things," said Steve.

"You say you have also heard that some people connected with the Stokes campaign may have been in contact with Russian authorities about how and when the hacked material could be released. Do you have any specific names?"

"None. I just know that it may be going on. Now I must go." She started to get up.

"Wait, there's something else you have to know. I've been ordered to return immediately to Langley to supervise the drafting of our final report."

Her eyes darkened. "So you are leaving again?"

"The irony is, it's because of you – because of the dynamite material you've given us." There was so much more he wanted to say. He wanted to reach across and embrace her, protect her, take her away from all this. Of course, with Langley listening, there was no way he could do any such thing. She gazed directly at him now with her pale blue eyes. Did she also feel a similar longing? There was no way to ask.

"Another thing," said Steve. "Phelps will no longer be your agency contact. I've made sure of that. Another person will be taking over. His name is Brian Hunt. I've worked with him for many years. You can trust him."

"What about your promise to me?" Again, she locked her eyes on his.

"Once our report is finished, we will never again ask you for information," he said. "That promise will be kept; I swear."

# CHAPTER FOURTEEN:

Langley

Astonishing how much had changed since he'd made that commitment to Maya just a few months ago, thought Steve. How could he have been so hopelessly naive? His mind in turmoil, he'd managed less than a couple of hours sleep on the red-eye from L.A. back to Washington.

He went home, showered, made a phone call, then headed for CIA headquarters at Langley. Depending on traffic, the drive took about twenty minutes. When he was not on assignment abroad, it was his daily route for almost thirty years. He could have driven it blindfolded. It was another bleak day, cold and rainy, spring still several weeks away. Though it was 10:00 a.m., his headlights were still on, traffic was crawling on the I-66, the windshield wipers beating a dismal tattoo. Talk radio was nothing but Stokes, Stokes, and more Stokes. Steve switched to classical FM on WETA.

They were half way through Mozart's "Requiem." He thought, what could be more appropriate?

Steve Penn's days were numbered. Stokes's private goons and his vast intelligence network would continue stalking Steve's every move, his emails, his conversations, his likeness, anywhere on the planet. And, inevitably, they would pounce at a time of their choosing, and eliminate him as easily as they murdered Brian Hunt. The conclusion was evident: There was no way the individual known as Steve Penn could lead Deep Strike.

He turned right onto Highway 123; the traffic was lighter, then right again on to Colonial Farm Road where the traffic sign baldly stated the "Central Intelligence Agency" lay ahead. That sign always amused Steve: to give the public a precise idea where the CIA was actually located was considered a highly controversial move back in 1967 when the sign was first posted; even though Soviet reconnaissance satellites were already mapping every square foot of the United States. Even admitting that the CIA existed was considered by some political hawks a breach of national security. For a long while, operators at the agency were instructed to answer "Executive 3-6115" instead of "Central Intelligence Agency." Today the organization was still so shrouded in secrecy that the precise number of employees, more than 15,000, and its ever-burgeoning budget, fifteen billion dollars, were considered highly classified secrets.

The U.S. also refused to publicly acknowledge the existence of the vast network of spy satellites covering almost every inch of the globe. Nor the fact, until revealed by Edward Snowden, that the mammoth National

Security Agency, with three times more employees than the CIA, was using technical means to sweep up just about every communication anywhere on the world including the United States. They were also the largest single employer of mathematicians anywhere.

When he first joined the CIA in 1983, Steve had hopes of playing a significant role in the global battle against the forces of evil. He really did. Over the ensuing years, however, he came to understand he was just a tiny cog in a huge, hopelessly bureaucratic mechanism. For the CIA was only one of sixteen American intelligence agencies, each with its own teeming bureaus and departments scattered across the world.

Even Steve had been taken aback in 2010 by a report in *The Washington Post* that there were 1,271 organizations and 1,931 private companies in 10,000 locations in the United States that were working on "counterterrorism, homeland security, and intelligence." The "intelligence community" – an expression that always made Steve wince – consisted of at least 854,000 people holding top-secret clearances. The total cost of all that was, of course, classified, but estimates ran up to eighty billion dollars.

The agency's sprawling headquarters buildings – called the CIA Campus, as if it were a bucolic sanctuary given to the study of poetry and philosophy – was on the right, not far from the Potomac River. He parked his car in the northern lot, opened his umbrella, and headed for the old headquarters building. He walked through the brightly lit marble lobby and past the biblical quotation etched in the wall: *"And ye shall know the truth and the truth shall make you free."* In light of what had happened to the Russian hacking investigation, he didn't know whether to cry or laugh aloud at the irony of those words.

He stood for a moment before the white marble Memorial Wall, with stars engraved for each of the 117 agents killed "in the line of service" since 1950. The names of eighty-four of those agents were inscribed in the Moroccan goatskin "Book of Honor" on a stand by the wall. The identities of the other thirty-seven remained secret, even after death. Steve had known fifteen of them. He wondered how many would make the supreme sacrifice a second time around, if they knew how their country was being run today. One thing was certain: there would never be a star commemorating Brian Hunt.

Steve walked past the uniformed guard, ran his card through the scanner, and took the elevator to the seventh floor. The hallway was decorated with large photographs depicting the progression of computers over the past seventy years. The sequence began with the mammoth ENIAC, built at the University of Pennsylvania during World War II, which needed 18,000 vacuum tubes and covered 1800 square feet. Forty years later came IBM's "Deep Blue," which vanquished world chess champion Gary Kasparov in 1997. Finally, there was the microscopic chip of D-Wave's newest quantum computer, 100 million times more powerful than the fifty-ton ENIAC. It would not be long, thought Steve before artificial intelligence and algorithms would completely do away with the need for analysts like himself.

At the end of the corridor was the office of Jim Page, head of the CIA's Directorate for Digital Innovations.

"Jim free?" Steve asked Page's executive assistant.

"You scheduled?"

"Called him an hour ago," said Steve.

The assistant checked his screen. "Go ahead, he just wrapped the morning briefing."

Page was sitting behind his large glass-topped desk talking quietly into a phone, as he read from a file. He waved Steve to the plastic and aluminum chair across from him, and raised two fingers to indicate he'd be just a couple of minutes more. Page was tall and thin, like a stork, with gray hair and wire-rimmed glasses perched on his large beaked nose. He had a short scraggly white beard, which he often ran his hands through when wanting to give the impression that he was pondering the weightiest problems.

There was an open book on his desk, a small, neat stack of files with the red classification label, a mug of coffee, a crocodile-framed picture of his wife and two kids, and four telephones. The orange one led directly to the CIA director's office. The bookshelves lining two walls were filled with abstruse tomes and academic journals covering every aspect of cyber technology. Steve knew that several had been authored by Page himself, though the bulk of his research was not available in open academic journals or textbooks, but restricted to a sophisticated elite with the requisite security clearances.

Page was the one who pushed hardest for the CIA to set up the new directorate in 2015. Its mission was to make sure they were at the cutting-edge of whatever was going on in digital and cyber tradecraft. After all, not just Russia and China, but nations all over the world were developing advanced cyber capabilities. The technology was relatively cheap; the potential threat, enormous.

A small group of dedicated military hackers, wielding sophisticated coding skills that were no longer the preserve of the developed world could take down a massive electrical grid, plunge an entire nation into darkness, destroy a country's ability to respond to a nuclear attack, or completely subvert the elections of the greatest democracy on earth as the Russian hacking investigation had shown.

The budget and staff of the DDI ballooned every year since it was founded. Page was fond of saying how there was definitely no end in sight to the expansion of his fiefdom. Steve had been his first choice to head up the Russian investigation. Back then, they both knew the issue would be sensitive, but they had no idea it would become as explosive as it ultimately did.

This morning Page was clearly uncomfortable; coiled, edgy, as he finished his call. He gave Steve a tight smile, but avoided his gaze.

"Get you some coffee?"

"No, thanks," said Steve.

"Looks like you're finally finished with the flu?"

Steve stared at Page bewildered for a second; then remembered the excuse he'd used to stay away from work over the past few days. "Yeah. Guess the flu comes with age."

"A lot of it going around," said Page. He paused, then leaned forward raising his eyebrows. "So, what's up, Steve?"

""That's what I was going to ask you."

"What do you mean?"

"It's pretty goddamn obvious from the way the hacking investigation is being buried that the career of anyone connected with it is toast. Certainly mine is."

"I'm not so sure," said Page, his eyes still elusive. "Jensen is still feeling her way around."

Monica Jensen, who Stokes had chosen to head the CIA, had formerly been a congresswoman on the Intelligence Community Oversight committee for three terms. Her picture was on the wall behind Page, next to a larger photograph of President Stokes.

"She doesn't have a clue about how we operate." said Steve.

Page gave a noncommittal nod.

"You managed to keep your job though," said Steve.

"What does that mean?" said Page.

"You played the game well, obeyed rules, kept your head down. Of course, you were director of the offending unit, but I was the one who wrote the report, who liaised with the other agencies, who briefed the congressional leaders. Once you sniffed which way the political winds were blowing, you didn't lift a finger to help. Hell, you were even too tied up last week to attend Brian's funeral."

Page stiffened but kept his expression neutral. "I had to go to the director's meeting. We sent flowers. But what exactly you getting at?"

"Tell me Jim, how do you go about briefing the guys from the White House?" said Steve, his voice rising. "These days they could be a direct wire to the Kremlin."

"I don't get it." Page's lips tightened, "You trying to talk yourself out of a job?"

"Let's not kid each other," said Steve. "It's obvious my career is deep-sixed. It's over. I'm not going to wait for a candy-assed executioner like yourself to tell me I'm fired or demoted to shredding classified garbage for the rest of my professional life."

Page raised his hand. "Steve, I highly recommend against doing anything precipitous. I understand your situation." But it was clear he was relieved by Steve's decision. He was suddenly solicitous, the tension drained from his face. "Why don't you take some time to think over your decision?"

"Thanks, I already have," said Steve. "Bottom line is I'm saving you the trouble of firing me outright. In return for going quietly, however, I want to make sure of a couple of things."

"What's that?" Page was abruptly suspicious again.

"First, that, despite what's happened to the investigation, Dancing Bear continues to get the regular payments we agreed upon as long as her daughter lives."

Page was silent for a few seconds, brow furrowed. He began stroking his beard.

Steve pulled a piece of paper from his inside jacket pocket. "I've got a copy of the email you sent to me with that guarantee," said Steve.

"That's classified," said Page sharply.

"I've still got clearance," said Steve. "Is the agency going to keep its word or not."

"We will, of course we will," said Page refusing again to meet Steve's gaze.

"If one day it does not," said Steve, "I warn you every major paper in the country will know about it. I'll blow this place sky high."

"Is that a threat?" Page's eyes darkened.

"It's a promise," said Steve. "Second thing, I'd appreciate it if the agency would give me a disability retirement, so that I can collect a decent monthly benefit and keep my medical insurance."

Page's brow was smooth again, the director obviously relieved that the conversation had returned to standard bureaucratic matters. "Should be no problem, Steve. I'm sure I can set that up. Can't say I blame you for your decision." He picked up a pen from his desk and twirled it in his fingers. "Sometimes I think I'd be happy to get out of this racket myself, but I've got a family to support. And I've signed so many secrecy agreements with the agency, I wouldn't be of much use in the academic or business world."

"C'mon Jim," said Steve. Your budgets are going to keep expanding exponentially. Cyber war is the flavor of the month. Your empire's going to grow and grow forever."

"Too bad you don't want to be part of it," said Page.

Steve leaned forward. "Between us Jim, I'm sick of it."

"Frankly," said Page, "I'd already heard via the grapevine that you wanted out."

"I haven't bothered to make a secret of it," said Steve. "I'm washed up. Why try to fight it?"

"Any idea what you're going to do?"

"Yeah, well, I thought I'd write a book about the inside story of the Russian hacking investigation, kind of an exposé? Already got a great agent."

Page smiled stiffly but couldn't hide his face turning white.

Steve shook his head. "Just kidding, I really have no idea what I'm going to do. Not having a family or real ties to anyone can be an asset when you're with the agency. When you're out..." He shrugged as his voice trailed off. "So how fast can you do the paperwork?

"A few days should do it. They'll of course be several documents for you to sign. Non-disclosure stuff, the usual. Any other forms we can always email to you, okay? And, uh, you'll return that classified email about Dancing Bear."

"Of course," said Steve rising from his chair, "Now I've got my house and furnishings to sell. Get rid of some other odds and ends. Then I'm gone. Frankly, I'll be delighted if I never see this part of the world again."

"Since that's what you want, consider it done." Page came around the desk to shake Steve's hand. "We'll miss you around here," he said with his best attempt at a smile.

"Sure you will," said Steve.

Page raised his hand, shaking his index finger in mock remonstrance, "But remember: no book."

"Don't worry," said Steve. "People wouldn't believe it, anyway."

* * *

That afternoon he phoned Gail Larsen, a real estate agent and also a neighbor. A few months ago, he'd invited her out for dinner a couple of times. She was a divorcée in her early forties, auburn hair, nice body, vivacious, easy to get along with. He thought it might lead to more; she certainly seemed interested. After the first two dates, she had invited him to her house for a candlelight dinner. She was wearing a simple black jersey dress that reached her knees with high neck and long sleeves that clung to her body, a long string of pearls, and high black heels. The spaghetti alle vongole was perfect. Steve had brought two bottles of Brunello. They finished them both. He felt very relaxed, secure, and happier than he'd been in a long time. After they'd eaten the dark chocolate mousse, he put his fork down and placed his hand on Gail's, the light from the candles reflected in her dark brown eyes.

"Why don't we have the next course upstairs?" he asked.

"Sounds like a good idea," she smiled, surprised by his unusual boldness.

They stood and embraced, their bodies pressing against each other, he slipped his hand under her dress, ran it up her leg and thigh, lifting the dress in the air. She was wearing black lace underwear. She reached for his belt. They began to undress each other even as they headed for the stairs. They tore off the rest of their clothes in the bedroom; then fell onto the bed and lay facing each other. "My God, you look like a twenty-year old," said Steve. She smiled then moved her eyes from his face to his crotch where his penis was wildly erect. "I could say the same for you," she said with a laugh.

They made love three times that night: twice before they went to sleep, once again in the morning when they woke. She made bacon and eggs for breakfast before they each hurried off to their own jobs. "It was marvelous," she told Steve before leaving, her eyes still radiant.

"I'd say fantastic," he said, as he headed for his car. He was humming to himself as he drove towards the highway and the road to Langley.

They never dated again. It was Steve who backed off, as he always did in such circumstances. There was a switch inside his skull; a switch he couldn't control. As soon as he got into a relationship that might actually go somewhere, that might demand he open up, lose his pervasive fear of getting too close, too intimate with someone else, he'd suddenly back off and run for the emotional hills. He'd done that with everyone except Maya. With her, it was the objective circumstances, not his own emotional scars that destroyed any possible future together.

Without mentioning Maya, he tried to explain his problem to Gail when she called him at home three days later, asking why she'd heard nothing from him. She was at first sympathetic. "We're so good together, Steve, I'm sure we can work this out," and then she became increasingly irate. He had to admit his excuses sounded lame even to himself. They finally met for coffee and, after a very long discussion, they agreed to remain "good friends."

But Gail was a successful real estate agent, and it made all the sense in the world for Steve to give her a call when he decided to quit the agency and sell his house. She was surprised at his decision. She never knew that he worked for the agency, just something to do with Homeland Security. She already knew his place; it was an ideal location, sound construction, and should move quickly.

"It's a good time to sell," she said, "but I'll miss you. Is it anything to do with another woman?" She asked cautiously. She had never lost a small hope that they could somehow come together again.

"Not at all," he said with a smile.

That evening, Steve got a call at home. "Steve, Ed Diamond. Sorry to disturb you outside of office hours. But I wanted to make sure to reach you." Steve immediately recognized the deep, portentous voice. Diamond was the lead reporter on *Focus*, the most watched news program in the country, broadcast every Sunday night. On the other hand, could someone at the agency be trying to set him up for a charge of leaking classified information?

"How did you get my number?" Steve asked.

"Can't really tell you," said Diamond. "One of my staff managed to dig it up. Again, sorry about the late hour. I wanted to know if I could come by to talk with you, informally."

"About what?"

"The Russian hacking investigation."

"Sorry, Ed, but no way. Everything is classified."

"Totally off the record?"

"Nope. No can do."

"You'd be doing a service to your country."

"Ed, I know all the arguments. Please, no."

"What about sometime in the future?"

"Who knows what the future may bring?" said Steve.

"Who indeed? At least let me give you my private number if case you ever change your mind."

Steve jotted it down.

Gail sold his house two days later to a couple who had just moved into the area, the husband working at the FDA. They also bought most of the furniture. Steve's car went at a bargain price to a neighbor who was a passionate hunter.

The rest Steve sold off at a garage sale that weekend, along with his mountain bike.

Gail Larsen dropped by. Steve absented himself from the sale for a couple of minutes, invited her into the kitchen, and poured them each a glass of wine. Her eyes were brimming as they toasted each other.

"You still haven't told me where you're going," she said, taking his hand.

"I'm not really sure," he said.

"Will you be back?"

He looked at her squarely, "Honestly? Probably not."

A tall, muscular man wearing a battered rain hat, yellow slicker, and jeans, wandered about the garage looking over various items. He finally selected several paperbacks at two dollars each. Steve looked over his choices: Le Carré, Furst, Deighton, Ludlum.

"You must be an espionage freak, like me. Enjoy."

"I plan to," said the man, handing Steve a $10 bill. He walked up the block, turned left at the corner, and headed for the gray Galaxy parked by the curb. He opened the front door and got in.

"Certainly looks legit," he said. "Selling just about everything he's got, telling everyone who'll listen he's leaving town for good."

"Maybe so," said the green-eyed woman at the wheel. Captain Jean Swanson turned to face the man. A large red scar disfigured her right cheek. "But I still think there's something going on," she said. "I'm sure of it."

CHAPTER FIFTEEN:

Cape Cod

The following day Steve took a cab to Reagan National Airport to catch the 2:00 p.m. Jet Blue flight to Provincetown on Cape Cod. He exchanged a few polite words with his seat neighbor, spent half an hour glancing through the *Times* and the *Post*, then fell into a profound sleep. He was dreaming about himself and Brian mountain-biking near Kabul—though they'd never biked in Afghanistan. In the dream, they were joined by Benjy, Steve's long-dead young brother. And then, suddenly there was Maya and her daughter peddling along, also part of the group. Benjy yelled that he couldn't keep up; they slowed down. Benjy still fell further behind. Finally, he began firing at them with an AK-47. As the bullets whizzed by, Maya was screaming, desperately trying to protect her child. Steve yelled at Benjy to stop, but the shots kept coming closer and closer. The nightmare abruptly ended when the plane bumped down at the Provincetown airport. Steve was breathing rapidly, his palms damp. What the hell gave rise to that God-awful dream?

He picked up a two-door silver Toyota at Avis, tossed his bags in the trunk, and drove half an hour along a narrow road to the town of Truro. There were dunes and wild grass on both sides of the road; the ocean and bay just a few miles away on each side. In the summer, the long white beaches attracted thousands of tourists. The pounding surf in some stretches made it a favorite of windsurfers. There was also a picturesque old stone lighthouse, humpback whale watching, and fishing; fishing was Truro's particular pride. It was also what brought Steve to the area.

Today, it was gray and cloudy, too early in the season for tourists or swimmers. A few hardy souls were surfing with wet suits. At 5:30 p.m. Steve checked in to the Alverton Inn, a 19th century gothic revival hotel, perched on a grassy hill above the town. The perfect setting for a dark Brontë novel, thought Steve as he walked along a dimly lit corridor to his room on the third floor. He ate by himself in the hotel restaurant that night. During the season, the tourists fought for reservations; this evening, the dining room was quiet, only two maroon-jacketed waiters on duty. Steve ate alone, reading the latest novel of Martin Cruz Smith. He ordered clam chowder, seared tuna, and a half bottle of Chassagne Montrachet. His waiter was a young man who also worked at the desk during the day. "First time here?" He asked as he brought the chowder.

"It is," said Steve. "Lovely spot."

"You should come again later in the spring. The wildflowers are sensational."

"Never too early for fishing," said Steve.

"You a big fan?"

"Did a lot when I was younger, around Seattle—mainly salmon," said Steve. "I've been hearing about the Cape for years. Finally got a chance."

Mercifully, there were no anguished dreams to trouble his sleep that night. He woke at 7:15 a.m. to the squawking of seagulls flying about the towers of the hotel. He opened the window, breathed in the salt air and gazed across the rolling green lawn of the hotel toward the ocean. The surf was light, the water slate gray like the sky overhead. He showered, skipped shaving, and dressed in a heavy plaid shirt, jeans, and sneakers.

The same waiter as the night before served him breakfast: coffee, grapefruit juice, two eggs sunny side up, crisp bacon, and toast. He downloaded *The New York Times* on his iPhone, checked the weather forecast: gusting winds in the afternoon but little chance of rain. He drank another cup of coffee and signaled for the bill.

"Thanks, good luck," said the waiter, pocketing the generous tip. "Watch out for the wind."

In the summer, the streets and sidewalks of Truro would be packed, but at this time of year, the village felt like a ghost town. Steve drove east along Main Street, turned right to Pamet Harbor and stopped in front of a one-story building facing the water. There was a large painted sign above the door: "Real Deal Fishing Charters." Steve had found the company on the internet, checked it out. It was ranked number one for activities according to Trip Advisor. He called to reserve a fishing boat for the day. He'd pick it up at 8:00 a.m.

It was warm and cozy inside the charter office. The morning news was being broadcast on the TV perched on the wall. A burly young man in jeans and a thick Hudson Bay sweater was behind the counter, just pouring a cup of coffee. Two walls were filled with photos of beaming fisherman of all ages displaying their shimmering catches.

"Morning," said Steve. "You're Randy?"

"Right. And you're Steve Penn?" Randy had long stringy blond hair that hung almost to his shoulders, blue eyes, and a gold ring in one ear.

"Your boat's tied up at the dock, all fueled and ready to go. Just like I promised."

"Great."

"Just need you to pay and sign some papers."

Steve filled out the forms for insurance and a waiver of responsibility, then handed the young man his credit card. The price for the day was $500, to be paid in advance.

"We're expecting it to blow a bit this afternoon, northeasterly," said Randy as he led Steve down to the wooden dock. Steve was wearing his backpack over a waterproof orange parka, and carrying a green canvas bag. The powerboat he'd rented, a white 22-foot Triton with black trim, bobbed by the dock. Randy jumped in first; Steve handed him his gear, then came aboard as well.

"Should be just what you want," said Randy. He pointed to the large red outboard clamped to the stern. "That's a 250-horse Merc; all the power you want. He indicated the controls. "There's your radio, compass, GPS, and radar fish-finder, CD player with an iPod input. All pretty straightforward. Here's the charts you'll need. Any questions?"

Steve took a moment to look over the controls. "Thanks, I'll be fine. Done a lot of fishing over the years."

Randy continued the briefing. "I've put a few rods for you to use over there, along with a box of lures. There's also a live bait well. Lifebelts, there. Life raft, just pull this to inflate. Here's the personal satellite locater beacon. You turn it on like this. In any case, it also goes on automatically in the water. There's the cooler. I put in a six-pack, some water, and granola bars like you asked. It's on the house."

"Thanks," said Steve.

"Wanna give it a try?"

Steve turned the ignition; the engine immediately roared to life. "Sounds great," he said, letting it idle.

"Well, good luck," said Randy as he jumped back on the dock. "Like I said, we're expecting a bit of a blow this afternoon. Seas can get a bit heavy, but you've got a great boat here, and you seem to know your way around. Any trouble, give a shout on the radio. We can get to you in a jiffy. Make sure you're back by 5:00 p.m. latest. Don't want you out after dark."

"Got it," said Steve.

"Should be good fishing. A guy last week caught a 90-pounder. Too bad you're going alone," Randy said as undid a mooring line and tossed it to Steve.

"Maybe next time," said Steve. "Sometimes it's just nice to get away by yourself."

"Sure, know what you mean," said Randy, tossing Steve the last line.

Steve stood, sheltered by the windscreen, feet planted wide and slowly backed the boat away from the dock. Once clear, he edged the throttle forward and turned to wave to Randy, still watching from the dock. Then he pulled the three white bumpers from the water and carefully stowed the lines.

Out of the harbor, he pushed the throttle further forward and the bow began thumping the incoming waves, then rose to plane, leaping from crest to crest. Steve breathed in the crisp, iodized air and turned to watch the foamy wake spread out behind him. The beach homes and trees and brown sandy dunes sank towards the horizon as he goosed the throttle and roared out to the open waters.

About a mile out to sea, at one of the spots indicated by Randy, Steve picked up some fish on the radar. He slowed to five knots, set out a couple of rods, and began trolling. He listened to Ella Fitzgerald from the playlist on his iPhone and watched the low gray line of the Cape slide past in the distance. After a couple of hours, he hooked his first tuna, darting silver in the dark waters beneath him. It was a strong fish and their struggle lasted more than twenty minutes, until Steve fought it to a standstill. He pierced it with a pike, hoisted it into the air and brought it down quivering to the deck, where he dispatched it with a sharp blow to the back of the head. Got to weigh at least forty pounds, he thought. Too bad there was no one to take a picture.

That was enough fishing for the day. The gray of the morning gave way to glimpses of sunlight and blue as the wind chased the clouds across the sky. Steve continued leisurely up the coast, ate the grilled chicken the hotel had prepared for him. Then he wiped his hands and wrote a short note on a piece of stationery he'd taken from his room the night before. He placed the note in a plastic folder, which he firmly taped to the inside of the windscreen. That done, he sat down to reread one of his all-time favorites, "The Polish Officer" by Alan Furst.

At 2:00 p.m. he was six miles east of Provincetown, approaching the prearranged GPS coordinate. The other boat was already there, a twenty-four-foot Harborcraft, white-hulled with green trim, a rental from The Boat House in Provincetown. The tall, lanky figure in the stern was wearing a blue woolen cap, a yellow waterproof parka and jeans. Charlie Doyle waved at Ed; then tossed a dingy into the water attached by a rope to Charlie's boat. Ed retrieved the dingy with a boat hook, then cut his own engine, lowered the tuna he'd caught into the dingy, then jumped in himself and waited while Charlie hauled him hand over hand back to Charlie's boat.

"Great to see you," said Steve, clambering up the swim ladder, then turning to pull up the tuna as well.

"What the hell am I supposed to do with that?" said Charlie.

"Thought your girlfriend might enjoy it," said Steve. "It's worth a fortune at today's prices."

"I love fish," said Charlie "Brenda hates it."

"Your problem," said Steve. "Now let's get going."

The blue sky had lost its battle with the dark gray clouds and a cold northeasterly blow was coming up. Charlie pushed the throttle forward and pancaking from wave to wave, the boat headed back toward the

Cape, leaving a wide, frothing wake behind in the darkening sea. Charlie pulled up to the private dock of a home south of Provincetown, made the boat fast with one quick loop around a cleat, and left the motor idling.

"You know your way around boats," said Steve

"Told you I did. Hell, I used to go fishing all the time in Detroit." He handed a key ring to Steve. "Car's parked in front, blue Chevy from Hertz. The house belongs to a friend of mine. It's empty, been on the market for a year. He undid the rope and backed away from the dock. "Bon voyage!" he yelled, as he pushed the throttle forward; the bow rose and he headed back up the Cape.

Later that afternoon, as Randy had warned, the Northeaster picked up, gusts reached thirty knots an hour, whipping up white caps on the dark jade rollers cascading in off the Atlantic.

At 5:00 p.m., when Steve was supposed to have returned his boat, there was still no sign of him at The Real Deal rental shop. At 6:30 p.m., he still hadn't shown. Randy had planned to cook dinner for his girlfriend – he'd bought all the ingredients – but was unable to close up shop. He tried to reach Steve via VHF, but got nothing but static in reply. At 8:00p.m., he called off his date and phoned the Coast Guard station at Falmouth.

Within fifteen minutes, their orange and white MH 60 chopper, with a two-man search and rescue crew, rose from the pad and headed for Truro. They ran more than two hundred and fifty such missions every year. The ocean was dark and storm-tossed, and visibility was poor. There was no sign of the missing boat: no flares, nor signal from the satellite locator beacon.

It was their radar that finally picked up the black speck, the boat, lying on its side in the surf twenty miles north of Truro. There was no trace of Steve. The life raft was still on board; it had never been inflated. They continued the search at sea and along the beaches for another three days but Steve's body was never found. What they did find was a message inside a plastic folder taped to the boat's wind-screen.

It was a simple hand-written suicide note, with the day's date noted on the upper right hand corner:

To whom it may concern,

I have decided to end a life that no longer has any purpose.

I know that the nice people who rented me this boat are covered with insurance. I apologize for any inconvenience this may otherwise cause.

I have used weights to ensure my body will come to rest on the bottom of the ocean. At least it will provide nourishment for the fish.

Steve Penn

When word of the note got out, most of those who knew him were not surprised. Once he left the agency, he really had nothing to live for. No other vital interests, no family to support him, always something of a loner. He'd sold almost all his belongings, like a man coolly planning to do away with himself. Despite the note, the Coast Guard continued their search.

Though the media on the Cape played up the story, Steve's disappearance was ignored by the rest of the nation with one exception: Martha Jenkins, a reporter with credentials from the Boston Globe, turned up the day after the search ended to write a human-interest story about the mysterious disappearance, she said. She was very thorough, spent two days retracing Steve's short stay in the area, talked at length with the waiter who'd served him dinner and breakfast at the hotel. She also spent an hour over coffee with Randy and interviewed the rescue crew at Falmouth, and even examined the wreck of Steve's boat, which had yet to be removed from the beach.

Randy and his girlfriend checked the *Boston Globe* each day for the next week, searching for the article on Steve's tragic disappearance. Finally, Randy called the features editor to be told that no such report was in the works. And when he asked to speak with Martha Jenkins, he was told that the folks at the *Globe* had never heard of her.

"Have to admit there was something a little weird about her," Randy told his girlfriend. "Fantastic green eyes but a red scar down the right cheek. Wonder what that was all about?"

* * *

Two weeks later, they held a memorial service for Steve. Ironically, it was at the same church in Arlington where the funeral was held a month earlier for Brian Hunt. The same small choir sang a medley of Steve's favorite Leonard Cohen songs. There were several bouquets of flowers – the largest a display of fifty-three roses, once for each year of Steve's life – that were sent by Steve's real estate agent, Gail Larsen. Brian's widow Joanne was there, along with Sarah Levin, Charlie Doyle, and a few other of Steve's friends from the agency, as well as Bob Peterson president of the local mountain bikers club.

Jim Page, Steve's boss at the agency, delivered a moving, if brief, speech praising Steve's patriotism and character, though he had to be short on specifics on what Steve actually did. Joanne spoke about what a wonderful friend Steve was to her and her husband and their family. Rather than speaking, Sarah Levin walked to the pulpit where her cello was leaning. "I want to express my sadness through music, not words," she said, taking a chair and draping herself and around her cello. The church was filled by the slow, wistful third movement of Dvorjak's Concerto in B minor. Afterwards, there was a pause. It was not clear that anyone else wanted to talk until Gail Larsen approached the pulpit. She had barely begun when she broke into sobs and was unable to finish. "It's all so sad," was all she could say.

No one noticed the woman sitting near the door in the last pew, with green eyes and the red scar on her cheek. She remained until the end of the service.

CHAPTER SIXTEEN:

Switzerland

Steve had had no trouble locating the car that Charlie left for him by the seafront home on the Cape. The drive to Boston's Logan Airport took about two hours. Steve could have made it quicker, but he was feeling weary and stopped at a diner in Hyannis for two cups of watery coffee. At the airport, he returned the Hertz car, unloaded the two suitcases packed with his belongings that he'd earlier given to Steve, and headed for the international terminal. The ticket for the Swissair flight to Zurich was in the name of George C. Hardy, as was the Canadian passport, which Charlie had arranged for $10,000 from a talented forger in Toronto, who used to freelance for the Canadian equivalent of the CIA. Steve slept for most of the seven-hour flight, until he was gently awakened before landing by the stewardess who served him yogurt, muesli, a croissant, and coffee.

The Zurich airport was crowded with early-morning passengers and Swiss anti-terrorist police, who patrolled the terminals in groups of three wearing bulletproof vests and carrying Heckler & Koch MP5 service rifles. They were on high alert; a suitcase bomb claimed by al-Qaeda had killed two and wounded fourteen others at the Geneva Airport just the week before.

Steve showed his Canadian passport at customs and retrieved his luggage. He then picked up a Renault Megane from Europcar and took the E-25 west. It was a wonderfully clear day; the kind that enables Switzerland to live up to its travel poster image. Just a few puffs of white veiled the jagged peaks of the Matterhorn and Mont Blanc, but the rest of the Alps rose breathtakingly stark and white against the cobalt blue sky.

He turned off the E-25 to the A7, took the Montreux exit, and followed the signs to Clinique La Prairie, a spa, and hotel. The complex sprawled over seven acres of green hillside that sloped to the eastern end of Lake Geneva. It was one of Europe's most prestigious centers for anything related to health and well-being, and included a five-star hotel where guests could rest after a hard day in hydrotherapy, mud baths, seaweed treatment, and deep muscle massage. What La Prairie offered most of all, however, was privacy and discretion.

Steve had decided the only way to carry out his mission – to survive in the post- Orwellian world where U.S. intelligence agencies vacuumed up every digital communication on the planet, and satellites and drones and millions of street cameras could identify individual faces hundreds of miles distant – was to disappear and recreate himself with a new face that even his former wife wouldn't have recognized. Which is why he'd come to La Prairie.

He dropped his car with the hotel valet, walked past a couple of elderly Germans in fluffy white Frette bathrobes on the way to the spa, and checked in at the registration desk. The bellboy escorted him to his room on the fourth floor overlooking the lake. He unpacked, showered, and dressed in a pink shirt with a blue cashmere sweater, light gray flannels, and loafers. At 10:55 a.m., he walked along a serpentine flowerbed exploding with yellow and red tulips to the three-story gray concrete building that housed the Centre for Plastic and Reconstructive Surgery. The office of the director, Doctor Neil Bilstrade, was on the third floor, with a stunning view of the Matterhorn and Jungfrau. The doctor greeted him with a dry, confident grip.

"Delighted to meet you finally, Mr. Penn," he said, clipping his vowels with a slight Scottish accent. He had curly brown hair, light blue eyes, and a ruddy complexion, thanks to regular weekends on the nearby ski slopes.

It was Sarah Levin who'd told Steve about Bilstrade. He'd been twice used by the agency to deal with difficult cases that had to remain confidential: one agent who'd had his jaw half shot off in the Ukraine, the other a former head of the Romanian secret police who needed to be furnished not just with new papers but a new face as well.

Born in Glasgow, Bilstrade studied medicine at Cambridge, specialized in plastic and reconstructive surgery. After his residency, he spent seven years in Rio perfecting his skills under Dr. Ivo Pitanguy. He came to La Prairie first as deputy director, then was promoted to director, a post he'd held for the past fifteen years. His discretion was as valued as his surgical skill, which was legendary and the subject of countless magazine articles and documentaries.

Behind him on the wall was a rogues' gallery of before and after pictures of patients he'd treated over the years. He was, of course, unable to reveal anything about his more illustrious cases. The leading European and British tabloids, the American movie magazines, and gossip columnists would have paid a fortune for such information. But no such leaks ever occurred, which was the main reason Steve was there. Just the same, he would be known by everyone at La Prairie, including Doctor Bilstrade, as George Hardy. There would be nothing in the file to connect Hardy to Steve Penn.

"I hope you had a good flight, Mr. Hardy," said the doctor. "Can I offer you a tea or coffee?"

"Coffee, thanks, and please call me George." The doctor passed the order to his receptionist; then looked brightly at his visitor. "It's nice to finally meet you in person," he said. Via an untraceable server, Steve had already sent the doctor pictures of his face taken from all angles, plus X-rays, scans with 3D reconstruction, and the results of a series of lab tests.

"So you want a total redo?" The doctor pursed his lips. "Despite the fact that you have no evident physical defects."

"What I'm after," said Steve, "is a radical change of appearance that will still leave me physically presentable, shall we say, but unrecognizable to my own mother, if she were still alive."

"And as I understand it, you want me to accomplish this miracle in a maximum of four weeks?"

Steve paused to accept a cup of coffee from the receptionist and waited until she'd left before he answered. "Unfortunately, that's all the time I can spare. I'm a man in a hurry, a lot of urgent things to attend to."

The doctor shrugged. He was used to not asking searching questions of clients who obviously didn't want to be probed. "If I may be very frank, Mr. Hardy, I am not a man to be pushed around. And I certainly don't need more patients. On the other hand, I find your case interesting. I enjoy a challenge." He turned to the wide screen on his desk and brought up two high-definition color images; on the left, a front and side view of Steve as he currently appeared, and on the right, a front and side view of another high-cheeked man, with a fleshier face, beard, large nose, and prominent chin.

"That's your before and you after—the you I am planning to create," said the doctor. He smiled and raised his eyebrows. "So what do you think?"

"That's me?"

"In four weeks."

"Impressive. Never mind my mother, I don't think I'd recognize myself. How are you going to do it?"

"It will involve a number of procedures. We will use rhinoplasty to change the shape of your nose – make it bigger – perhaps somewhat Roman.

"How?"

"We make all the incisions on the inside of the nose, little cuts, lifting the soft tissues away from the skeleton," he pointed to the image on the left of Steve as was. "That allows us to open the nose like you would open the bonnet of a car, and then build up the bone and cartilage.

"As for your cheeks and jaw and chin, we will make them more prominent. We'll use custom-made synthetic implants designed from the CT scan data you sent me, here and here, along onto the cheek bone area, and there, at the point of the chin. We can also take fatty tissue from other parts of your body and flesh things out a bit here and there. We'll also change the angle of the jaw to make a wider mandible."

"Mandible?" asked Steve.

"Jaw bone. We can do all that with incisions in the mouth, so we don't leave any scars on the outside."

"No telltale scars?"

The doctor shrugged, "There'll be some swelling and bruising of course, but that will only last a couple of weeks. The injured tissue will slowly go through the color of the rainbow; like this." He digitally manipulated the image of Steve on the right-hand screen. "Dark purple then red and blue and yellow green. Then the discoloration descends with gravity, like this, down through the tissue down into the neck, until it disappears.

"As for changing your hair style and color, obviously no problem there. I'll make an appointment with one of our beauticians. The optometrist in the clinic can deal with the color of the eyes with contact lenses. And the shape of your body? If you were grossly overweight, we could of course do something surgical about that, but you're not. So it depends on how much exercising and dieting you're willing to put up with. The spa is fully equipped and we've got two professional dieticians on staff.

"Of course," said the doctor, "we could do more."

"What do you mean?" said Steve.

"I don't want to get into matters that don't concern me, but if your worry is to totally insulate yourself from modern facial recognition technology—well, that would be a much more radical procedure, and could never be done in just a month."

"What kind of procedure?"

"I'll show you," said the doctor, pointing again to the image on Steve's face on the screen and moving the cursor between Steve's eyes. "You see the distance between your eyes is--uh--60 millimeters. That's a key measurement for sophisticated facial recognition technology. That's something we could only change by moving your orbits, or eye sockets. We call that a 'box osteotomy.' Unfortunately, that could put your vision and other nerves at great risk.

Steve shuddered inwardly.

The doctor continued, "You're also talking months of very sophisticated procedures."

"I'll skip that."

"Of course, there is also gait analysis."

"Gait analysis?"

"It's how you walk. Each of us has our own unique way. And now there are sophisticated cameras and computers that can identify someone based on that characteristic alone."

'How do I change that?"

"You don't. We're stuck with it."

As the doctor continued talking, Steve gazed out the window, across the lake to the mountains, where the sun was bright on the peaks of Mont Blanc. He'd gone skiing there once many years ago with Marilyn, his first wife, for their honeymoon. The conditions were perfect—blue skies, deep powder. They'd spent the days with a guide exploring the endless slopes. In the evening, they drank white wine from Neuchatel, ate fondues, escargots, and raclette. Later they made love, and talked excitedly about plans for a family, for their future; a future that never happened.

He suddenly felt a vast emptiness in his gut, a surge of fear. He'd forfeited everything from that past. Now here he was so many years later planning an even greater loss by ceding his identity to the strange, unfamiliar face peering at him from the right side of the screen, the visage he was about to become. It was as if he were consigning his real self to oblivion.

The doctor brought him back from his reverie. "You also said you wanted to change your voice. Is that still the case?"

"If it can be done within the time span I've set."

The doctor stroked his chin. "I've spoken with a couple of colleagues who specialize in that region of the throat. It is possible to feminize a voice; that is, make it higher pitched by splitting one of the cartilages in the voice box. That shortens the vocal chords reducing the wave length and making it higher."

"Not what I'm after," said Steve.

"I assumed that. It's difficult to make a voice deeper but we could inject filler, hyaluronic acid, to roughen the voice or make it more hoarse."

"How would you do that?"

"Endoscopy, a tube down the throat. Again, no external cuts on the body. A colleague would be doing it, not me."

"Tell your colleague I'm game," said Steve, letting out a deep breath, "So, doctor, when do we start?"

"This afternoon, after lunch. As we originally planned. If you're not too tired, of course. In any case, over the next few weeks, you'll be asleep much of the time."

CHAPTER SEVENTEEN:

San Francisco/Washington, D.C.

It was about five weeks later and five weeks after the memorial service for Steve Penn, that Doug Robb, a tall, broad-shouldered man, rented a three-room apartment in the Jasper Building at 45 Lansing Street in the Rincon Hill neighborhood of San Francisco. The Jasper, with 320 residential units and thirty-nine floors, was one of several spectacular new high-rise apartments that shot up like a giant steel and glass forest in San Francisco over the past few years.

They are home to many of the Internet technology warriors, who have invaded San Francisco, swarming north from Silicon Valley; young men and women who pulled down huge salaries and/or hold stock options from absurdly successful companies with names like Uber, Facebook, Netflix, Google, AirBnB, most of which manufactured nothing but boasted net a worth greater than General Motors or Ford or General Electric and offered services that weren't even dreamt of a decade ago.

Doug Robb was paying $8,000 a month rent for his apartment. It was on the 29th floor, with a stunning panoramic view of the city, day and night. It was equipped, of course, with all the magical accoutrements required to attract discerning young residents. Doug was in his early 50's and older than most of the other tenants. He had hazel eyes, a strong roman nose, full cheeks, and a prominent chin. His black hair was graying at the sides. Gray also flecked his light moustache and neatly trimmed beard.

"I'm here to reinvent myself," he told Ronnie, the bartender, who offered him a free welcoming beer the day after he moved in. Doug was polite and well-spoken with a deep resonant voice, but tended to keep to himself much to the disappointment of several female tenants, who regularly worked out alongside him in the gym or watched him swim laps in the 20th floor pool.

He'd been an investment consultant back East, he told Ronnie. "Got left a pile of money by an aunt because I was her only living relative. So I decided I could afford to come to SF and try to strike it rich." He was investing for himself and a few friends, running his own start-up fund. "I'm in it for the thrill of the chase," he chuckled, accepting another beer. "But I'm not kidding myself about the chances. It's like the Gold Rush all over again. It's the people who sold the miners their supplies who got rich; almost all the miners went broke."

His business card stated simply, Douglas H. Robb, President, DHR Investments. There were a PC and a couple of laptops on the glass-topped desk in the second bedroom, which he had converted into an office. There was also a printer, but no files, not even sheets of paper. He was rarely on the phone, spent hours every day taking long walks through the Presidio or along the beach toward Crissy Field. After a week, he bought himself a mountain bike and every few days would head off in his Toyota to explore Mount Tam and the hills of Napa on the other side of the startling blue bay.

In his desk drawer, he had his American passport and birth certificate. In his crocodile wallet were six credit cards, a driver's license, social security card, health insurance card, membership in the Harvard Club, and a CV that went back fifty-three years to his birth in Brookline, Massachusetts. It was backed up by framed degrees from Harvard College and Wharton Business School and membership in the Society of Financial Analysts, which hung on the wall by his desk – all in the name of Douglas H Robb.

In fact, the real Douglas H. Robb had passed away forty years ago. He was hit by a car in Brookline while riding his bike home from school. About half a century later, his identity was usurped by another man who apparently committed suicide in the waters off Cape Cod, Steve Penn. From Switzerland, Steve had Fed-Exed a passport picture of his new self to Charlie Doyle, who then completed the application for an American passport in the name of the hapless Baltimore teenager, Doug Robb.

For the rest of his life, however, Steve could never rid completely banish the occasional twinges of disbelief when he looked at the person staring back at him in the bathroom mirror.

* * *

The Eisenhower Executive Office Building, in Washington D.C., is located just west of the White House on 17th Street between Pennsylvania Avenue and New York Avenue. It was completed in 1888, in the grandiose French Second Empire style, with curlicues and gables, a brassy intruder to the austere neoclassic world of federal Washington. For years, it was the world's largest office building; it was also considered a monstrosity. Mark Twain referred to it as "The Ugliest Building in America." The architect ended his life by suicide. As time passed, it became increasingly inefficient and outdated, a huge rambling artifact. But then in 1969, it was rescued and transformed from a Washington eyesore on life support, to a National Historic Landmark, and a fortune was spent to resuscitate the vast, quaint structure.

One of the officials working there in a subdivision of "the Office of the President," was George Ramos. He offered a crisp "good morning" as he showed his pass to the female marine guard at the Pennsylvania Street entrance. She smiled warmly in return, and why not: Ramos was forty-two years old, a strikingly handsome man with glossy black hair, arched eye brows, and an athletic build. Added to that, a jutting metallic jaw, sensuous lips, and flashing white teeth that could have honored an Hermès perfume ad.

There was also the way he strode down the entrance hallway as if he owned the place, past the busts and portraits of fifteen presidents and a host of legendary military commanders who once also had their offices here. Indeed, George's career was definitely on the rise again. He was rubbing shoulders every day with the movers and shakers in the government. Not bad for someone who less than a year earlier thought his professional career was washed up.

He scurried up the marble staircase to the second floor, walked along the marble corridor to a large door with a bronze plaque on which was engraved "Executive Liaison Office." The door opened to a suite of offices. His was the largest, with a commanding view of Pennsylvania Avenue.

On the wall were various pictures: one of himself in Special Forces battle dress with a group of Afghan soldiers at a fire-base near Kandahar; another of him standing before a tank in Fallujah, with cheering Iraqi soldiers after they'd just retaken the city. Behind his mahogany desk, hung an AK-47 mounted on a plaque. His team discovered it in a cave in the Tora Bora Mountains where the embers of the abandoned cooking fire were still warm. The weapon had actually belonged to Osama bin Laden; they'd found his prints on it.

The largest photo was of Ramos standing beside a beaming President Stokes in the Oval Office, just after he'd appointed George to one of the top posts in the Executive Liaison Office (ELO). Stokes's signature was scrawled across the bottom of the photo, along with the dedication: "To George Ramos – with thanks in advance for all the things you're going to do for me."

Actually, few people knew the ELO even existed. It was set up two days after Stokes became president.

Those who worked for the outfit, or were high enough in the president's entourage to be informed about it, referred to it as the "S Team" – the "S" standing for Stokes, of course. It was, in effect, the president's private intelligence force; his own CIA/Special Forces/Delta team. Its existence was rumored, but never officially acknowledged and certainly never challenged by the Republicans in congress who were still too cowed to take on the president on such a sensitive issue.

Its budget, hidden in a line item of the Department of Transportation, quickly expanded, as did its staff, now including another forty-five offices in the cavernous basement. There were also independent contractors who were paid under a different black ops budget and worked out of their own offices in Washington and Virginia. The total was more than 500 people, almost all with elite military and intelligence experience. The idea was that, when necessary, they would also have access to more redoubtable weapons systems: drones, helicopters, even fighter jets, surface craft, and submarines

They worked under the direct control of the president, the line of command passing through Cliff Dayton, his "Senior Counselor, who also secretly headed the ELO. The S Team was split into several groups with different purviews. George was commander of the Operations Division, recommended for the job by one of the retired generals on the transition team. Dayton summoned George to personally interview him for the post.

George had been making $150 a day as a "private contractor," essentially a night watchman, for a small Virginia security company. He was told to show up at

Dayton's transition office on K Street the next day. He'd no inkling what the job was about. All he knew was that— at just thirty-five years old,--Dayton was supposed to be Stokes's most influential advisor. He received George in his sprawling office. He had an aquiline nose, jutting jaw and a two day Italian-look beard, looking and dressed like he'd just stepped out of Vanity Fair.

He began scrolling though the file on the screen of his PC. "Ramos--your training, fighting experience, bravery, etc., all excellent." His voice was keen, precise. "Early promotion to colonel, great efficiency reports, etc., etc. But then in Afghanistan, you were apparently implicated in what was called "mistreatment of detainees" at Bagram Air Base." He turned to look squarely at George with piercing brown eyes. "What was that all about?"

"Sir, we needed to get intelligence in a hurry. We caught these three guys and needed to make them talk."

With meticulously manicured hands, Dayton continued scrolling. "So," he said "you hung them by their wrists from the ceiling for several hours and then water boarded them, among other things."

"Yes, sir." I can forget about this job, thought George.

"Did you ever get the information?"

"No, sir. But they were bad dudes, very bad dudes, believe me. What I did was to try to save the lives of my fellow soldiers." Why the hell did this jerk call me in to be interviewed to begin with?

Dayton's stern gaze didn't waiver. "Two months later you were involved in an action near Kandahar that resulted in a very high number of civilian casualties." He pursed his lips. "Your version?"

There was a trickle of perspiration now running down George's back. He wondered if he should just get up and leave. "Sir, I was advising a battalion of Afghan soldiers tracking down one of the main Taliban leaders near Kandahar. We got a tip that he was holed up in a house on the outskirts of this village. A major meeting was planned for that night. The intelligence looked solid."

"Yes?"

"So we surrounded the place, broke down the doors, threw in concussion grenades, and charged in."

"And," said Dayton reading from the record before him, "Turned out not to be a Taliban meeting but a wedding reception."

"Yes, sir."

"Ten civilians killed, including four children. Six others seriously injured. An entire family wiped out."

"Sir, it was the intelligence. The man who fed us the information had it in for the family we hit."

"Something you found out afterwards."

"Yes, sir." Fuck this noise! George thought. I don't have to stay for this.

"Actually, according to the investigation, you'd also become infuriated and lost control of yourself after one of your buddies was hit. Turns out that fire came from your own men. But it was seeing your buddy get killed that led you to order your men to seek revenge."

"I'd had three tours in Afghanistan. I'd been in country for five months. It was pretty brutal."

Dayton stroked his chin. "You were finally given the choice to face court martial or resign." George's face was burning now. He'd had it.

"That's right. I resigned." Suddenly he stood up, glaring at Dayton. "Look, I don't know what this is all about, but I don't have to go through all this shit again. I resigned. I'm out. Those bastards from Human Rights Watch and Amnesty blew what happened out of all proportion. We are fighting bad, evil people who think nothing of using women and children as cover. But back here, civilians who could care less about America, who have never seen battle or a buddy blown apart, those creeps are second-guessing people who are putting their lives on the line each day for our country. That's bullshit, but that's what it's come to. Now, if you'll excuse me, I'm out of here."

"Hold on, soldier," said Dayton, smiling for the first time. "Sit down." George hesitated, took a deep breath; then sat down heavily.

Dayton raised his hands, "Can we get you something to drink: coffee, beer?"

"Water's fine, thanks."

Dayton walked to a small fridge by the wall and returned with a bottle for George. He was wearing tight-fitting jeans, a trim light blue jacket, and moccasins. He seemed conscious of every move he made.

"Thanks," said George, still trying to control of his breathing. He took a large sip of water.

"Look, Ramos," said Dayton back in his seat. "We know you're good. We've seen your efficiency reports. You're one of the best. We also think you were unfairly treated. We're looking for someone like you: someone with the experience you've had, the ability to give and take orders; someone who will be loyal to the president above all. You will have to organize and oversee difficult missions. These missions that may involve skirting normal rules and regulations, but they may have to be carried out for our country's security." He gazed again directly at George. "Do you think you could handle that?"

George took another drink of water and cleared his throat. "Sir, my father was in the Bay of Pigs invasion. He was captured on the beach and spent three years in a Cuban prison, but he never gave up. When he heard what happened to me, how I was punished, it broke his heart, literally. I would like nothing better than to be able to serve my country again and to serve the president. It would be an enormous honor. Believe me. I would be forever grateful to you and to the president."

"You know, I believe you would," said Dayton. "Consider yourself hired."

The same day that president Stokes moved into the White House, George Ramos moved into his new office at the newly minted ELO. His major duty was to supervise domestic security and monitor threats to the president that went beyond the purview of the FBI or the Secret Service. It was understood that might entail offensive operations that could not be legally carried out by normal U.S. forces.

It was also understood that the president was never to be explicitly informed of such operations. "In the unlikely event of any investigation or inquiry," Dayton ordered, "there must be a mile-thick wall of deniability between the Oval Office and the actions of your team."

The water boarding and murder of Brian Hunt had, of course, been one of those missions. With the silencing of Hunt and the suicide of Steve Penn, the threat from any remaining members of the CIA's Russian hacking team seemed to have subsided.

But this morning Cliff Dayton had called George at home on his mobile.

"Ramos, a heads up, the president asked during his briefing this morning about whatever became of those CIA agents who'd investigated the so-called Russian hacking. I told him it was all under control as you assured me it was. But you know how paranoid the boss can be. Get back to me so I can close the books on this."

"Consider it done, sir," said Ramos. He immediately ordered his assistant, to track down Captain Swanson and have her report soonest to his office. She arrived at a little after 10:00 a.m..

"Send her right in," said George. Captain Swanson, like all the members the S Team, wore no uniform or insignia of command. She was dressed in a black pantsuit, with a white blouse, that didn't emphasize but also didn't hide her curves. Still, she moved with an erect military bearing, a no-nonsense manner about her.

"Good morning, sir," she said precisely, refraining from any salute.

The first time he'd seen Swanson's startling green eyes, Ramos had been aroused. It was only when she twisted to consult a file in her attaché case, that he was confronted with the stark red scar disfiguring her right cheek. That apparently turned off most people. For Ramos, however, it was a definite turn-on. This morning he wondered again what she might be like in bed, then immediately banished the thought: any advances on a female subordinate would be fatal to his resuscitated career. Plus, his performance was once again on the line because the president himself was concerned. Ramos gestured for Swanson to take the chair across from him.

She sat crossed her legs and looked at him expectantly

"It's about the Penn case," he said.

"I just did an update four days ago," she said. "A month after his disappearance."

"I need to run through it with you."

"Any particular reason, sir?"

"The president brought it up in the morning briefing."

"Any idea why?"

He had no idea why, but he didn't like the way this woman subordinate felt she had the right to probe.

"Just answer my questions, captain." He drummed his fingers on the desk.

"Yes, sir." Her lips tightened.

He read from the paper in front of him. "First, your bottom line is that you'd like to keep the investigation open."

"Yes, sir."

"Why is that, Captain? Penn quit his job, wrote a suicide note, sold off all his belongings, etcetera, etcetera. It's true that his body was never found. But there's a lot of ocean out there, am I correct?"

"Yes, sir. But if Penn wanted to kill himself, why go all the way to Cape Cod to do it? Why make sure the body can never be recovered? Maybe because there is no body."

George continued, "You also say there is not a trace of him on any surveillance reports. The agency provided a recording of his voice to the NSA. They put him on high-priority search, but have picked up nothing – zilch – anywhere. Also, you say absolutely nothing has been turned up from a face recognition search: CTV images, drones, overhead reconnaissance. Nothing."

"Correct, sir."

"And the other two agents Penn was close to. They've both quit the agency, but that's not at all surprising. There was no future for them there and they knew it. You say they've all set up elsewhere on their own." He continued reading from her report, "Sarah Levin. Still lives in Virginia but has a small office in D.C., on New Jersey Avenue. Consulting in her specialty: machine learning, also teaching and doing independent research for a paper for MIT. Plays cello with a local chamber music group. What's the paper for MIT?"

"Just more about a new development in deep learning," said the captain.

"Nothing to do with the White House? The Russians?"

"No, sir, definitely not."

"Any Russians in her chamber music group?"

"No, sir."

"Sex life?"

Jean's lips tightened. "She's gay."

"Hah," George snorted. "Would've bet on it. Playing around or a regular partner?"

"Living with Sylvia Hendrix, big time gay rights activist."

George pursed his lips. "OK. Charlie Doyle has his own cyber security company in London. Consulting for wealthy clients in the Gulf. Seems to be doing very well. Already helping to coach a local British basketball team."

"Yes, sir, we actually thought he might go back to the dark side, hacking for personal profit So far no sign of that."

"He also nothing to do with the White House, Russians, etcetera?"

"No sir, not that we know of."

"So, again, nothing to do with what interests us." He put down her report and glared at her, his brow furrowed. "Bottom line, Captain, this all looks pretty tame. I'd like to be able to send word to the president this thing's wrapped up."

"Yes, sir," she sat expressionless.

George suddenly brought his fist down on his desk. "But goddamn it, Captain. That's not your conclusion. You're saying we should stay on top of them, keep the taps going, keep looking for Penn. You don't seem to realize we've got plenty of other stuff on our plate."

"Just a feeling I have, sir."

"A feeling?"

Impassive, she met his gaze. "It's all too neat, sir."

He looked at her. She was one tough broad, he knew from her record: massive injuries in some attack on a firebase near Kabul. After she recovered, she was just as fierce. When she'd been given the order to finish off Hunt, she'd done it without flinching. This was not someone who would be pushed around.

"So what more are we supposed to do?" he said. "We silenced Hunt because we had to. All the alarm bells were ringing. The president was adamant. Now you want to silence the other three also, just to make sure. Though you have absolutely no evidence that they're up to anything?"

"No sir. I just can't believe they backed off that easily."

He'd made his point, but she still sat there, her eyes filled with defiance. And goddamn it, he was still incredibly aroused by her, by that scar, by the disfigured beauty of her face. He rose from his chair and began pacing the office.

"What were the other officers who were close to Penn supposed to do?" He asked as he walked behind her. "They lost. Their so-called investigation into Russian hacking was crap. Hunt is dead. Penn committed suicide and the others are off on their own making money." He changed to a gentler tone. "You know, Jean, there are a lot of other things you could be helping me with," he leaned forward, placing his hands on her shoulders.

He felt her immediately stiffen. He knew he was on the verge of a fatal move.

"Captain, stop," she said.

But the heat from her skin under her thin blouse turned him on even further "I need a personal assistant. It would mean more pay, higher rank."

"I said stop!"

Despite himself, he ran his left hand down the front of her blouse towards her breast.

"You sonofabitch," she exploded. She reached back and seized his hand with hers, pinning the back of his hand with her thumb into a wrist lock. Then she twisted his wrist violently clockwise, flipping him over and sending him crashing to the floor. Stunned, he lay looking up at her as pain throbbed through his shoulder and arm. He was unable to move as she kept an iron grip on his hand.

She was livid. "Don't you ever fucking do that again," she hissed. The next time you try it you'll wind up without any balls. She was breathing hard, fury radiating from her eyes. "When I was a teenager I was gang-raped by a bunch of assholes like you. No one ever took me again. Now get the fuck up and start playing macho leader again.

Staring wide-eyed at her, he slowly rose to his feet. His shoulder felt like it had been dislocated. He circled warily back behind the desk. She sat stiffly back in her chair, facing him.

"Let's get things straight," she said. "I still want this job. If you fire me now, you can be goddamned sure everyone will know why. I'm here to defend President Stokes. He's out to save our country. And no limp dick like you is going to fuck things up. Now let's get back to our roles."

He couldn't believe the scene he was playing. They glared at each other until his breathing became more normal, his adrenalin slowed. Then, he shook himself and leaned forward, his brow furrowed. "Captain, I take note of your report today, but until you come up with something that proves me wrong, I'm telling the president the threat is over. But, OK, go ahead and keep an eye on Penn's friends. Meanwhile I'm also putting you on another investigation."

"Yes, sir," she made no effort to hide her scowl. "He's out there. I know it."

CHAPTER EIGHTEEN

Moscow

Two men in jogging suits were walking in a birch and willow forest twenty-two kilometers west of Moscow. On the left was General Artyom Borovik, fifty-eight years old and commander of all Russian ground forces. It was a warm spring day, the trees budding, the woods filled with birdsong. It was General Borovik's favorite time of year, heralding renewal, rebirth, new possibilities.

With him was his former superior, long-time friend, and mentor, General Sergei Petrov, sixty-eight, who'd retired from the army three years ago. There was no question Petrov was ailing. He was panting rather than breathing and his pale skin was like parchment stretched over his narrow, heavily lined face.

The two generals were neighbors, their dachas within two miles of each other. Borovik's two-story wooden vacation home had been in his family for three generations. It was his sanctuary; a haven to escape from the endless intrigues and pervasive terrors of Moscow. It was a place to enjoy snow-shoeing and cross-country skiing in the winter and long hikes and swims in the lake during the hot summer months. It was also a sanctuary for his family. His daughter would be visiting this weekend with her two children. Normally the expectation of their boisterous presence put him in good spirits, but for the past few months he'd been unable to shake his foul mood.

"Cheer up, for God's sake, Artyom," said Sergei. "It's April. You're going to be seeing your grandkids. You're healthy, your wife is healthy."

"I know what season it is," Borovik snapped, then felt further annoyed that he'd replied so sharply.

Petrov had been diagnosed with colon cancer last January. He was undergoing radiation but had been told he probably had less than a year to live. But Sergei Petrov had never been one to surrender. He'd survived the ruthless ins and outs of politics in this country for decades. He was walking slower than usual, stopping every now and then to catch his breath, but he kept up a steady stream of chatter.

"Look, Artyom, what's done is done. You can't let it get under your skin. You'll destroy yourself and your family."

"For God's sake," said Borovik despite himself, "please stop telling me what I already know."

What was incessantly gnawing at Borovik was what he viewed as the reckless decision by Russian President Vasily Vasilovich Kozlov to order his military hackers to attempt to influence the American elections.

"I told Vasily Vasilovich he was playing with fire," said Borovik, "It's asinine."

"I know that's how you feel," said Petrov, raising his arms. "Everyone knows. But Vasily Vasilovich didn't heed your great wisdom. And it looks like he was right; Stokes won."

In fact, both the generals knew that Kozlov never expected that Stokes would actually win. The Russian president's idea was to disrupt the America's so-called democratic system and undermine the leading candidate, whom Kozlov detested. He wanted to make Americans lose faith in their political parties and institutions. In this case, however, he outperformed.

"Vasily Vasilovich is still crowing like a rooster," said Borovik. "To anyone who will listen. He doesn't care if the Americans know what his hackers did. He's proud of it. He wants everyone to know what he and Russia can do. Vasily Vasilovich and Stokes deserve each other."

What infuriated General Borovik even further was that the man who'd convinced Kozlov to hack the U.S. was Borovik's rival, General Alexei Abramovich, the brilliant, fast-talking head of Russia's cyberwar division. Under Abramovich's leadership, the division's staff and budget had skyrocketed over the past few years. They now had the effrontery to run recruiting ads on television showing a smiling Russian soldier laying down his rifle to pick up a laptop computer. They'd also recruited hundreds of programmers and hackers from private industry and even criminal gangs to come and work for the military.

General Abramovich argued there was no way Russia, with its tattered economy, could keep pace with the extremely sophisticated new weapons America was developing. Cyber war was a much cheaper but extremely effective method of wreaking great damage on the enemy. And Kozlov had agreed. In one heated session, he ridiculed General Borovik as an "old woman" for his tiresome warnings about the threat of U.S. reprisals. "The U.S. president," said Kozlov, "has no balls."

"You have to agree that Vasily Vasilovich was right." said Petrov. "It's been a huge success."

"You are wrong, Sergei. In the end, it will backfire."

"Admit it, what upsets you the most is that it is Alexei Abramovich, getting credit for it."

"He is a turd!" Borovik spat onto the ground and turned to face Petrov. "A corrupt, lying piece of shit."

Ivanov knew better than to respond, but he and everyone else close to Borovik also knew that what infuriated Artyom the most was that General Abramovich had once been his son-in-law. He'd dumped Borovik's frumpy daughter and their two children five years ago for a leggy blond Russian model who seemed to have been born behind the wheel of a jet-black Maserati.

"Vasily Vasilovich may once have been a great KGB officer, a true patriot." Borovik continued. "But he's become like the rest of them. He could not bear to stand by and watch all the other sharks tear away their pieces of our country. Vasily Vasilovich had to get the lion's share for himself, billions and billions. He's one of the richest man in the world today." Borovik's voice rose with indignation. "And you and I stood by and watched. We were honest fools."

Reflexively, Petrov put a finger to his lips and looked around them. "You know how dangerous it is to talk this way, Artyom. Especially a man in your position. Me, it doesn't make any difference, but you've got a wife, a family."

Borovik wasn't listening. "Did you see Alexei Abramovich just bought a dacha in the Rublevka for sixty million rubles? And that's not to mention his ski chalet in Sochi and his waterfront mansion in Palm Beach. Everyone knows about this. Where in God's name does he get such money? And that is nothing beside the wealth of our other kleptocrats. And it's all done in the open – they, with their supermodels and Ferraris and mansions all over the world."

Petrov took a seat on a moss-covered log, extracted a couple of pills from his chest pocket, and swallowed them with water from the thermos he was carrying. "I know. My wife is always reading the gossip pages about the new trendy Moscow nightclubs and restaurants. Imagine! One is even called Siberia! All the incredibly expensive new fashions – all the coming and going – it is obscene."

"Now with Stokes in power in the U.S." said Borovik, "there's no limit to what they can do, the deals they can make. Their fortunes will become even more outrageous."

"But neither I nor you can do anything about it," said Ivanov wearily. "We can only sit and watch the rot. The press is silenced; the opposition leaders have been bought off or murdered or imprisoned. And the others…"

"Everyone is too scared to move," said Borovik. "It's like the Americans who know what is going on with Stokes. They are also sitting and watching and letting Stokes have his way, just like we're doing with our own crooked leader. But I am not going to just sit and watch."

"What else can you do?"

Artyom paused, considering whether to confide in his friend. "This is obviously not to be told to anyone else," he finally said.

"Agreed," said Petrov, "though I'm not going to be around much longer to talk to anyone about anything."

"I have established a very small group of computer experts on my staff, hackers – two men and one woman, responsible only to me.

They are all very good, all very upset with what is happening. They are using their talents to, shall we say, map out the wealth of our rulers: their real estate interests, their companies, their bank accounts, their offshore holdings."

"And what will you do with this great prize?" asked Petrov. "Who will pay any attention?"

"I don't know that I'll ever be able to use it," said Artyom quietly. "Right now, it would bring nothing. Vasily Vasilovich and his people control the courts and the investigators and…"

"If he ever found out what you were doing," said Petrov, "you'd be a dead man, liquidated along with all your evidence."

"But I have to do something. Keep gathering this information, keep my head down, watch, and wait. I may not be able to undo what is done, but that does not mean I have to accept everything until our homeland is totally destroyed."

Petrov smiled with thin gray lips. "The only blessing from my illness, Artyom, is that I will never live to see that day."

CHAPTER NINETEEN

Manhattan

Outside in the skies above Manhattan, there was the crack of thunder, and the storm that had been threatening all day finally struck. Inside, sitting in his office, Charlie Doyle heard the wind and rain beating against the window. A half-filled glass of single malt stood on the desk. The nimble fingers of Charlie's left hand were drumming to the beat of Kendrick Lamar's latest rap. A pile of back issues of the hacker's favorite, "2600" were on the floor under the desk.

In front of Charlie was a cluster of three thirty-two inch monitors. The current on-line edition of "Hack!" was on the left screen. On the right, the website of Kane & Levin, a prominent Manhattan tax law firm whose offices were about one hundred blocks away on 57th Street. On the center monitor was the computer screen of Geraldine Brail, a leading partner in Kane & Levin. Charlie's computer was mirroring every one of

Brail's key stokes. In San Francisco, on the other side of the continent, Steve Penn was patched in to the same transmission. This might be pay dirt, he thought: Kane & Levin were the tax attorneys of President Walter Stokes.

Their goal was to come up with the evidence to convince a Republican-dominated congress to impeach the president of the United States. Using a sophisticated encryption app, they began discussing strategy as soon as Steve returned to the U.S. with his new identity.

Stokes tax returns were the obvious target. The president had to be concealing some disgraceful acts. Why else would he categorically refuse to make public his returns? But how to get hold of them?

"I could hack into the IRS at some level," said Charlie "but to actually get Stokes's tax returns, that's something else."

"If that were doable," said Steve, "they'd have been hacked by now. Every investigative reporter in the country is after them."

"Security at the IRS is tighter than a drum," said Charlie. "Believe me, I've checked them out more than once. They went ape-shit a few years ago when several hundred thousand returns got hacked, but they've really tightened up since."

"What about the possibility of someone in the IRS going rogue?" said Steve. "Someone high up who has been canned by Stokes and would be pissed off enough to help us?"

"Possible," said Charlie, "but if anyone in the organization goes digitally anywhere near those files, it sets off alarms all over the system. The hard copies are kept in a vault. Also, the penalties for revealing data from the IRS are enormous. So yeah, we might spend a few months at it, but we'd probably be wasting our time."

"So let's go directly after Stokes's tax attorney," said Sarah. "He prepares the returns, so he must have copies."

"Maybe," said Steve. "In any case, their security can't be as solid as the IRS."

"Surprising no one has already done it," said Charlie. He'd always thrived on such challenges. Early on, he'd hacked into the Pentagon and the NSA, but he became legendary among hackers when he took over a 737 in flight, hacking into its controls via the electronics of the entertainment box beneath his economy class seat. Later he claimed he'd warned the airline in advance about the dangerous gap in security.

For Charlie, hacking the data of the president's tax attorney was definitely doable.

A Google search produced the name of the firm handling Stokes's returns: Kane & Levin on West 57th Street in Manhattan. K & L's website provided the names and emails of 110 members of their staff, from principal partners to the paralegals and receptionist.

But Charlie wanted a way into the firm. The answer was the Starbucks located just half a block away from K & L's offices. It was a gathering place and coffee route for the firm's lawyers and staff. Charlie had no problem taking over the Starbucks' Wi-Fi, then pay-loading the laptops and electronic devices of everyone who logged on.

The next step was to program a tempting "clickbait" for unwary users. That came from Sarah: an alarming headline that appeared to be from the front page of the *Wall Street Journal*: "PC's around the globe hit by new hack." According to the breathless account, unknown cybercriminals had penetrated millions of Apple and Android devices with "a vicious new Trojan horse that once activated, would encrypt all the contents of the victim's computer." The hackers then demanded four hundred dollars from each victim to deactivate that malware. Luckily, there was a new free fix to remedy the problem. All you had to do to get that patch was click on the link embedded in the article, and follow instructions on the screen.

At 7:00 a.m., the next morning, Sarah emailed that fake story to the entire list of 110 employees of Kane & Levin. By 8:14, the first musical alarm went off on his computer indicating a hit. "Show time," yelled Charlie. The new Trojan horse instantly infiltrated the workstation of Geraldine Brail, a senior partner in the firm. She had, of course, been cautioned by K &L's security maven never to click on a suspicious link, but this was an article from the *Wall Street Journal*. In the next hour, three more alarms went off. The malware was now embedded in four K&L computers. It was, the experts later agreed, a very elegant hack.

Linked in from San Francisco, Steve watched on his own computer screen, as Charlie focused on Geraldine Brail. It took only a few minutes to discover her login and password and obtain instant access to K & L's general directory. Charlie then intercepted the two-factor authentication password required to enter the higher realm of security, supposedly protecting the client files. In the meantime, Geraldine Brail thought she had typed the challenge password required to login to the file-viewing application.

Charlie scrolled through the files in alphabetical order until he reached "Walter Stokes."

"Bull's eye," he said.

"Let's see what you got," said Steve, following the action.

When Charlie clicked on "Walter Stokes," the file opened to reveal hundreds of sub-files. One of them was labeled "IRS returns." When he clicked on that, further sub-files appeared, each marked with a date going back twenty years.

"Pay dirt," said Charlie. He clicked on the most recent file.

In far-off San Francisco, Steve held his breath. But instead of a tax return, a single notice came up. "For security reasons – no digitized IRS returns available. See M. Kane."

"Shit," said Charlie. "They've taken them completely off-line, probably on another computer not linked to the Internet."

"Or stored in M. Kane's safe," said Steve.

Charlie continued to click on each of the other dated sub-files; they all produced the same infuriating message.

"It would have been too easy," said Steve. "But there's got to be something else we can work with, some kind of lead."

"I'll check through the whole goddamn thing" said Charlie. He spent several hours prowling Stokes's files. There were bills of sale and purchase, contracts, mortgages, entertainment expenses, even Christmas cards. There was also a file called "Businesses & Misc."

"Could be interesting," said Steve, as Charlie opened the file. It contained a three-page double-spaced list of 256 different names, apparently belonging to companies, some with Stokes's name in one form or another; some that appeared to have nothing to do with Stokes. Nine of them had the name followed by an initial. Charlie and Steve copied the list.

"That may still give us something to chew on," said Steve.

Charlie closed down the malware on all the Kane & Levin computers and instructed the intruding droppers and Trojans to self-destruct and wipe all network and system logs. The IT security folks in the firm would never realize they'd been hacked.

Over the next two days, Steve, Charlie, and Sarah ran through the list of 256 company names they'd copied. Eighty-nine of them no longer existed; they'd gone bankrupt or simply folded. Many of the others were U.S.-based, most of them connected in some way with Stokes.

Nine of them, however, didn't show up on any list of anything to do with Stokes, nor were they incorporated or registered in the U.S. They each had an initial after the name: BSP-P, Highflyer-P, West End BV, Pyotr1C, Kalinka C, Krypto C, Styx C, Arbat C., Rivka1-C.

"Any ideas where we go from here?" said Steve after they'd looked over the list.

"Sleep on it," said Sarah.

They did. Steve woke early the next day in San Francisco as dawn began to penetrate his bedroom.

He prized these moments. He would lie there, running through events of the past day, going over ideas for the future, examining problems still unresolved. It was a time when his brain was sharpest. And then it was all so clear.

As planned, the members of Deep Strike held another encrypted call at 7:30 a.m., San Francisco time. "It's simple," Steve immediately began. "Those nine companies are all offshore. I should have realized it right off. P stands for Panama, BV for the British Virgin Islands."

"And the last six companies, all C's" said, Sarah.

"Could be the Cayman Islands," said Steve. "But I don't think so."

"Why?" said Sarah.

"Most offshore venues tell you nothing about who are the real owners of the companies based there. But at least they do publish a list of those companies. I've already checked Panama and the British Virgin Islands. Turns out that BSP, Highflower, and Westend are all listed there. They've also all got the same corporate officers. All of them are with the same Panamanian Law Firm—Rodriquez & Baltra in Panama City."

"Those sleazebags!" said Sarah. "They're money launderers for crooks all over the world. Not to mention the CIA. You won't get anything out of them. But those last five companies—the ones labeled at the end with C's. That C's gotta be for Cypress."

"That's my bet," said Steve, "particularly where Stokes is concerned. It's THE center for Russian money laundering."

"So then, what's the next step?" said Sara.

"I've been trying to figure that out," said Steve. There was a reason he had undergone plastic surgery and adopted a completely new identity. It gave him the freedom to move around that the other members of the group didn't have. But he needed to make each move count.

"One option," he said, "is go to Panama and see what I can pry out of Rodriquez & Baltra."

"Good luck on that," said Charlie.

"Agreed," said Steve. "On the other hand, the Russian-sounding names from Cypress are tantalizing. I could go there."

"And run headlong into another wall of corruption and secrecy," said Charlie.

"Exactly," said Steve. "Why jet off to Panama or Nicosia when the question of Stokes's ties to Russia is really our target? I think we can short-circuit the investigation if I go directly to Moscow. If that doesn't pan out, then I'll head for Nicosia or Panama. But Moscow comes first. I'm leaving soon as I can."

He didn't tell the others about what – really, who – he was counting on most in Moscow: Dancing Bear.

CHAPTER TWENTY:

Moscow

It was noon when Doug Robb, aka Steve Penn, walked cross the glittering marble lobby of the Four Seasons in Moscow and registered, giving his profession as "Private Investor." He had flown all night on Lufhansa from San Francisco via Frankfurt. The lobby was crowded with people on the make from all corners of the globe, like the five young Qatari princes in jeans and t-shirts with their veiled wives and elder daughters. They mingled easily with elegant members of the Russian elite, sporting their leather coats and bodyguards and tall, long-legged blonds.

Those Russians were the new *nomenklatura*, the immensely privileged, immensely wealthy few, victors of the so-called "open lottery" that transferred the resources and industries that had once – in theory at least – belonged to all the Russian people. Instead, they were sold off at bargain basement prices to a favored few: billion-dollar industries going for a fraction of their real worth, massive fortunes created overnight. It was known that Russian President Kozlov got a piece of just about every deal that came down the pike.

With the scandalous help of compliant institutions, like Germany's huge Deutsche Bank, Russia's new billionaires were converting their ill-gotten rubles into hard currencies to be parked in safer havens abroad. Trophy real estate holdings in places like Palm Beach and Belgravia and Gstaad were particularly prized. That huge capital flight was a major reason that Russia, with a population more than twice that of France, had a gross domestic product only one quarter that of the Gallic state.

Moscow changed with every visit, thought Steve as he took the elevator to the 14th floor. His room looked out over the 18th-century spires and domes of the Kremlin and across the new cityscape of Moscow – a forest of towering cranes and skyscrapers, glitzy restaurants and apartment buildings and expressways – and enormous traffic jams. A brownish pall of smog hung over the city.

It was such an amazing contrast to the Soviet capital that he'd first come to almost thirty years ago as a twenty-three-year-old agent for the CIA. This was long before he'd met Maya. It was his first overseas posting, and was considered a plum assignment. It was due largely to his grandmother who'd been born in Kiev and emigrated to the U.S. She brought Steve up in Seattle to speak Russian even before he learned English.

He'd been assigned to the U.S. embassy in Moscow under cover as an agricultural attaché. His wife, Marilyn, had come with him and found the Soviets and their capital superb subjects for her watercolors. Those were exciting times. With his policies of *glasnost* and *perestroika*, Mikhail Gorbachev was sabotaging the foundations of the old Soviet Union. It was as if spring had suddenly come to a land frozen for decades in glacial silence.

His mission was to learn what was really going on under the surface, to find out whether real change was on the way and what form it would take. His team's first major breakthrough came when they used Moscow's decrepit sewer system to gain access to cables transmitting the most highly classified Soviet military messages.

His main efforts, however, were to maintain contact with the few valuable human intelligence sources who had been developed by his predecessors. He was also to generate and then run new ones, as he had with Maya Chertkova. It was an extremely difficult task: as an American diplomat he was under surveillance every time he left the embassy. Breaking free of his shadows to retrieve information from a dead drop, or to actually speak directly with one of his sources, was an extremely time-consuming and fraught endeavor. Much more perilous, of course, for the Russian source, than for Steve, who enjoyed diplomatic immunity.

As the station chief in Moscow explained to him, "In the event the KGB discovers what you're up to, just remain cool. You can expect to be picked up, held for a few hours of relatively civilized questioning during which you reveal nothing. You'll then be released to the custody of one of our embassy officials who will maintain you have nothing to do with the agency. And finally, the

Soviets will order you to leave the country. The likely fate of your Soviet source, on the other hand, will be quite different. If they are lucky, they'll be sentenced to some freezing shithole in Siberia from which few ever return. If they are not lucky, they'll get a bullet in the back of the neck in the basement of the Lubyanka."

Steve remembered that advice now, returning to Moscow as an agent running his own minuscule spy team. He could forget about diplomatic immunity. He was also going to confront not just the Russian secret police, but America's vast intelligence network as well; both of which who would view him as an enemy to be tracked down and eliminated.

He unpacked, showered, and took a taxi from the hotel. Out of habit, he changed cabs three times, exiting one to flag down another going in the opposite direction. He was alert to cars and faces in the crowd, to patterns that most people would miss. The last taxi deposited him on Petrovka Street in front of TsUM, one of Moscow's most elegant department stores. It was built in a six-story Gothic Revival style, and had been refurbished to befit the ostentatious tastes of the new generation of Russians and foreigners who flocked to its counters and restaurants.

He took the elevator to the sixth floor, then got out and took the staircase immediately on his right, went down one floor and waited. Finally satisfied that no one was following him, he went to the pay phone in the back of the store's cafeteria and made a call. He let the phone on the other end ring three times; then hung up and repeated the same process again. After a snack in the cafeteria, he took a cab to the sprawling State

Tretyakov Gallery. He'd spent a lot of time there during off hours with his wife Marilyn when he'd first come to Moscow, wandering through its galleries, savoring the finest collection of Russian art anywhere in the world. He returned to the hotel at six and had an early dinner, reading a selection of the daily newspapers.

The weather was at the top of the headlines. It was the fourth day in a row that Moscow residents had reported unusually thick smog and the smell of burning, "with some complaining of ashes falling from the sky." The environmentalist group Greenpeace claimed that the smog was a result of forest fires in Siberia. Other environmental groups blamed climate change. Typically, the government had released no health warnings in relation to the smog, although some Muscovites had chosen to wear protective masks when outdoors.

The Russian government was brushing off the threat of climate change just like Stokes and his gang, Steve thought. Man was destroying himself and evidence of it was everywhere. Some philosopher had presented the theory that, although there are an infinitesimally great number of planets in the universe that could theoretically support life, we've so far seen absolutely no sign of intelligence out there because every potentially sophisticated civilization annihilated itself by war or wanton destruction of its own biosphere as we now seem on the verge of doing.

The next day was Saturday; there was still a shroud of smog over the city. Again taking a circuitous route, Steve went to Sokolniki Park, rented a bicycle, and rode along one of the shaded paths. He stopped by an old cast-iron bench under an elm tree. He sat down, unfolded a newspaper, and felt underneath one of the slats until he retrieved a small black box taped to the bottom. There was a piece of paper inside with the number "2" written on it.

He then continued biking for another hour, had a light lunch, and took the Northern Metro line to the crowded Smolenskaya Station. He walked south for three blocks, entered a small café, waited for a couple of minutes, and doubled back on his route. There was no one following him. He continued to a large, grey cement apartment building at 86 Shabolovka. He rang apartment 254 from the directory at the main door, was buzzed in, took the elevator to the third floor, exited, and took the steps down to the second floor. He recognized the musty smell of stale cigarettes and old carpeting as he walked along the dimly lit corridor to the apartment at the end and rang the bell. He could see someone examine him through the peephole in the door.

"Steven?" she asked.

"It's me," he replied. She opened the door just a few inches, leaving the security chain in place and peered at him startled with wide, pale-blue eyes.

"Who are you?" she asked.

"For God's sakes, Mayushka, it is me," he said quietly in Russian, afraid of alerting the neighbors. He used the name he called her when they made love. "It's me, Mayushka," he repeated. "Let me in, I'll explain everything."

She hesitated, then undid the chain and opened the door but continued to gape at him in disbelief. She was wearing a blue denim shirt open at the neck and jeans, her red hair tied up in a bun on the back of her head.

Steve felt his pulse quicken. It was just a few months but it seemed many years since he'd last been with her. Seeing her out of uniform, with her slim white neck and the mole on her right cheek, it was hard to believe that she was one of the CIA's most valuable assets in Russia.

She pulled back when he tried to take her hand. "How can you be Steve?" she said. "Your accent sounds like his, but your voice is deeper. It's different."

"Are you alone? And did you do something to your hair?" Steve used the secret code between for "Are you certain we are clear?"

"Yes. My mother is out with a friend. I just gave my hair a complete do-over, thanks for asking." But despite the exchange of secret phrases, she continued staring at him.

"It is very complicated," he said. He led her to a dark green sofa in the small living room. There were several icons and a few family photos on the wall, a framed display of military decorations, and a large picture of a Russian officer being decorated by Stalin. There was a copy of the current edition of *Pravda* and a bowl of apples on a wooden table covered with a white lace doily.

Steve took a chair facing her. "It's a very complicated story," he said.

"You already said that," her mouth tightened.

"But it's true," he said and then launched into an account of the extraordinary things that had happened since they'd last met. The report on Russian hacking had been openly derided by the new president, who now was the ultimate boss of America's intelligence community. Brian Hunt, who for several months after Steve left had been Maya's Moscow contact with the agency, had been murdered. The other agents who had worked on the investigation had quit their jobs rather than waiting around to be fired. The Republicans, who might have been expected to howl in outrage at Russia's blatant actions, were groveling in silence. "If anyone had told me this was going to happen six months ago, I'd have said they were crazy," said Steve. "But, so far, our country's accepted it--eyes wide open."

"I can't believe it," she said. "It's terrible what happened to Brian. He was a good person. He brought me a special gift for my daughter when he went back. Your country has become just like Russia." She gazed at Steve for a long moment. "I understand you are the person that – that was Steve." she raised both hands. "But it is still very strange to be with you like this."

"Strange for me too."

"Would you like some tea?" It was the first time she had smiled since he arrived.

"That would be very nice." He remembered when she made him tea in a glass with a lump of sugar, after the first time they'd made love. As their affair continued, it became something of a rite, "our tea ceremony," he'd joked, "though the Japanese usually do it with their clothes on."

After finishing the tea, he said, "Despite all that's happened, you're still getting the medicines, aren't you?"

"Yes, thank God."

"Before I left, I did my best to made sure they'd continue."

"Thank you," she smiled slightly.

Now comes the tough moment, Steve thought. The abrupt change of course. "But the way things are going, you can't count on anything."

"Despite the promise?" She raised her eyebrows.

"Anything could happen with Stokes. He's a madman surrounded by pygmies. Your daughter's not the only one at risk. The whole world is. That's why I've come back here." I also longed to see you again, he almost said but didn't. Things were complicated enough.

"But your investigation was finished," she said.

"Yes, but not yet for me. I'm not going to let them get away with this."

"But you're only one person."

"The information to destroy Stokes – to reveal the game he's been playing with Kozlov – it exists. I'm sure of it." He looked directly at her. "But I need your help again."

She raised both hands. "No, Steve, Dancing Bear is over, finished. You promised."

"I'm not asking for information about your country. I need to make contact with one or two very good hackers here. The best."

"Hackers?"

"I've got a job for them".

"But you're not with the CIA."

"It's for me."

She shook her head, "You're crazy,"

"Perhaps. But who would you suggest?" he said. "I know the best hackers also work at times for Russian intelligence."

She paused. "There are the Sirotskys."

"They'd be available?" Steve was surprised. Olga and Boris Sirotsky were two of the most notorious hackers in Russia. In one coup alone, they'd made a fortune hacking the accounts of ten million subscribers of NetChat, then peddling terabytes of personal data on the dark web to criminal gangs. They also worked on occasion for Russian intelligence, which, in return, closed its eyes to their larcenous doings.

"They worked with my unit for a while," said Maya. "But no more. I'm not sure what happened. Kozlov or someone close to him wanted a cut of their business. Half of everything they have made, in the past and going forward. In return, they will be allowed to continue to operate."

"Like a tax," said Steve.

She laughed bitterly. "They don't see it like that. Now they hate Kozlov as much as the rest of us."

"Can they be trusted?"

"Absolutely," she said. "It may surprise you but they have a strong sense of professional honor."

"Will you put me in contact with them?"

"You are really serious?" said Maya.

"Tell them it's for a few days of research work."

"They will be very expensive. How will you pay?"

"Just put me in touch," said Steve.
"Will it help my daughter?"
"It will."

CHAPTER TWENTY-ONE:

Moscow

It took Maya less than twenty-four hours to set up a meeting with the Sirotskys. At noon on Saturday she passed the time and address to Steve as he gazed at the Picassos in the Pushkin Museum. But he would go to the rendezvous by himself; he didn't want Maya any more involved than she had to be.

Befitting their lofty status, the Sirotskys maintained their own safe house in the Patriarshiye Ponds, one of Moscow's elite residential areas. They regularly swept it for hidden cameras and listening devices. Steve, aka Doug Robb, arrived precisely at 8:00 p.m. Boris Sirotsky opened the door and extended a thick hand, "You are Mr. Robb?"

"Doug Robb," answered Steve. Sirotsky had the iron grip of a prizefighter.

He was a tall, broad-shouldered man with thick lips, narrow eyes, and a light black beard. He ushered

Steve into a spacious living room. Olga Sirotsky rose from a white suede sofa to greet him, and then stood beside her husband as if they were posing for a cover of *Moscow Life*. They were both in their early thirties. Olga was a strikingly beautiful woman with light gray eyes and blond hair that fell to her shoulders. She wore a white dress shirt, tight black Prada jeans, and crocodile moccasins. The top three buttons of the shirt were open, exposing the soft swell of her breast. Boris was more laid back in a black t-shirt, jeans, Gucci loafers, and a diamond-studded Rolex glittering on his wrist.

To prepare for this meeting, Steve had read the profile the *Financial Times* had written about the couple two years ago. They were very open about their wealth: vacation homes on Korfu and in Gstaad, a five-story apartment in West Kensington in London with three Rothkos and two Chagalls. That surprising candor about their success was before Kozlov decided he would also like a piece of the action.

Steve accepted a glass of Glenfiddich from Olga and then sat in an armchair facing the Sirotskys on the couch. Olga's shapely long legs were curled beneath her.

"Thank you for meeting with me," said Steve. "I speak Russian."

"We were told," said Boris, spreading his arms. "So here we are. What can we do for you?"

"I am working on a research project," said Steve, taking a sheet of paper from his breast pocket. "I have the names here of six Russian-controlled offshore companies registered in Cypress. I need to know who the real owners are, what businesses they are in, and what records you can get of their transactions. I am particularly interested in real estate purchases they have made in the United States through certain other offshore front companies. I have those names also here. I suspect that many of those purchases were for properties owned by Walter Stokes or his family. Many of the loans were probably also to him.

"Can I see the paper?" said Olga.

He passed it to her then took another sip of scotch. She read through it with Boris, pointing her finger at some of the entries. Boris raised his eyebrows. "Interesting list," he said. "Who are you working for, Mr. Robb? May I assume that is not your real name?"

"Robb will do," said Steve. "I am working for a very small private group. I can't go any further than that."

"You are not CIA?" asked Boris.

"I am not. Another thing: It is highly likely these companies I am giving you are also connected in some way with Kozlov, or people very close to him."

"So that would link Stokes and Kozlov," said Olga.

"And perhaps destroy them both," said Boris with a slight smile.

Steve nodded. "That is a possibility."

"By when do you need this information?" asked Olga.

"Shall we say one week?" said Steve. "You can always follow up with additional information as you get it."

Olga and Boris raised their eyebrows and looked at each other.

"Please excuse us for a few minutes while we discuss this," said Boris. "Feel free to have another drink." He and Olga walked into the kitchen and closed the door.

Steve refilled his glass and waited. He thought about Maya and her child and Brian Hunt and how it had all come down to this: on his own in Moscow, trying to hire a pair of millionaire Russian hackers to destroy the presidents of the U.S. and Russia. He could hear raised voices coming from the kitchen. They weren't arguing in Russian but in some other language he didn't recognize. After fifteen minutes, they took their seats again facing Steve. Olga was scowling.

"We have decided to discuss accepting the job," said Boris. Olga said nothing. Her lips were tight. "

"Discuss accepting?" Steve looked puzzled.

"Yes. First of all, we are only agreeing to talk with you because of the person who sent you to us. We have grown to respect her – unlike many of her colleagues. We have no doubt that we could do what you are asking; we have the skills and the contacts. But we are not sure if you will be able to afford our services."

"Try me," said Steve.

Boris nodded. "You are asking us to undertake a task that will be – shall we say – very risky. It may involve the most powerful interests in our country. As we are sure you know these are very strange times here. Three people known to be connected with our country and your elections have met untimely deaths in Moscow over the last two months. You have read about them."

"I have," said Steve.

"That risk necessarily affects our price," said Boris.

"I understand."

"You are asking us to get very sensitive detailed information on six different companies?"

"That is correct."

"We will require from you two million American dollars."

"Two million; that should be...."

Boris interrupted, "Two million dollars for *each* of those companies."

"That's twelve million dollars!" Steve's eyes widened.

Boris raised a hand, "Plus – three million dollars more."

"More? For what?" asked Steve.

"You can call it 'good will,'" said Boris, with a tight smile. "We have excellent contacts in the government, in the major banks, and so on, but we need to keep the people who help us happy. For you that is just money. For us, it might be our lives." He pointed his index finger at Steve. "Fifteen million dollars. Half is to be paid in advance and the rest when we deliver the information."

"No disrespect meant," said Steve, "but how can I be sure you won't just take the seven and half million dollars you're asking for up front and disappear?"

"A very good question," said Boris. "You might also ask how you will know that the information we give you is true and not just something made up. You won't, Mr. Robb or whatever your name is. Except that we have a reputation in this country. We do not operate like that. I am sure your friend has told you."

Steve nodded grimly.

"So then," said Boris, "you have our offer. We are not carpet merchants. You can take it or you can leave it."

"Thank you," said Steve. "It's now my turn to absent myself to consult my team. You will have an answer within twenty-four hours."

Boris gave a thin smile and nodded. He handed Steve a card with the couple's confidential contact details. "This is our 'open' contact. We are sure you know that we will not communicate anything pertaining to this matter on this channel."

Olga shook hands with Steve stiffly and remained in the living room, a worried frown on her face, while Boris walked him to the door.

Prior to this trip, Steve had spoken with Jake Pearlstein, his deep-pocketed backer in Palm Desert, and explained he would be trying to recruit one or two of Russia's top hackers.

"I don't know if it will work, Jake," he'd said. "But, considering the risks involved, I do know it will be expensive."

"How much we talking about?" said Pearlstein.

"I'm flying blind," said Steve, but anywhere from $5 million to $20 million, even more."

"Sounds like an expensive ballpark," said Pearlstein. "I could probably handle it. I'll wait to hear from you."

After talking with the Sirotskys, Steve returned to his hotel room and sent an encrypted email to Pearlstein, "Hi Jake, weather's fine here in Moscow, they're saying it might be 15 degrees tomorrow. Miss you. Best, Doug."

Afterwards, Steve soaked in a hot bath for almost an hour, then wrapped himself in a thick terry robe, and lay on the bed watching Russian television. They were broadcasting a Russian classic: *Alexander Nevsky* by Sergei Eisenstein. Steve became so enthralled by the great black and white film that he never realized when Pearlstein's answering message arrived.

"Temperature sounds fine, Doug. Envy you, best Jake."

CHAPTER TWENTY-TWO:

Moscow

The next morning, Steve approved the transfer of $7.5 million from a British Virgin Islands account controlled by Jake Pearlstein to an account in the Cayman Islands indirectly controlled by the Sirotskys. Thus began a nail-biting week. Steve had no enforcers at his command. There was absolutely nothing to prevent the Russian hackers from absconding with the funds, except their own definition of honor.

To maintain his cover as a wealthy independent investor, Steve spent his waiting time trolling Moscow's most promising hi-tech startups. At the top of the list was a company called Way-Ray located in a townhouse in the eastern part of the city that had long ago seen better days. The living room resembled the set up a low-budget sci-fi thriller. The centerpiece was a holographic projector mounted on a car dashboard. It emitted beams that would look to a driver as 3D arrows glowing over the tarmac, indicating the way to go. "This will change the way the world drives," said Way-Ray's gangling twenty-two-year-old founder, Vitaly Ponomarev. "In three years, we will be a billion-dollar company for sure."

"A billionaire by thirty?" Steve smiled.

"Exactly," said Ponomarev, aping his Silicon Valley cyber heroes.

"What are your sales figures to date?" asked Steve.

"Nothing – yet. But we have fantastic interest from many companies. We are poised to take off."

After another half hour of talk, it turned out that though Way-Ray had a very long shot at success, the world of hi-tech startups in Russia was even less impressive. What surprised Steve as he made the rounds of new companies over the following few days was that, for a country so large there were so few like Vitaly Ponomarev around.

Kozlov might be strutting on the world stage, but the country that had put the first man into space years ago was a pygmy as far as private high tech was concerned. As Vitaly Ponomarev had finally admitted to Steve, "Most of the billionaires in this country, earned their fortunes by using their connections and bribery. They took over companies that used to belong to the state. They did not build them up themselves. We have no tech heroes in this country. No Elon Musk or Mark Zuckerberg. In any case, people with money here are not interested in investing in startups. They would rather spend it on their wild lifestyles: on women and yachts and foreign mansions."

Steve was surprised when the Sirotskys sent him a coded message to meet at their safe house one day before their week was up. He arrived at eight in the evening, as requested. Again, it was Boris in black t-shirt and jeans that let him in. Olga sat on the sofa in the living room, still looking sensational with her blond hair tied back in a bun and a form-fitting black Lululemon yoga outfit with sequins down the side. She nodded when Steve took a chair across from her. On the coffee table were several black file folders and a large porcelain bowl of pistachios.

"Before we get to business, can we offer you a whiskey again," said Boris cheerfully, "or perhaps vodka?"

"Thanks," said Steve. "I'll try vodka this time."

"And, please, help yourself to the pistachios," said Boris. "They're very fresh."

Boris poured vodka for the three of them; then raised his glass to toast, "Na Zdorove." Steve took a sip of the burning liquor. Boris emptied his entire glass, then patted Olga's shapely butt to indicate she should make room for him. He plopped down on the sofa and smiled broadly at Steve.

"So here we are," he said, pointing to the files on the table between them. "One folder per company. As you suspected, the real owners of the companies are very close allies of Kozlov. My wife will begin."

Glancing coolly at Steve, Olga picked up the top folder. "This one, Rivka I, is controlled by General Anatoly Popov, one of the rising stars in the Russian military."

"I've heard of him," said Steve. It was the first time Olga had spoken since Steve offered them the work. She had apparently become reconciled to the fifteen million dollars.

"Also," said Olga, "Popov is the former son-in-law of the deputy commander of the Russian armed forces. These pages give a list of his holdings outside Russia," she said, flipping through the file, "in Athens, in London, in Paris, and Mallorca – a five-bedroom vacation home overlooking the water at Deia. There are pictures for most of the properties.

"He bought a new shopping mall from Stokes a year ago in Houston, Texas. Also, he seems to be in partnership with BST, one of the Panamanian companies you gave us the name of, which is controlled by Stokes. They have an investment together in a new five-star hotel in Malta. It is called Seabreeze. What is interesting is that Stokes's company only put up 20% of the capital for that hotel, but was credited with 49% of the investment."

"Fascinating. Good work," said Steve. Olga awarded Steve a slight smile. The fear that had been hanging over him for the past week – that he might have thrown away fifteen million of Pearlstein's dollars – was beginning to dissipate. He took a large sip of vodka and picked up a handful of pistachios.

Boris refilled his own glass before he opened the next folder. "This one, Arbat, is owned by Alexei Petreykin who controls the cement industry in this country. Actually, not by Petreykin himself, but by his wife and two sons, seventeen and nineteen years old, obviously brilliant business people," he raised his eyes to the ceiling then thumbed through several pages of their property holdings, stopping at one. "Here you can see he bought a property in Dallas, Texas from Stokes for three hundred million dollars, a 200-unit housing complex. We checked. A year earlier Stokes bought the same property for one hundred fifty million. Doubled his money in a year."

"Either Petreykin was very stupid," said Steve.

"Highly unlikely," said Boris.

"Or something else was involved here," said Steve.

"You should look for the something else," said Boris as he picked up the next folder.

"This company called Kalinka," he continued, as if he were giving a guided tour of a posh Moscow suburb, "is owned by another of our biggest oligarchs, Fyodor Lebedev. Interesting history--he came up through the ranks of the KGB with Kozlov, then just happened to be in the right place when they sold off one quarter of the country's natural gas. And voilà," he snapped his fingers, "an overnight billionaire. And we're the ones who are considered the crooks." He gave a mirthless smile, "At least Olga and I work for our profits." He riffled the pages and stopped at one. "Ah yes, among other things, we see they are partners in a new residential development in Kuala Lumpur, with Westend—another of the Panamanian companies you gave us owned by Stokes."

Olga took over again with a folder for the company called Styx. "It is owned by the wife and three children of Dmitri Morozov," she said. "Also apparently wonderful business people. Morozov started as steelworker, from somewhere got the money to invest in several iron and steel firms, a mobile phone company called Norstar, and a newspaper, *Sparks*. He also owns the Cosmos Bank and the Sloane Titans soccer club. He bought three properties from Stokes, in Memphis, Houston, and Los Angeles. All the details are here," she said.

"Again, my congratulations on your research," said Steve.

"Thank you," she smiled. Her earlier hostility seemed to have vanished as she continued, "This last company – Krypto – belongs to Sasha Volkov. He made his fortune also overnight when he was handed control of Russia's potassium mining industry. He added oil and coal, the Bourneside Chargers Soccer Team, and a couple of banks. He also bought a number of overseas properties." She flicked to a marked page. "These two condominiums in Austin, Texas total a hundred million dollars." She turned to another page, "Another interesting note, one of Volkov's banks, Argo, made a loan of four hundred million dollars to Stokes five years ago."

"That's when Stokes was teetering on the edge of bankruptcy" said Steve.

"A true friend in need," said Boris.

"Okay, that's five companies," said Steve.

Boris looked uncomfortable. "The last one you asked about was Pyotr1," he said giving a huge shrug and glancing at Olga. "Unfortunately, there we have to admit defeat. We were able to find nothing on it, other than the address that you already had. It is in Novosibirsk. It is a vacant lot. I swear to you, Olga and I spent many hours trying to hack into the company. But there was nothing to hack into. It is a totally empty shell. We have checked with all our contacts. No one has heard anything about it."

"How could a company be totally empty?" said Steve.

Boris raised both hands, "In this country, anything can happen, believe me" he said. "Olga and I may earn our living by hacking, but you must believe us, we are scrupulously honest in dealings with our clients. You can ask anyone."

Steve stood staring at the couple, not knowing how to react. "Please, have another vodka," said Boris, refilling Steve's glass. He poured another round for himself and Olga, who again was giving Steve a grim stare.

"You don't know the risks we are taking!" she exclaimed. "We could be…"

Boris raised his hand. "Wait, Olga. She is right, but to prove our honor and sincerity, we have deducted two million dollars from the amount you still owe us." He picked up a slip of paper from the table, and handed it to Steve. "Our bill. We have also deducted one-sixth from the charge for good will. So that means you owe us only three million dollars more. Once we have received notice you've transferred the funds, we'll hand over these files to you."

Steve realized they had him stymied. They might or might not be telling the truth about not being able to find out anything about the sixth company, Pyotr1. There was no way to challenge them. In any case, the data they'd gleaned about the first five companies and their links with Stokes was already very impressive.

"Too bad, you couldn't find out something about Pyotr1," said Steve.

Boris shrugged again, "Yes, that is too bad. But it sometimes happens even to the best of us. Just the same, you will admit that the material we have developed is most interesting."

"Absolutely," said Steve. He'd made his disappointment about Pyotr1 clear enough.

"So now," said Boris with a hungry smile, "It's just a question of the three million."

"I'll do it right now," said Steve. He picked up his iPhone, launched an enciphering app, and typed in a brief text message.

"Would you like some *piroschkis*?"; asked Olga, no longer the ice queen now that the money was on its way.

"Thanks," said Steve. "I've worked up quite an appetite."

She disappeared into the kitchen to return with a platter of pastries and three bowls of soup. "You should try my borscht, as well."

The soup and *piroschkis* were excellent. Steve hadn't realized how hungry he was. "We're going to miss all this," said Boris gesturing with his soup spoon. "You should see our house in Moscow and the dacha. We have some wonderful art. We would have been honored to have you over, but considering the circumstances, it would not be wise."

"You're going somewhere?" said Steve.

"I think it is time for us to leave the country," said Boris. "At least for a while."

He looked at Olga, who said nothing. Steve wondered which one of the couple was pushing to flee the country.

Olga's mobile signaled an incoming text message. She looked at the screen, typed a short reply then nodded to Boris. "The payment has arrived," she said.

"Actually," said Steve, "I feel uncomfortable about having these large files with me in Moscow. Could you give them to me on a smaller digital format instead?"

Boris smiled one more time, "We had the same thought," he said, taking two USB sticks from his pocket. "I've made two copies, just in case. All in-app view only and here's the password." He handed Steve a small slip of paper. "We will have the original files Fed-Exed to you by an associate in Frankfurt. Just tell us where you want them sent. But first, finish your dinner."

Ten minutes later, Steve shook hands with Olga, who insisted he take a couple of *piroschkis* with him in a bag to the hotel, and Boris led him to the door. "A pleasure doing business with you, Mr. Doug Robb, or Doug, if I may call you that. We wish you the best of luck with your project."

It was drizzling, but the traffic was relatively light when Steve left the Sirotskys' safe house, hailed a cab, and told the driver to take him to the Four Seasons Hotel. He slumped back in the seat and closed his eyes, still wound-up after his meeting with the Sirotskys. He went over in his mind the things he had to do now: contact the team back in the U.S. to start checking out the mountains of data he'd just been given. But that would have to wait until he was out of Russia. He'd call Pearlstein to thank him, figure out a safe place to conceal the two USB keys while he was still in country, and set up a meeting with Maya again before he left. Out of common courtesy, he owed her thanks for having set up the Sirotskys, but the heart of the matter was he simply needed to see her again though he had no idea where yet another encounter might lead.

He got out of the cab in front of the Four Seasons, and walked through the lobby, nodding to the concierge. He would treat himself to a steam and a massage he thought as he entered the elevator. Just as the doors were shutting, two men wearing black leather coats entered behind him. The taller one, standing near Steve, had the acrid odor of garlic on his breath. When Steve got off on the fourth floor, the two men exited behind him. He walked down the hallway, the back of his neck tingling with the knowledge that the two men were just behind him and the two USB keys were just waiting to be discovered. When he reached his door, he wheeled to face his followers.

"Go ahead," said the tall man, "Let us in."

"By whose goddamned order?"

"Russian Army Intelligence," said the tall man. He thrust a large gold badge in Steve's face, "You are under arrest on suspicion of being an American spy."

CHAPTER TWENTY-THREE:

Moscow

Steve was in the rear seat of a black BMW, handcuffed, and wedged between the two plainclothes men from army intelligence. Both of them, he now discovered, stank of garlic. They had ransacked his room, confiscated his laptop, attaché case, and the two USB keys in the false heel of his shoe. They then led him out of the hotel and into the waiting car, where they'd manacled his wrists and tied a blindfold on his face. His mind was in turmoil; an hour ago, he'd been elated by the information from the Sirotskys. Now, everything was shot to hell, his mission destined for ignominious failure. And his own fate?

Without diplomatic status, Steve had no idea what awaited him: brutal interrogations, years in prison, or execution in some dank, underground prison. So this is the way it all ends, he thought. Steve Penn exits stage left, leaving nothing and no one behind.

They drove for about an hour through heavy traffic. The three Russians listened to Moscow's twenty-four-hour sports news station and talked among themselves – shop gossip, retirement benefits, children, girlfriends – then turned off on what seemed to be a dirt and gravel road. They continued for another fifteen minutes before the car came to a stop. Thankful for the fresh air, Steve was taken out of the car and hustled along a path into a building, down a flight of stairs, and finally, prodded into a chair.

What interrogation techniques would his captors use? How long could he resist? Had he left any trail that might lead them to Maya? As for the Sirotskys, they'd be able to fend for themselves. Perhaps they'd already left the country.

The blindfold was suddenly removed.

But instead of a hulking inquisitor from Russia's security services seated across from him, there was a florid man with piercing gaze and bushy white eyebrows in the uniform of a Russian general. He looked sternly at Steve, then ordered the two plainclothesmen to wait outside. Only after they had left, did he spread his hands in welcome and introduce himself in Russian,

"I am General Artyom Borovik, commander of Russian Land Forces. And you are?"

"Douglas Robb," said Steve. Of course, he knew who Borovik was. But why the hell was one of Russia's most powerful generals concerned with Steve Penn?

"You can speak freely," said the general. "This is my private office outside Moscow. I use it for my own purposes. I have it regularly swept. The people who brought you here are completely loyal to me."

"My name remains Douglas Robb," said Steve, still trying to fathom what has happening.

The general shrugged, "As you wish. I am not going to tell you how I learned of your presence in Moscow, but I decided to have you picked up before less sympathetic authorities discover you and put a bullet in the back of your neck." He smiled slightly and gestured to a side table where there was a bottle of Stolichnaya, an ice bucket, and three crystal glasses. "Whatever your name, I imagine you might like a drink," he said.

Still dazed, Steve nodded silently.

The general filled two of the glasses, handed one across the desk to the American, and raised his glass to toast, "Na Zdorove."

"Na Zdorove," Steve replied, lifting his own glass. What the hell kind of interrogation was this? He took a large sip. Only a few hours before, he'd been toasting two notorious Russian hackers. Now he was drinking with one of Russia's most formidable generals.

"You probably need an explanation," said Borovik, settling into his seat.

"Probably."

The general knit his heavy brow. "None of what I am going to tell you can go beyond this room. I have been told that I can trust you."

"You can," said Steve. He had no idea who spoke so favorably about him to the general nor what Borovik might say next.

"The reason you are here," said the general, "is that I am very interested in what you are doing and wish you well. There are others in our armed forces who feel the same way." He stood and began pacing behind his desk holding his glass of vodka. "We would like to see your President Stokes out. We also want to cut our own president down to size. We were against his meddling in your elections. We were against his intervention in the Crimea. But his head is swollen with what he thinks is success."

He stopped pacing to have another large sip of vodka then continued, "Kozlov listens to no one. Like Stokes, he is a dangerous narcissist. Thanks to him, corruption is destroying our country. It will destroy yours if you let it. If you get rid of Stokes, that may help us get rid of Kozlov and his rotten gang."

He returned to his seat and leaned forward, gazing directly at Steve. The shadows from the overhead light played across his face. "You want information about Kozlov and his billionaire thieves and their ties with Stokes. I already have that. We've been collecting it for years, but we have not been able to do anything with it. We will give it to you."

He picked up a brass paperweight on his desk in the shape of Sputnik, turned it over in his hands, and looked at Steve with a sly grin. "It will be interesting to see how our information compares with the information you got from the Sirotsky couple."

Steve blanched.

"I assume you haven't had time to look at that yet," said the general. "I am curious; how much did it cost you?"

"You mean there is something you don't know?" said Steve.

The general made a disparaging wave of his hand. "I would imagine many millions. In any case, it is irrelevant. Here is one of the USB keys they gave you. If you don't mind, I'll keep the other for myself. I assume they are both the same."

"I believe so," said Steve.

"You can pick up your laptop and other material from my men when you leave," said Borovik. "Now go back to your hotel and be quiet. Wait for a day for someone to come and give you what you need."

Steve shook his head in disbelief. "That's it? I just walk out of here a free man and wait for your gift package? And no one says anything?"

"I told you the people who picked you up work directly for me, they are completely loyal."

"Then how do you or I explain their arresting me to anyone at the hotel, for instance, who might have seen what happened. Surely, the FSB and the other services have agents there. The lobby and sidewalk must be crawling with them."

"My men didn't arrest you," said the general, continuing to turn the paperweight. "They brought you in for questioning."

"On suspicion of being an American spy," Steve added.

"Exactly," the general brightened. "Our story is that we had been following you as you contacted various hi-tech start-ups in Moscow. You had long, detailed conversations with them about their advanced technologies. All very suspicious. Which is why, when I found out, I immediately ordered you to be picked up so we could find out what you are up to," The general smiled and raised his hands. "I see now that you are exactly what you claim to be: an independent investor looking for possibilities in Russia. A totally reasonable activity."

He finished his glass of vodka. "So that's it. My driver will take you into Moscow. You will get a taxi back to your hotel, and you will wait there for a day or so as I asked. Someone will contact you.

"One more thing, Mr. Robb – or whatever your name is." The general leaned forward and fixed Steve with his dark piercing eyes. "You must never reveal to anyone that you've ever met me. Never. I have too many enemies. I am putting my life in your hands. Now go."

CHAPTER TWENTY-FOUR

Moscow

So all Steve had to do was sit back and wait to be contacted. But there were other intelligence agencies out there, and as long as Steve remained in Moscow, he had his cover to maintain. The next morning, he visited two more start-ups: a food delivery service programmed to bombard you with menus curated to suit your specific tastes, and a bicycle-sharing app modeled after one that had made already made billions in China. The problem was that the first company had no real business plan; as for the second, well, Moscow wasn't Shanghai.

Afterward, Steve swam in the hotel pool, had the steam and massage he'd been planning to enjoy the day before, and then ate alone at Olivio's, a trendy Italian restaurant up the street from the hotel. Who was it, he wondered as he ate his spaghetti alle vongole, who was it who tipped General Borovik to his secret mission in Moscow? The Sirotskys? They had worked with military intelligence in the past. Were they playing both sides? What about Jake Pearlstein? His financial interests spanned the globe. Did they include connections with the Russian military?

He gazed at the couple loitering under the lamp across the street. Had he seen them earlier in the day? Maybe. He took another sip of the Brunello. There was also Maya. But with her background spying for the CIA, there was no way she would risk revealing her current contacts with Steve. Her image floated before him. He could almost smell her perfume. It was frustrating to know she was only a few miles away. But contacting her at this point would be far too dangerous for both of them.

The next morning he awoke at eight. He had only a couple more start-ups on his list, but absolutely no appetite to deal with yet another young billionaire wannabe. He sprawled in bed zapping idly between news channels on his TV, then walked towards the bathroom to take a shower. It was then that he saw the envelope that had been slipped under his door. The message on the one sheet of plain paper inside was typed in Russian:

"Good morning. There is a very nice new shopping center in the Crocus City Mall in Krasnogorsk. You should go to the Lapidus watch store (next to Louis Vuitton) and admire the new Rolexes in their window.

"You should be there at precisely 12:30. Wear a coat and carry today's *FT*. Someone will bump into you and place something in your left pocket. It will be encrypted. The password is xyz8v9b. Make sure you are not followed. We will also check.

"Signed, Your new friend."

Krasnogorsk was a western suburb of Moscow. Steve took a circuitous route, backtracking a couple of times, before getting off the metro at the elegant new Myakinino stop, the first station to be built outside of Moscow. He crossed the street to the hulking new exhibition center and entered the Crocus City Mall. It could have been any thriving mall in any prosperous city on the planet. All the global glitz was there: Armani, Aquascutum, Calvin Klein, Prada, and on and on. It was Saturday and the mall was thronged, the excited burble of the crowd mingled with whatever was the latest Russian rock hit being blasted throughout the sprawling complex. Everything here, thought Steve, belied the stories that Russia was facing severe economic problems. But who knows?

He waited until 12:27 before pushing his way through the jostling crowds toward the Lapidus jewelry store, the *Financial Times* under his right arm. He then stood in front of the window, gazing at the shimmering display of gold and diamond-studded watches. "Don't hog the space," said a burly man beside him, reeking of garlic. He butted Steve out of his path as Muscovites were wont to do. Instinctively, Steve shoved back. Then he felt a hand in his left pocket. Turning quickly, he got a quick glimpse of the retreating man's face before he disappeared in the crowd. It was the same hulking agent who'd "arrested him" at his hotel two days earlier.

Steve then walked to the nearest bathroom, entered one of the stalls, and removed the small plastic envelope that had been placed in his pocket. Inside was a USB key. He took it out and placed it inside the hollow heel of his left shoe. Then he continued browsing the shops. In case anyone was following him, he wanted to make it look as if the visit to this new mall was for idle sightseeing, rather than the clandestine passing of highly secret information. After lunch at a Lebanese restaurant, he took the metro back to his hotel. Once in the room, he inserted the key into the USB port of his laptop and entered the password that had been on the note slipped under his door that morning. Several PDF documents appeared on the screen. He opened the first. It was written in Russian.

"Summary. Here you will find the information promised. Checking the data on the USB key you provided us yesterday, it seems your hacker friends have given considerable material on many luminaries of our new *nomenklatura*. The case of the offshore company Pyotr1 which you asked them about, however, is another story. The person listed as the owner of that company, Alexander Vasiliev, is a well-known Russian violinist and also one of our President Kozlov's oldest friends. He is, of course, the owner in name only. The real owner is Kozlov himself.

"You will see that the holdings are very extensive. You will also see the many financial ties with your President Stokes. That includes purchases of several U.S. properties for amounts far above their market value. Also there are listed loans by two banks controlled by Kozlov: The Alpha Trust and Atlantis Group. Those loans were to Stokes for a total of nine hundred million dollars. Finally, there are three partnerships between Stokes and Kozlov's offshore companies for construction of a new port in Colombo, Sri Lanka, a shopping mall in Nairobi, and a superhighway in Taiwan. You will find extensive back-up documents confirming all those holdings.

"Remember our agreement!

"Your new friend."

Steve's heart beat wildly as he opened the rest of the documents: sales records, bank statements, confidential memos. It was all there. The Sirotskys had screwed him—well, not entirely. They'd made a cool ten and a half million dollars in exchange for damning information about the links between Stokes and top Russian oligarchs. But when it came to taking on Russia's president, revealing the activities of Kozlov's own holding company, they'd backed off in fear. And they'd gotten away with it.

But assuming the information General Borovik just gave him was for real, he now had the evidence he needed. Ironically, it had cost him (and Pearlstein) nothing. He could only imagine the frustration – the bottled-up fury of Borovik and other Russian military officers – he could only imagine their outrage, compiling this information, piece by sordid piece, over the years; knowing the depths of Kozlov's corruption but unable to do anything about it.

Early that evening, he walked down the street to Olivio's, the Italian restaurant where he'd eaten the night before. He ordered fettuccine Alfredo with another bottle of Brunello and considered his next steps. First, he had to arrange for the damning information on Stokes and Kozlov to be broadcast nationwide in the United States. Once aired, there was no way the Republicans could avoid launching the impeachment process any longer. In fact, like Nixon, Stokes might even be forced to resign of his own free will before Congress acted.

But proceeding to that next stage, checking out the information he'd been given and arranging for the broadcast, could not be done in the Russian capital, blanketed by the FSB and other intelligence agencies. The U.S. would also be risky. He would leave immediately for London, where Jake Pearlstein had already offered him the highly secure facilities of his Belgravia residence. That would be the perfect spot.

Steve was just finishing his pasta when the headwaiter came to his table. "Excuse me, are you Mr. Robb?"

"Yes."

"A young man just gave me this. He told me to hand it to you."

Steve thanked him, opened the envelope, and removed the typewritten message inside. Who would believe this? He thought, today is turning out to be like a scavenger hunt, one secret typewritten message after another.

This one, to his surprise, was from Maya. "Taking the children to see the penguins at the Moscow Zoo tomorrow. 10:30 is the feeding time. I thought you would enjoy the outing. Dancing Bear."

His heart was beating quickly again as he returned to the hotel. She must have followed him to the restaurant and then had someone else deliver the message. Or perhaps the concierge, who had booked the restaurant for him, had told her where Steve was eating. If she hadn't found him, would she have slipped the message under the door of his room? He hadn't wanted to risk contacting her, but now she was contacting him. Was there some emergency? The medicine for her daughter cut off? What?

Back in his room, he booked himself on the 5:00 p.m. British Airways flight the next day to London. That would give him time to go to the zoo, return to the hotel, check out, and take a taxi to Sheremetyevo.

He woke early the next morning, packed his bag, and took two hours to travel to the zoo via a serpentine route, constantly on the alert for anyone who might be following him. What would it be like, he wondered, studying the crowd, as he exited the Barrikadnaya Metro Station, to move around normally without worrying about somebody tracking your every move or attempting to intercept your every communication.

The Moscow Zoo was one of the capital's sights he had never visited before. Once notorious as a slovenly, dilapidated residence for thousands of unfortunate species, the Moscow government had taken over management from the state and spent several million rubles on restoration with partial success. Steve eyed the result skeptically as he walked through the fake stone entrance designed to look like a fairy tale castle with a waterfall and watchtower. It was a feeble attempt at a Disneyland, Steve thought, and it stank like a filthy barnyard.

Just the same, the paths were thronged with families on a Sunday outing with their children, complete with ice cream cones, hot dogs, and cotton candy. Amazing how many of them were already overweight, even the kids. A sign indicated the penguins were up the path to the right. A crowd was already gathering before their enclosure. A group of the black and white sea birds, absurd as always with their tuxedo vests, were waddling about the gray granite rocks. Others darted about in the water then also clambered up on the rocks, instinctively crowding to where the morning feeding habitually took place.

Steve spotted Maya sitting on a wooden bench, across the path. Without any sign of recognition, he walked casually towards her. Expressionless, she moved her bag so he could sit down.

"Nice day," he said, as if chatting up an attractive stranger.

"Yes," she smiled slightly, turning her pale blue eyes towards him. He could smell her perfume. He wanted desperately to take her hands, to touch her, but nothing could be less appropriate. He noticed there were fewer people further up the path where there was an empty enclosure.

"Why don't we move there," he said quietly.

"Let the children finish watching the feeding." she said.

"Which one is Sonya?" Steve asked.

"On the left with the yellow top and red jeans."

Steve looked across the way and turned back to Maya. "I still don't see her," he said.

"Sonya," Maya shouted and waived. A young woman by the railing turned her head briefly and waived back with a quick smile. She had her mother's long red hair, blue eyes, and the burgeoning figure of a future beauty. Steve suddenly realized he hadn't seen Sonya since she was three years old. She must be fifteen now, he thought, amazed at the passage of time. Sonya was holding the hand of a gangling boy with long brown hair. He was wearing a white Chelsea football shirt and jeans.

"Who is the boy?" Steve asked.

"My son," Maya smiled.

"Your son?"

"That is what I said."

"I didn't know you had another child."

"I do."

He felt a sudden surge of anger, jealousy. Maya had never told him there had been another man in her life. It was like an ice shower.

"Oh, I see," he said, feeling abruptly disconnected from her, an outcast. He was overwhelmed by a feeling of bitterness.

The feeding ended and the crowd began to disburse, the children tugging their parents toward the aquarium beneath the penguin enclosure.

Sonya and her brother scampered back across the path to where Maya was sitting with Steve. "Sonya," this is Mr. Robb," said Maya. "He is an old friend of mine." The girl looked at Steve with a smile. Steve smiled back. She leaned down and gave him a peck on the cheek.

"Thank you, Sonya," said Steve. "You are very pretty – just like your mother." The girl blushed.

"And this is Evgeny," said Maya, beaming at her son. "Evgeny, shake hands with Mr. Robb."

The young boy with long brown hair and hazel eyes shyly extended his hand looking curiously at Steve. Funny, thought Steve, as he shook the hand, he looks so familiar.

"Mama, can we get a strawberry ice?" asked Sonya.

"It will be my treat," said Steve, handing the girl a hundred ruble note.

The two children scampered off to the kiosk.

"You are lucky," Steve said, "to have two children."

She looked up at him solemnly. "You were afraid to ask who the father was," she said.

"I didn't want to pry." He felt the stirrings of jealousy again. How stupid of him not to have realized that she might be sharing her bed – sharing her life – with another man. "After all, I don't own you. You are not mine." Though I wish you were, he wanted to add, but didn't.

"Steve, you are Evgeny's father."

He stared wildly at her, his heart racing. "What?"

"I said, you are Evgeny's father. Evgeny means 'child of a noble man.'"

"How could he…"

"Don't talk so loud," she said looking around her. "He was conceived the last night we were together in Moscow, before you left to join your wife."

A son! He had a son! "All those years…how could you never have told me?" asked Steve.

"Because I thought you were married," said Maya. "It was only two years ago you told me what happened to your wife. By that time, I was used to raising Evgeny by myself, used to not having a father around."'

Steve started to interrupt.

"Also," she continued, "you know there was no way we could have lived together. You could not have lived here. I was not going to leave my mother in Moscow.

"And I have my pride. I was not going to use my child as a way to catch you. I had already prostituted myself for the medicines."

Once again, Steve's head was whirling. He had undertaken this mission because he thought he was alone in the world – no wife, no children. Now everything had changed, but there was no dealing with all that now.

He wanted to take Maya's hands but didn't. He couldn't. Not here, not in public, not in Moscow. "Maya, this is fantastic, wonderful news. I am so delighted, believe me."

"But…" she said and waited.

"But I am reserved on a five o'clock flight to London. I have to finish my mission. I would love to stay with you and the children. But I can't. Not right now. But we are going to manage this, somehow. I swear. I just need a few weeks."

She looked at him, soberly, "You really think it could work?"

"Would you really consider living with me?" He asked.

"You are so blind," she said angrily. "Why do you think I put you in contact with the Sirotskys? Only because I was afraid the medicines might end if Stokes continues in power?"

Steve stared at her, dumbly.

"And who do you think told General Borovik about you?"

"You?"

"Who else? And you, the smart CIA agent, couldn't figure that out?"

"How do you know Borovik?"

"He served in the army with my dad. He's been like a father to me since my own father died. I know how he feels about Kozlov and the scum running this country. I didn't know he was actually tracking Kozlov's finances."

The children ran back with the ice cream cones. "We brought one for you, mama, and for Mr. Robb," said Evgeny, handing one to Steve. "Can we go to the aquarium now?" said Sonya.

"Of course," said Maya. "But I'm not sure if Mr. Robb can stay."

Steve licked his cone and looked at his watch. "I would love to join you," he said, "but I have to catch an airplane in a few hours. I have to go back to the hotel first."

"I've never been on an airplane," said Evgeny.

Steve tousled his hair, "Maybe one day I will take you," he said.

The boy looked at Maya, then at Steve, "You promise?" said the boy, wide-eyed.

"I promise," said Steve.

CHAPTER TWENTY-FIVE:

London

When King George IV decided to make Buckingham Palace his permanent residence in 1825, Richard Grosvenor, the 2nd Marquess of Westminster, saw a smashing opportunity. He commissioned architect Thomas Cubitt to transform a swath of his country property into exclusive housing on this suddenly very fashionable land. The development would come to be known as Belgravia. It consisted of majestic enfilades of four- and five-story white stucco mansions, built around a series of regal squares and resplendent gardens. It soon became the favored address of the British elite.

No longer. Belgravia today has been transformed into an international ghetto of the world's super-rich – Russian oligarchs, Gulf sheikhs, Greek shipping magnates, Indian nabobs, and Italian tycoon – all seeking safe haven on Belgravia's shady streets. The quiet, stately

Georgian facades belie the seamy fraud and corruption underpinning the fortunes of many of their venerable proprietors. A good number of the dwellings, in fact, are vacant for much of the year. They are personal trophies, a store of value, not permanent abodes; places to stash wealth of questionable origin, which also serve as a *pied*-à-*terre* for occasional shopping sprees at Aspreys or Harrods, or a week of fancy restaurants and West End musicals. There are also scores of embassies and ambassadorial residences located here, watched over by bevies of unblinking CCD cameras.

Arguably, the most eminent addresses of Belgravia are around Belgrave Square. None are more splendid than Number 51, the detached white mansion at the Northeast corner. It was built in 1852 specifically for Lord Thomas Rathbottom, who made a fortune selling munitions to the British army in India. He and his descendants lived there until 1905. There followed a series of sales to other prominent British families, until 2010, when the property was purchased for fifty million pounds by American start-up billionaire, Jake Pearlstein. Pearlstein then spent ten million pounds to transform the mansion, while constantly struggling against Belgravia's rigid zoning regulations. The hidden underground excavations were as spectacular as the mansion itself. They contained a fifty-seat theater, a twenty-five-meter swimming pool, and a large cantilevered room, balanced on huge springs and totally protected by the most sophisticated electronics. Like the installation in Pearlstein's home in Palm Desert, it was designed to shield the billionaire from unprincipled competitors and intelligence agencies that might attempt to penetrate the technologies he was developing or the financial moves he was plotting.

It was to use those facilities and escape the omnipresent intelligence services of Russia and the United States that Steve Penn came to London. It was here that Jake Pearlstein invited him to continue his campaign to take down the American president. "It's all yours," Pearlstein wrote in an encrypted exchange with Steve in Moscow. "My wife's cousin was supposed to be using the place next week. I'll inform her it's no longer available. She can always get a suite at the Dorchester. Two members of our housekeeping staff will remain. They can be totally trusted. My butler, Mike Rourke, has also been specially trained."

Steve arrived at Pearlstein's mansion around 8:30 p.m. after the three-and-a-half-hour flight from Moscow. Mike Rourke answered the door. He was a brawny, sandy-haired Irishman, from Dublin; in his forties, with gray, twinkling eyes and an easy smile. He wore a striped vest under a black cutaway jacket, and made it clear he could shift from Belgravia formal to Irish charm at will. Waiting in the hallway was the head housekeeper, Edith Jones, sturdy, dark eyes, brown hair done up in a bun; wearing a black dress with a white apron. "Can I fix you something to eat, Mr. Robb?" She asked with a light Welsh accent.

"Thanks, I ate on the plane," said Steve. "Frankly, I'd just like to get some sleep."

"Certainly. You're to have the blue guestroom. It's on the third floor." She led Steve to the elevator; Mike followed, insisting on carrying the suitcase. The spacious bedroom was decorated with Austrian art deco furniture and oriental silk carpets; its windows overlooked the square and park below.

"Shall I unpack for you, sir?" asked Mike.

"Thanks, I'll handle that myself," said Steve. "By the way, Mr. Pearlstein told me you've had 'special training.'"

"Right, sir. Twenty years with the SAS."

"Afghanistan? Iraq?"

"And a few more places as well. Also some background in surveillance."

"We should be able to trade a few stories," said Steve.

"I look forward to that. What time would you like breakfast tomorrow?"

"Eight would be great," said Steve.

"Good night, sir," said Mike, closing the door behind him. Fifteen minutes later, Steve was asleep on the fresh, lilac-scented sheets.

The next morning after breakfast, he asked Mike to take him to the secure bunker in the basement. It seemed indeed to be an identical copy of the facility in Pearlstein's mansion in Palm Desert, down to the encryption facilities and reinforced blast walls in case of a terrorist attack. Though windowless, it was large and well ventilated. It was the perfect workspace for what Steve hoped would be the climactic chapter of his mission.

The only way to convince reluctant Republican leaders to impeach Stokes was to create a tsunami of popular outrage. It would be generated by the startling facts Steve had uncovered about Stokes and Kozlov. One way to put them out would be via the social networks: YouTube, Facebook, Twitter. But a much more potent way to present that information was via *Focus*, the leading TV news magazine in the United States. It was broadcast every Sunday evening at six on the NBS Network. Even the president, it was said, never missed it.

The chief reporter on *Focus* was Ed Diamond, one of America's most aggressive, yet trusted newsmen. When Diamond had contacted Steve just after he quit the CIA and asked to talk to him about the Russian hacking investigation, Steve had turned him down, but left the door open for the future. Now was the time. But it was too risky for Steve to contact Diamond directly: Stokes's intelligence agencies would be alerted instantly.

Instead, Sarah Levin would make the approach. She and Steve had already talked about that eventuality before he left for Moscow. She was currently working between Washington, D.C., and New York, consulting, teaching, and doing research on artificial intelligence. She also had a previous connection of sorts with Diamond. She had been profiled by him when she was eleven years old, for a program on child prodigies.

Steve waited until noon in London before he called her on an encrypted line. "The message for Diamond is we've now got the facts to take down Stokes," he said. "It's a huge story, but you've got to get him to move immediately. Once things start rolling, Stokes's goons will be after us with everything they've got. I've asked Jake Pearlstein to call to prepare the way for you. Diamond did a profile of him two years ago."

Pearlstein's call worked. When Sarah called Diamond that same morning in New York, she was immediately invited to his office. An hour later, she took the elevator to the headquarters of *Focus* on the ninth floor of the Ford Building at 557 West 57th Street. Producers' heads turned as the stunning Asian American was ushered into Diamond's corner office. The floor-to-ceiling window behind him looked out over the Hudson River.

The reporter looked up from a script he was writing on his laptop, smiled broadly, and stood to shake her hand. "Well, hello, again. I don't think I would have recognized you if I hadn't been warned you were coming," he said, still not releasing her hand. "You've certainly changed from the skinny eleven-year-old cello player." Diamond was tall, with graying hair and dark, brown eyes. He moved with the assurance of someone used to being recognized anywhere he went in the United States. His walls and bookcases were filled with awards and trophies and pictures of him with the last five presidents.

"Thanks for agreeing to see me so quickly," Sarah said, taking a seat across from him.

"It was Jake Pearlstein's fault," said Ed. "He told me I'd be getting a call from someone about what could be the major scoop of my career. Hard to resist."

She looked around, "Is your office secure?"

"Very. For the last two years, things being what they are, our offices are swept every week."

"What about the windows?"

"The windows?"

"Listening devices could pick up on those."

"I could lower the blinds and close the curtains," he said half in jest.

"That would help," she said. "What about your mobile?"

"You mean this?" Now, obviously becoming annoyed, he picked up the iPhone on his desk.

"Right, would you mind removing the batteries while we're talking, and then put it in that small fridge you've got in the corner. You should also not just unplug your laptop, but put some tape over its camera. That's right. And disconnect your TV monitors."

"You've got to be kidding," he glared.

"Not at all." She smiled sweetly and waited until he'd complied, before continuing.

"If you didn't have such a pretty smile, I'd have already tossed you out," said Ed.

"And, if you make a remark like that again," she said gently, "I'll be out of here in a flash."

He raised both hands in surrender.

"Now before we proceed," she leaned forward, "these are the ground rules. You take no notes. You tell no one on your staff – no one – about what I am about to tell you. And you tell absolutely no one where you are going. You'll be gone for a few days."

* * *

London Thursday-Wednesday

At 9:30 a.m. in London the next morning, a black BMW driven by Charlie Doyle, another member of Deep Strike, pulled up in front of the mansion at 51 Belgrave Place. Ed Diamond emerged from the back seat and Doyle escorted him to the front door. Mike Rourke let them in and then retrieved Ed's bag and laptop from the car.

Steve was waiting in the front hall. He shook hands with the reporter.

"You're supposed to be dead," said Diamond.

"I know," said Steve.

"In fact, you don't sound at all like the man I spoke with by phone after you quit the agency."

"That's the whole idea. I had my vocal cords modified."

"So how do I know for sure you really are Steve Penn?"

"For starters, when you phoned me at my home in Falls Church you apologized for calling so late. You also refused to tell me how you got my number. You said someone on your staff had found it. You argued I could be doing a service to my country by talking. And then you gave me your private number."

"All true."

"Also I imagine that Sarah Levin when she spoke with you must have vouched for me."

"She did."

"Charlie Doyle here also worked with me in the agency."

"That's what he told me on the way in," said Diamond.

"I didn't recognize Steve at first either after his makeover," said Charlie, "But, yeah, this is the real article."

Charlie pulled out his wallet and extracted an old picture. "Here's the two of us together in Red Square a couple of years ago."

Diamond pointed to Steve, "And this is the same man?"

"It is."

Diamond shrugged, "OK, just had to ask."

"Now that's out of the way," said Steve, "why don't we all have some breakfast?"

While they were eating, Diamond probed Steve about his decision to quit the agency and go rogue. Steve talked for about twenty minutes, then looked squarely at Ed. "The bottom line is I'm determined to finish the investigation we started." he said. "I hope you're interested. If not, there are plenty other news broadcasts."

Diamond furrowed his brow. "Why do you think I dropped everything to come?" He put down his fork and stared back at Steve. "I've taken all the security precautions Sarah demanded. So far, I'm the only one at *Focus* who knows about this meeting. Everyone thinks I left to do a crash story on a scandal involving the U.S. ambassador. No one knows where I'm staying, and certainly no one knows anything at all about you. And, yes, I also took the battery out of my goddamned iPhone when I left Heathrow." He was still looking directly at Steve. "I assume this will all be worth it."

"It will," said Steve. "Now, you must be jet-lagged. We've got a room here for you."

"Yes, Sarah informed me," said Ed grimly. "No one leaves this place until the broadcast is done."

"Those are the ground rules," said Steve. "We have to assume that everyone is looking for us."

"So let's get it done," said Ed. "I slept for a couple of hours on the plane. Let me just grab a shower first."

Over the next few hours in the basement bunker, Steve laid out the case he'd amassed on Stokes's illicit financial dealings with Kozlov and the Russian oligarchs. It was mindboggling in scope: the emphasis not so much on influencing American foreign policy, as enriching Stokes and Kozlov and their billionaire cronies.

First, aided by additional research of his colleagues, Steve went through an itemized run-down of purchases of Stokes's properties by Kozlov and several of the Russian *nomenklatura*. There were fourteen major properties in all, totaling more than two billion dollars. Checking the records, Charlie and Sarah had found that in every case the properties were purchased by the Russians for multiples of the price that Stokes had originally paid, at times just one or two years before.

"The Russians wanted to transform as many of their ill-gotten Russian rubles into U.S. dollar assets as fast as they could," said Steve. "They didn't care about the price. Dirty money like that is pouring out of Russia."

"For instance, in one deal," said Charlie, "this guy Alexei Petreykin, who took over the Russian cement industry, bought a share in a new housing development in Dallas from Stokes for three hundred million. Stokes bought the same property for a hundred fifty million just a year earlier. Doubled his profits in a year."

"And that help from Stokes" Charlie added, "enabled Petreykin and his family to convert three hundred million dollars' worth of grotty rubles into bright shiny U.S. currency, with no one checking where it came from."

"Which brings up another interesting question," said Steve. "Why didn't the American bankers who handled those transactions make a thorough check on the source of that money? They're supposed to know their client, according to U.S. Treasury rules. But when Sarah Levin asked the manager of the Republic Bank of Dallas what kind of background check he had done, all he had was a letter from Stokes vouching for this slimeball Petreykin: 'I have been doing business with Vasily for years. Wonderful guy! Honorable man--without question, the greatest!'

"The U.S. would never let a foreign bank get away with such bullshit," said Steve. "But this one note from Stokes was enough to convince the folks at the Republic Bank. Stokes, after all, was its major customer. Apparently, no one from Treasury ever asked any questions."

"But at times," said Charlie, "there was a variation on the theme. When some properties were purchased, the Russian buyers first siphoned off twenty-five percent of the price to be sent to Stokes's offshore company and presumably never declared."

"How do you know?" said Ed.

"Here," said Charlie. "These are the records from the Russian company which Steve got in Moscow. In this case, you can see that the larger amount in rubles was paid to Stokes's holding in Dallas. But you see on the next line, in brackets, the remainder in rubles, about twenty-five percent, was paid to Highflyer, Stokes's Panamanian company."

"Another damning tidbit," said Steve. "In 2009, when Stokes was on the edge of bankruptcy, his ass was saved by loans from two offshore banks. One bank controlled by Kozlov loaned Stokes four hundred million. Another, owned by the Russian petroleum monopoly, provided five hundred million. Both loans unsecured."

"Something else we learned from Kozlov's offshore company files" said Steve. "There's a contract for a huge new port and railway facility in Colombo which Stokes and Kozlov's companies cornered, thanks to a fifty-million-dollar kickback to the president of Sri Lanka."

The briefing went on for another couple of hours. "Okay, enough," said Diamond. "I'm convinced." He put down the last document and raised his eyes to the ceiling. "This definitely calls for a drink."

"As a matter of fact," said Steve. "There are supposedly several bottles of *Dom Perignon* in Pearlstein's wine cellar. He told me we should feel free to help ourselves." A few minutes later Mike Rourke emerged from the elevator with two bottles on ice, some chilled champagne glasses, and a tray of hors d'oeuvres.

"You do things in style," said Ed, raising his glass. "Steve, I have to say I thought at first you might be a bullshit artist. But this stuff is a bombshell. It'll blow Stokes and the Russians out of the water!"

"That's the idea," said Steve. He wished that somehow Maya could be here to share in the triumph.

"Before we go any further," said Diamond, "I've got to make a call to our local bureau."

Steve looked up abruptly.

"Don't worry," said Diamond. "I need a tape editor for this project. But you can calm down. I know the ropes." He phoned the London bureau of the NBS network and was put through to Dave Turecamo, a very talented editor he'd worked with on several occasions.

"Dave, I'm going to be needing your services. It's for a crash report on-uh-the U.S. ambassador here."

"Sounds interesting," said the editor. "When and where?"

"Immediately. A man called Mike Rourke will arrive shortly with all the info. Pack whatever you need for a few days away. See you."

Ed finished his champagne, then turned back to Steve and the others. "Of course, we're going to have to check out everything – every goddamned document and fact – to make sure there's no mistake. We'll be crucified if we fuck up." He paused and looked fixedly at Steve, "And I have to know who your sources are, just for me. You understand."

Steve slowly shook his head. "I can't tell you our sources," he said. "Their lives are literally on the line. They could be dead within a day after the broadcast. You say it's just for you, but I have no idea what kind of pressure you might come under. I swore I'd tell no one. I'm keeping that promise. In any case, we've already shown you these documents are legitimate. They check out. The original purchase price of the properties, the price the Russians paid. It's all there. It doesn't matter who they came from; they're the real thing."

Ed paused. This was the biggest story of his career. Penn was right. Knowing the sources wasn't key. He nodded. "Okay, but, like I said, we are going to check everything with a fine-tooth comb. We're also going to want to interview you, Steve."

"I don't think so," Steve grimaced.

"You'd better get used to the idea," said Diamond. "I understand your face can't be shown, but we can block it out digitally. You're key to the report. We can't get your sources. We need to have you. The story is as much about you as about Stokes."

"Okay," said Steve.

"We also have to go to the White House and the Kremlin and the oligarchs we name for comments."

"Of course," said Steve. "But once you do, they'll know what's up."

"Can't be helped," said Diamond flatly. "We're going to have work full-blast now. We've got three days. I want to feed the report in time for this Sunday's broadcast.

"Just understand they'll do everything they can to stop us." said Steve. "They've already murdered one of my friends. Right now, they don't know where we are. That may not last long."

* * *

Executive Liaison Office (S Team) Operational Memo:
From: Captain Jean Swanson
To: George Ramos, Operations, Executive Liaison Office (S Team)

Cc: Cliff Dayton
File: 178/2506
Subject: Steve Penn & Associates Update: Sara Levin--
Something stirring?

It's been more than a month since Steve Penn disappeared. Despite blanket surveillance by NSA and sister agencies in Europe, the U.K., Canada, and Australia, no indication whatsoever that Penn is still alive and operational. Absolutely nothing has been picked up by key words, voice, or facial recognition. Also no suspicious activity from any of Penn's former close associates connected with the Russian hacking investigation. We were ready, in fact, as per instructions (see GR 320) to reduce to a minimum all further activities in that area.

That was until yesterday when we received word of several abnormal, possibly coordinated actions; though none involving Penn himself.

1. One of Penn's former associates, Sara Levin, went to the offices of Focus on 57th Street in Manhattan at 9:12 a.m. We do not know for certain whom she saw, but suspect it may have been Ed Diamond.

Levin was interviewed by Diamond almost twenty years ago on the subject of child prodigies, but it is doubtful this visit would have anything to do with that. (Checking further with our source at Focus.)

2. Diamond left the building at 3:47 p.m. in a Skywards limousine. After questioning the driver, we found he took Diamond to the United Terminal at JFK. Driver had no idea where Diamond was headed. There were flights departing around that time for several major European and Asian cities. Currently checking video from surveillance cameras at the terminal, as well as immigration for all international departures.

No way of knowing if Levin's visit to Focus had anything to do with Diamond's late afternoon departure. We do know, however, that two days after Penn resigned from the CIA, Diamond phoned Penn in an attempt to set up an interview. At that time, Penn turned down Diamond's request, but seemed to suggest there might be a possibility in the future

(ref: ED 1597). We know of no contact they had after that. Currently retrieving the record of all communications to Focus for 24 hours before the Levin visit.
3. Charles Doyle, another of Penn's former confederates, is known to be in London, where he moved shortly after Penn's "death." He apparently told friends there he was leaving town for a few days, but gave no indication where. He does have a girlfriend in Cornwall. Following up with GCHQ in London.
4. Viewing this fast-moving situation, request urgent permission to go to London myself to liaise with our local partners.

* * *

Executive Liaison Office (S Team) Operational Memo:
From: George Ramos, Operations Captain Jean Swanson
To: Captain Jean Swanson

Cc: Cliff Dayton
Subject: Re your File: 178/2506.

Request to travel to London granted. Keep us posted on every development.

CHAPTER TWENTY-SIX:

London

It took a day and a half working almost round the clock in the bunker for Diamond and Dave Turecamo, his editor to assemble a rough cut of the report. They hunched over Dave' s laptop editing system at one end of the room. At the other end, Steve and Charlie hovered around a large glass-topped table, scrolling through other documents on their laptops, occasionally consulting a large white board above them filled with scrawled organizational charts, photographs, and scribbled notations. Mike Rourke and Edith Jones kept them supplied with food.

During the few breaks, Ed entertained them with accounts of his various reporting adventures: his classic interview with Saddam Hussein, when he asked the Iraqi dictator why he had pretended he had weapons of mass destruction.

"How do you keep it together when things get really tense?" asked Charlie.

"Old yoga technique," said Ed. "I take a deep breath, count to five when I let it out. Then take another breath and do the same. Works all the time."

Steve was interested in a different subject. "What about the problem of corporate control of your broadcasts?" he asked. "I mean, the great majority of media outlets in the United States are owned by mega-corporations. And it's only getting worse. How can you maintain your independence?"

"I won't kid you," said Ed. "It's a huge challenge."

"Your network is owned by Riggs Entertainment, correct?" said Steve.

"Since two years ago."

"Any idea what the company is worth?"

"About three hundred billion dollars, give or take a few billion."

"What else do they own?" said Charlie.

"I have trouble keeping track myself," said Ed. "The network's just a small part of an empire. Riggs also has a movie studio which streams video, and Vibe, which streams music. There's also Pixtalk on social media."

"I didn't know Pixtalk was owned by Riggs," Charlie said.

"There's also something like eight independent TV stations, a separate sports network, fifteen cable companies in the U.S., Japan, South Korea and, I think, Turkey, plus a bunch of newspapers, but the papers don't make much these days."

"Does that mean you've sometimes got to pull your punches in the reports you do?" said Steve.

Ed paused. "So far, no. We did hold off a few years back on a report about the heads of U.S. cigarette companies lying under oath."

"I remember."

"Also held back for a while on a story about U.S. torturing prisoners at Abu Ghraib in Afghanistan. Another correspondent got fired when he screwed up on a document regarding the Pentagon. So far, that's it. But we've never put together anything this strong about a sitting U.S. president." He shrugged. "Always a first time I guess."

By Friday afternoon London time, they had finished the rough cut. Exhausted, Ed's editor stumbled off to his bedroom on the fourth floor of the mansion. For Ed, however, it was time to start contacting the outside world.

The first call was to Josh Kantor, the executive producer of *Focus*. Before scurrying off to catch his flight to London, Diamond had ducked into Kantor's office with Sarah Levin just behind him, closed the door and said, "Josh, I'm leaving for a couple of days. If it works out, we've got a sensational broadcast, biggest scoop in years."

"About what?" said Kantor, removing his reading glasses to look up at Ed and Sarah. The bookcase behind him held almost as many broadcasting awards as Ed's.

"I can't tell you what it's about," said Ed.

"Gotta be Stokes," said Kantor.

"You didn't hear it from me," said Ed. "But if it's as good as my source says, it'll be dynamite. I'll have it ready for this Sunday."

"You going to introduce me to your charming friend," said Kantor looking curiously at Sarah.

"This is Sarah, Sarah Levin. Sarah, Josh. She's going to be installing an app on your laptop."

"Sounds like fun," Kantor smiled. "I was thinking you could just use my Skype account. It's encrypted, right?"

Sarah scowled. "Not encrypted enough to block the NSA and whoever is after us. This app will allow you two to have encrypted phone conversations over the next few days," she explained. "The calls will be routed through a very sophisticated anonymous relay. Anyone intercepting them will have no idea where on the planet they're coming from."

"Great, but just so I'll know, where the hell will it really be coming from?" said Kantor raising his hands.

Sarah shook her head, "Can't tell you," she said. "And you'd never understand the geeky gory details." The previous day, she'd made a quick round trip to Washington to set up the same secure facility on the private line of Senator Bill Gurd.

"Ed, wait," said Kantor, raising his voice. "As your supposed boss, I at least get to know where the fuck you're going."

"Sorry, Josh, I'll be in touch by Friday. You gotta trust me on this one. If anyone asks what I'm up to, just tell them it's something to do with corruption in a U.S. embassy somewhere."

Since arriving in London, Ed had called Josh once over the encrypted line to assure him that everything was on track, but he still refused to give any details on the report. Now, two days later – early Friday afternoon in London and Friday morning in New York – Ed put in an encrypted call to Kantor's *Focus* office.

"Josh, the story is for real. A major scoop, believe me. It will be the *coup de grace* for Stokes. It's about his illicit financial dealings – hundreds of millions of dollars – with Kozlov and a handful of Russia's biggest billionaire crooks. It's dynamite. Also a great personal bravery/crusading story about the former CIA agent who cracked this whole thing wide open. We've got him exclusive. I'll be sending you an encrypted script, but here's the details."

Diamond continued for the next fifteen minutes to outline the report to Kantor, interrupted by the executive producer's increasingly wary questions. "Sounds like it could be a winner, Ed," said Kantor cautiously. "But between thee and me, taking on Stokes with these kinds of accusations could be a real challenge."

"Not when you've got the kind of ammunition we do," said Ed.

"Who are your sources?" asked Kantor.

"I told you," said Ed. "This former CIA agent, Steve Penn. He was the one who headed the goddamned CIA investigation into Russian hacking. He's handed us a pile of documents. We've been checking it all out over the last couple of days. Everything's fine."

"Where do the documents come from?" said Kantor.

"From the agent's sources."

"And who are they?"

"He can't say. Their lives would be on the line. But they're all legit. Believe me."

"I'll have to let the lawyers look at them," said Kantor.

"Fine. We can encrypt the main ones and send them to you, along with our translations. The lawyers can also go over the script. But they will have to read it live in front of you, I don't want a copy floating around even for a second before we air it."

"So, finally, where the hell are you?" asked Kantor.

"Still can't reveal that," said Diamond. "Every bloody intelligence agency in the U.S. and Russia is going to be looking for us if they aren't already. Everyone here is restricted to base until we feed the piece."

"This isn't the way we operate," said an exasperated Kantor.

"And this isn't the usual piece of fluff we turn out," said Ed testily. "Listen, Josh, calm down, pop a Xanax; everything's going to be fine. The next call I place is to the White House, to Stokes's press guy. You can expect an immediate explosion, with more fireworks to follow. I'm also calling Kozlov's office in the Kremlin and contacting his fellow Russian oligarchs."

"Ed, I've never heard you so hopped up," said Kantor. "What are you smoking?"

"Nothing. Just into a sensational story," said Diamond. "What's wrong with you, Josh? This isn't the first time we've gone after the White House."

"But nothing like this," said Kantor. "Don't forget how Rather at CBS got his head handed to him for making a mistake about George W. Bush's service in the Air National Guard."

"Yeah, he screwed up on one document. But we've got scores of documents, and they're all solid. "

"Ed, in case you've forgotten, Stokes is a very different animal than the presidents we've had in the past."

"Are you saying the network won't broadcast this despite what we've got?"

"I'm just saying Stokes is going to play a new kind of hardball: vicious and brutal. You can bet on it. I'm going to alert corporate to what's up."

"Be my guest," said Diamond. He knew there was no way around that. "Tell them it's going to be a sensational report. The ratings will be sky high. They'll be delighted."

"Glad you think so," said Josh.

Diamond ended the call, took a deep breath, then punched in the number of Tony Crawford, the White House press secretary.

* * *

Twenty minutes later, Crawford scurried into the office of Cliff Dayton, President Stokes's chief advisor. Three minutes later, they went together to the Oval Office. Standing in front of the white velvet curtains, wearing a dark blue blazer, Stokes was recounting to his son, Ronnie, the meeting he'd just had with the visiting British prince. "He's a wimp," said Stokes, "But a sensational wife, let me tell you!"

"Sorry to barge in Mr. President," said Dayton. "But Tony just got a call. I thought you should know about it immediately." Stokes looked sharply at Crawford. "So, tell me."

Crawford flushed. "Sir, I just got off the phone with Ed Diamond."

"Great reporter. Great show." Stokes commented. "Been on it twice. Everyone said I was great."

"Diamond says he's going on *Focus* this Sunday with a broadcast that accuses you of billions of dollars of illegal dealings with President Koslov and five other Russian billionaires."

Stokes dropped into the seat behind his desk, "That dick said what?" For the next ten minutes, Crawford read aloud from the transcript of the conversation he'd just had with Diamond. According to the reporter, it was former CIA agent Steve Penn who came up with the documents to support the accusations. Playing with a gold letter opener on his desk, Stokes interrupted Crawford's account every few sentences with explosive assessments of Diamond: "cocksucker," "asshole," "shithead" and Steve Penn: "fucking liar," "goddamn traitor."

By the time Crawford had ended, Stokes's face was beet-red. "Give me that fucking transcript," he said. When Crawford approached, Stokes ripped the papers from his hands, glanced at them briefly and put them on his desk. Then he grasped the letter opener and brought it down so savagely it pierced the transcript and embedded itself in the teak desk that had served ten American presidents. "This is fucking outrageous!" Stokes bellowed. "It's treason! How the fuck did he…"

"Mr. President," said Crawford cautiously, "Diamond wants to know if we – if you – if the White House has any reply."

"No fucking way." Stokes yanked the letter opener from the desk. "It's all lies. Fake news on top of fake news. Pure bullshit created by my enemies. They're everywhere, believe me."

He wheeled on Crawford. "And what brilliant answer did you have when he told you this?"

"You shouldn't dignify any of this with a response," said Stokes's son. "What would be interesting to know though is how this disaster happened." He stared at Cliff Dayton.

"Yes, exactly," said Stokes, also turning his livid gaze on Dayton. "How the hell did this happen? When we won, you asked for a special intelligence operation of our own – off the books. And you got everything you wanted! Five hundred people working for you—a secret budget of hundreds of millions. Add to that, the shitload we spend on all that other stuff--the CIA, NSA, satellites. All that and this dickhead – what his name?"

"Steve Penn," said Dayton,

"This dickhead, Steve Penn, still gets through! It's fucking unbelievable!" He seized the letter opener again and pointed it at his advisor. "Goddamn it, Dayton, you were supposed to be on top of this. If you haven't the balls – if you can't do it – someone else will. Now get this," his tone suddenly became ice cold, "I want Penn and that whole goddamned *Focus* operation shut down. Now!"

He put the letter opener down. "The *Focus* broadcast, I'll take care of. We'll see if the guys who own Diamond's network have the balls to stand up to the White House. There's plenty we can throw at them. They've got a big business. *Focus* has gotta be just a pissant detail to them. They can't go around attacking me. I'm the president of the United States. It's treason." As Dayton and Crawford left, Stokes picked up his phone and ordered his secretary to call the White House Counsel and the Secretary of Commerce. "Tell them to get their asses right over here."

Meanwhile, a fuming Cliff Dayton returned to his office and immediately called George Ramos, head of operations of the secretive Executive Liaison Office.

"Ramos, you and your people have fucked up big-time," Dayton exploded.

"Sir?" Ramos gut instantly tightened. He had just returned from a lengthy, lubricated lunch at The Palm.

"You guys were supposed to be tracking the opposition," said Dayton. "You're supposed to be on top of everything. You've got a staff of 500, access to everything from every one of our goddamned agencies. We spend hundreds of billions on knowing what's going on and yet you let one former CIA agent make fools of us all, of me.

"Who are you talking about?" asked Ramos, his stomach still churning.

"Steve Penn,"

"The prick who wrote the Russian hacking report?"

'You told us he was dead. He drowned."

"He did."

"Did he? He's turned up very alive on a report that Ed Diamond is going to broadcast this Sunday!"

"I don't understand," said Ramos.

"Of course, you don't," said Dayton. "You'll be getting a transcript of Diamond's call to the White House press office. This is strictly confidential, but Stokes wants Penn and that whole goddamned operation shut down immediately, wherever they are. Those are your marching orders. And I don't give a rat's ass how you do it."

* * *

From: Captain Jean Swanson
To: George Ramos, Cliff Dayton
Subject: urgent call re former CIA agent Steve Penn and possible Focus broadcast.
Confidential:
I don't know how to reply to the comments you relayed from the White House. We are also surprised to learn that Penn is alive. As you know, however, we had our suspicions all along that his "suicide" might not be what it seemed. We also did issue an alert two days ago that something might be in the works. (see JS 51)
We have no excuses, but we do have further results that will lead to our locating Penn and/or Diamond.
Our search of records at JFK indicates that Diamond flew to London on UAL flight 46, arriving Terminal 2 at 9:00 a.m. British intelligence agency BCHQ informs that CCTV cameras at the airport show Diamond getting in a black BMW 25 minutes later. However, a check of the owner of the license plates indicates that they in fact are counterfeit.
There has also been anomalous traffic which likely are encrypted communications to the office of Focus's executive producer in Manhattan using unconventional protocols and moving relays, whose whereabouts we are unable to track.
I would respectfully draw your attention to the fact that, anticipating these events, I requested and received permission

to fly to London. I am now in an ideal position to liaise with British intelligence. Have already been given working space at the offices of MI5.

With full cooperation of BCHQ, we are focusing all efforts on tracking down any member of Penn's team and Ed Diamond in London. A big city, but we'll find them.

* * *

Immediately after contacting the White House, Ed Diamond called Sergei Markovich, the rotund spokesman of Russian President Vasily Kozlov. If Ed was going to broadcast charges against the Russian leader, he had to also give him a chance to respond. It was six in the evening in Moscow. Markovich was just getting set to go home, but when his secretary told him who was on the phone, he immediately took the call. He had been stationed for five years at the Russian embassy in Washington. He knew the name Ed Diamond and the impact of *Focus*. Later, however, he regretted his decision to speak with Diamond that evening. It had provoked a serious bout of heartburn and cost him a night's sleep.

Kozlov was already in a foul mood when Markovich walked into his office. The president had just received the latest confidential statistics on the Russian economy: unemployment was up, automobile and electrical power production in decline. The U.S. stock market was also down. As a result, the portfolio held by Kozlov's offshore company had just been shaved by ten million dollars. Muslim dissidents were still raising hell in Chechnya and the Caucasus.

Then in waddled Sergei Markovich to tell Kozlov about the call from Ed Diamond of *Focus*, that weekly purveyor of American lies and anti-Russian propaganda. "The bottom line is Diamond is charging you have made billions of illegal rubles in various Russian enterprises," said Markovich.

Kozlov shrugged and looked towards the ceiling. "People are always charging such things. I ignore them."

"But in this case," said Markovich, "Diamond says he has the documents to prove it. He claims you have an offshore company in…" He glanced at his notes. "In Cypress and Panama. It is called Pyotr1."

Kozlov's eyes narrowed. Unheeding, Markovich went on "Diamond also claims a bank you control called the Argus Bank made a loan of three hundred million dollars to President Stokes several years ago and that you are also in partnership with him in several other deals."

Kozlov leapt from his desk and crossed the room until his face was just a few inches from Markovich. "This is outrageous," he exploded.

"Diamond is asking if we have any statement," said Markovich fearfully.

"Tell that prick it is all lies! Lies from the usual sources, our enemies in the United States and other countries. They want to destroy us. This is an insult not only against the president of Russia but against all Russians."

Markovich was scribbling furiously.

"So," said Kozlov, returning to his chair, "that's the official statement." He thought for a moment. "Now", he said, "get me the FSB. I want to know how those fuckers got that information. I want to know now! And get Stokes on a scrambled line."

Over the next hour, Kozlov received calls from five other Russian oligarchs, also just contacted by Diamond. On the record, they were outraged. "The charges are a pack of lies," Alexei Petreykin had responded to Ed. "You broadcast this at your own risk," blustered another.

When they spoke with Kozlov however, they were panicking. As Petreykin warned the Russian president, "I'm not going to go down alone."

Meanwhile back in London, Steve made a call from the bunker to Senator Bill Gurd in Washington on the encrypted line that Sarah Levin had set up. "Senator, I'm not going to get into details, but we've got the goods on Stokes and his ties with Kozlov and the Russian oligarchs.

"I'd been wondering what the hell happened to you." said Gurd. "When's the broadcast?"

"This Sunday. There's no way your Republicans can refuse to act once this is out."

"I agree. A lot have been wavering. Where are you?"

"Can't say. Just watch Sunday."

Less than five minutes after that call, *Focus's* executive producer, Josh Kantor, called Ed Diamond on the encrypted line. "Ed, we've got trouble," said Kantor.

"What's the problem?" Ed put the call on speakerphone so that Steve and the others could listen. They were part of this battle.

"Your call to the White House has ignited a firestorm at corporate," said Kantor. "Chairman Riggs is up in arms."

"I figured it might provoke something," said Ed.

"I warned you about taking on Stokes," said Kantor.

"They're not really going to cave, are they?"

"It doesn't look good," said Kantor. "Stokes just called Riggs. He's threatening to use every means at his disposal to destroy the corporation if your broadcast goes on."

"The president had the guts to call himself?" said Ed. "Have to make that part of our report."

"You're out of your mind," said Kantor. Steve watched as Ed's face reddened. "Riggs wants to talk with you directly," said Kantor.

"Just a min…." Ed began to protest.

"Ed," another voice cut in, "this is Mark Riggs."

"Hi Mark," said Ed. He'd met the CEO only six or seven times over the past couple of years since Riggs had purchased the network.

"Josh, you still on the line?" said Riggs.

"I am," said Kantor.

"O.K. This is all obviously between us; it's very confidential." Ed made no move to turn off the speakerphone in the bunker. Steve moved in closer to listen as Riggs continued. "I just had a call from the Oval Office, from Stokes."

"Josh told me," said Ed.

"Stokes is threatening to bring down the wrath of his entire administration on us."

"I told Josh we should put that in our report," Ed said. Steve wanted to cheer Ed's bravado, but he suddenly felt a huge black pit open in his stomach. He'd put himself totally on the line to get the material for this report. Sacrificed everything. Risked Maya's life. Now it looked as if it all could be coming apart.

"Diamond, you really have lost touch," said Riggs. "You think you're back in the glory days of Woodward and Bernstein and Watergate. Well, think again! You don't know Stokes. He's a totally different."

Ed began taking deep breaths as Riggs raced on, "Your broadcast could be not just the end of *Focus* and the network but of the whole goddamned corporation." The chairman's voice now was trembling with anger and fear. "You don't realize how many ways the government's got us by the balls: licensing, cable permits, TV broadcast rights, not to mention a massive libel suit. All for the sake of one shitty report on *Focus*."

"And what happens with the next shitty report on *Focus* that takes on Stokes?" asked Ed.

"There won't be one," said Riggs. "At least nothing like this." He paused, as if listening to a nearby advisor. "I understand you won't reveal the source of your information," he continued.

"That's not entirely right," said Ed, frowning. "Our main source for this is Steve Penn, the CIA agent who led the Russian hacking investigation."

"The former agent," Josh Kantor interjected.

"The former agent," said Ed, "who has risked his life to get at the truth about the corrupt relationship between Stokes and the Russians." Whose side was Kantor on?

There was a pause again as Riggs was fed another question. By whom? By a corporate lawyer? By Josh? "What about Penn's sources?" asked Riggs.

Ed glanced at Penn. Steve shook his head firmly.

"Since the beginning Penn has said that he cannot reveal his Russian sources," said Ed. "It would be like pinning a target on each of their backs. He swore he'd never reveal their identities to anyone. That includes me. But, after going back and forth over the documents, we're convinced they're for real. And by the way, Woodward never revealed his key source to the editors of the *Washington Post*."

"I don't give a shit about Woodward and the *Post*," Riggs was yelling now. "I want to know Penn's Russian sources." Steve again vigorously shook his head.

"No way he'll reveal them," said Ed. "Not even to you. But, like I've said, everything he's given us checks out a hundred percent." He paused, took a deep breath and then added quietly. "But, you know what, Mark, the bottom line is you should never have bought the network and put yourself in the news business to begin with."

"Ed, wait!" Josh tried to cut in.

"No, Josh, you can't deprive me of my heroic last lines," Ed said. "Mark, for you, news is just a product to sell and make money from, like anything else. All this talk about needing Russian sources. You could care less about them. You're just looking for an excuse not to broadcast this report. You're scared shitless."

They could hear Riggs furious breathing on the line, "The broadcast is cancelled," he bellowed. "And you, Ed, are on the verge of being fired."

"As a matter of fact, Mark, I quit."

CHAPTER TWENTY-SEVEN

London

"That son of a bitch," said Ed after he ended the call." He paused, shook his head, "Deep breathing doesn't always help," he said. There was a funereal stillness in the room. Everyone avoided each other's gaze. "I was thinking it was time to make a career change," Ed finally said. "But what happens to you, Steve? You put everything on the line for this."

Steve remained silent, but the fear he'd felt a few minutes ago – that everything had been in vain – hovered again on the edge of his consciousness, a black depression waiting just off stage. He couldn't give in to it. "Why don't we broadcast the report ourselves?" Steve said. "On YouTube."

Ed paused. "Why not? Better than throwing it in the trash heap."

"Better? Hell," said Charlie, "This report will go viral in minutes. How many watch *Focus* each week?"

"Ten to fourteen million," said Ed.

"On YouTube this will get just as many viewers; probably more." said Charlie. "The most popular ones are getting billions of views."

"They star pet cats and naked pop singers," said Steve "but, just the same, with luck, we could certainly get tens of millions."

Ed turned to his editor. "Dave, how long will it take you to upload the report to YouTube?"

"Maybe ten minutes. But tagging it so it goes viral will take up to an hour."

"Let's do it," said Ed. "I'll write a new intro about how Stokes blackmailed Riggs to keep this report off the network. We'll spread this goddamned story all over the world."

"I'll also put up a Facebook page," said Charlie, tapping away at his laptop. "After that come Twitter, Instagram, Snapchat, and on and on."

In less than an hour after the report had been uploaded to YouTube it had hit 100,000 views and was climbing vertiginously. It was then that President Stokes also launched the first of several furious Tweets from the White House.

"Laughable, absurd, don't waste time watching this crap. No wonder Focus wouldn't broadcast it. @ PresStokes"

"Lies, all lies from the lying media. Everything made up. OUTRAGEOUS! @PresStokes"

"This is treason, traitors & terrorists wanting 2 destroy us & all we hold dear. DEATH TO TERRORISTS @PresStokes"

Russian President Kozlov also joined in the Twitter attack from the Kremlin: "More American smears and lies against the Russian people. We will no longer stand for it. @VKozlov"

After he had dictated the last of the Tweets, Kozlov bellowed at Markovich, "Get me Stokes again on the line." He'd already sent a blistering order to the head of Russia's Cyber War Command.

Meanwhile, the numbers of viewers on YouTube and Facebook continued soaring, and #Stokes&Kozlov became the trending hash tag on Twitter, Instagram and Snapchat.

Steve broke out the champagne again. "With so many people watching this," he said, "there's no way the U.S. Congress will not move to impeach."

Then, suddenly, all across YouTube, the broadcast simply vanished. A variety of different messages appeared in its place: "Error loading. Tap to retry." "There is no network connection." "This material has been removed because of obscene content." Links to the report also disappeared from Facebook, to be replaced by a similar slogan. All Tweets linked to the show also mysteriously evaporated.

"What the fuck?" said Charlie, staring at his laptop.

Indeed, within minutes the report had completely disappeared from millions of sites across the planet. Only copies of snapshots with transcribed text remained on rogue channels or conspiracy theorists' pages, most had been edited to sound like they were penned by some teenage prankster and most were peppered with commentaries dismissing the credibility of the source. A transcribed copy on *The Onion* didn't help at all.

"It's as if it never existed." said Ed. "How the hell can that happen?"

"It's obvious," said Steve grimly. "Our intelligence organizations and military have developed the capacity to rule the Internet. They've made no secret that was their goal."

"It's ironic," said Charlie, "I actually worked on that project with the NSA when I was at the agency. Nothing is as important as the Internet. We wanted to destroy all enemy communications and capacity to react instantly."

"Yeah, but this isn't war," said Ed.

"It is to Stokes," said Steve.

"And to the Russians," said Charlie. "From what we heard they were out to do the same thing to us in a fraction of a second, censor whatever they chose anywhere. And instantly control everything. They were supposed to be a couple of years ahead of us. I'll bet Kozlov and Stokes made this a joint cyber operation."

"Great," said Steve, "I can already hear the White House line at the press briefing-- after all the squabbling between Russia and America, it took Stokes and Kozlov to make a major step forward in their combined fight against terrorism."

Though he was certain it would be of no use, Steve put in another encrypted call to Senator Gurd in Washington.

"What the hell happened to your broadcast?" said the senator. "I'd alerted our key guys in Congress, told them they had to watch this piece. They were finally going to get the truth on Stokes. I went way out on a limb for you."

"Senator, they've totally blocked us from the network and from all social media."

"Outrageous!" said Gurd. "But that doesn't do us a rat's ass bit of good."

"But I can still make the report available to you," said Steve. "You could show it to the congressional leadership."

"Forget it," said Gurd. "If it had been on *Focus,* we might have had a chance, though I doubt it. Now it's on *The Onion.* Big fucking deal. You don't understand what's happening here. People are terrified of Stokes. They're like deer trapped in the headlights. They're paralyzed by fear. They're not going to move."

Steve clicked off the call and slumped in the chair staring at his laptop. As he feared, this indeed had been a trip to the bottom. He'd sacrificed everything on a gamble that he could defeat the American president. And he'd lost.

But there was a bitter irony to all this: He'd taken the lead in the fight against Stokes because he felt he had nothing to lose: no relations, no wife, no children. But by undertaking this mission, he'd discovered he was not alone. He did have family. But he'd failed them too.

"So that's it?" said Charlie Doyle. He took one of several organizational charts from the wall, squeezed into a paper ball, and tossed it into the nearest waste basket. "Too bad, too late for me to turn pro," he said.

"So what will you do?" asked Steve.

"Hell, I don't know. Guess I'll stay in London. The consulting business is good; lots of money, regular trips to Abu Dhabi and Qatar. The sheiks don't seem to mind if I make my base here. Ride around in a red Ferrari. Got a great girl – really hot." He stood and picked up his laptop. "In fact, now that it looks like we're not going to be locked up here for the weekend, guess I'm free to join her in Cornwall. Her family's got a farm there. I'll go home, pick up the car, and I'm off."

He shook hands with Steve and the others. "I'll miss you guys," he said, ducking his head as he entered the elevator, "but we'll stay in touch."

Steve stared as the elevator doors closed on the lanky figure. A good man, he thought, like Brian Hunt. Again that feeling of guilt as if he'd let the whole team down.

He had dinner with Ed and Dave Turecamo, the first meal they had in the formal dining room of the Belgravia mansion, with its Regency furniture and Venetian chandeliers. Edith Jones insisted on preparing a farewell banquet of sorts. "Something really English," she said bringing in a platter of roast beef with Yorkshire pudding. Then came apple pie with a wedge of cheddar. There were also a couple of fine bottles of Chateau Talbot.

Despite half-hearted attempts to join in the conversation, Steve's thoughts kept returning to the categorical menace of Stokes's last Tweets: "Death to Terrorists and Traitors. Hunt them all down. Every last one!" Would a vicious man with such a twisted outlook on the world – a dangerous psychotic – would he feel he'd settled the score by simply ensuring that their broadcast was never seen by the world?

No. Stokes would be like an enraged beast that's been slightly wounded; rendered even more ferocious as a result. Some of the team were more at risk than others.

Steve's own identity and his new appearance were still secret. His face was not shown in Diamond's report. As for Diamond, he was too well known, too high a profile for Stokes to make people believe that he was some kind of terrorist. Sarah was still in the U.S. presumably not in Stokes's sights. Charlie had taken precautions to make sure he wasn't t tracked to 51 Belgrave Place, but what about now? They should talk about that. But Charlie had already left.

* * *

Action Memo:
Urgent, Urgent.

From: Jean Swanson
To: list.
Re: Charles Doyle Location.

Though we still have not found Penn and Diamond and their operation center in London, we have located one of the co-conspirators: Charles Doyle. A listening device placed by MI5 in Doyle's residence in Notting Hill picked up a call from him to his girlfriend in Cornwall. He will be driving there tomorrow morning, leaving approximately 8:00 a.m.
Predators available at USAF bases at Croughton and Welford. Await instructions for action.

* * *

Early the next afternoon, Ed dropped by Steve's room in the mansion to say goodbye. Steve was watching CNN. They were both a bit hung over from the two bottles of Bordeaux the night before. Abruptly, Chris Pappas, CNN's White House correspondent, cut in with a breaking story. The screen was filled with an image shot from far above of a sports car driving along a country road. The camera zoomed in and there were crosshairs on the car and occasional comments from the impassive, metallic voice of whoever was guiding the drone.

"This sensational footage," said the breathless CNN reporter, "was just released by the White House. "These events happened within the last hour."

"Target acquired," said the lifeless voice, "Locked on target." The crosshairs continued to follow the car as the lens zoomed in even further on the Ferrari and its driver. "And firing".

There was a pause of a couple of seconds then the vehicle was engulfed in an enormous ball of flame. After a few more seconds, when the flame and smoke had cleared, there was nothing but charred black remains where the Ferrari and its driver had been.

The image dissolved to the face of President Walter Stokes in the White House Situation Room surrounded by somber members of his cabinet and his national security team. Stokes seemed mesmerized as the scene of destruction and death was rerun on the huge screen before him. "Watch closely, folks," he beamed. "This is how we deal with traitors. Watch closely. Wham! Now look. Nothing left of him. Nothing. Just what we want."

Stokes turned to the camera: "The man just executed was, uh," he paused and looked at a paper in his hands, "Charles Doyle. Until a few seconds ago, Doyle was a leading member of a secret, underground terrorist organization. We now know they are linked to the same lying agents who did the so-called investigation of Russian hacking before the elections. We also have new very solid evidence – very solid, very solid – that they are tied to ISIS. Their purpose is to destroy our democracy and our American way of life. We don't know who all their members are yet. But our wonderful intelligence agencies are on their track. We will hunt them down and wipe them off the face of the globe.

"A further warning. They have sympathizers everywhere in the lying media. And in the very heart of our Congress – the very heart. Traitors who want to impeach me because of the courageous stand I am taking against terrorism and all those who want to destroy our beautiful democracy. I know loyal Americans won't be taken in by their fabrications and lies. I will deal with those vipers as well, I promise you. All of them. I will do everything to defend the good people of our wonderful, wonderful country. God bless America."

Steve was still staring in shock at the screen when he received an encrypted message on his laptop. It was from Sarah Levin. She still had a line into the CIA – an old colleague in the director's office. "Stokes apparently has just called the director on the carpet. He's outraged that the agency knew nothing about the preparation of the *Focus* broadcast. Also furious that they didn't know you're still alive and kicking. He's just upped the ante. Wants the identities of everyone in Russia who was a CIA source for the hacking investigation."

A knife twisted in Steve's gut. The key CIA source was Maya Chertkova. Handing over her identity to

Stokes was the equivalent of a death sentence. The American president would immediately relay the information to Kozlov, who'd have her shot as a traitor. Her children, including Steve's son, would be confined in some bleak state-run orphanage, lost to Steve forever.

Sarah's message continued: "The director has requested the names of the Russian sources from his staff. Already a lot of grumbling from career types, but no way the director can refuse POTUS demand. Best guess is he'll be turning names over to Stokes within the next twenty-four hours."

CHAPTER TWENTY-EIGHT:

Moscow

Steve managed to get to Moscow by midnight that evening. After Sarah's alarming message, he'd quickly packed an overnight bag and secured a seat on the afternoon BA flight from Heathrow to Sheremetyevo. Luckily, on his previous trip, he'd requested a multiple-entry visa for Russia.

He tried to sleep during the flight, but couldn't. He was obsessed by the sense of failure. He was beaten by Stokes at every turn. And now the American president had the gall to characterize the cold-blooded killing of Charlie Doyle as a blow against international terrorism. Equally outrageous was the full-throated support of Stokes's claims by so many in the media. They were led by Fox News, with its mindless array of "terrorism experts." They parroted Stokes's outlandish charges and Tweets as if they were gospel.

But it wasn't just the media. Steve still couldn't get over the tremulous voice of Senator Gurd on the phone a few hours ago, claiming that even the most influential Republicans in Congress were powerless to do anything to reign in Stokes. Eyes wide open, Americans were repeating a process some compared to the rise of the Nazis in Germany in the 1930s. Unless someone had the guts to stand up to Stokes and to take him down, the country was lost. Was there no way to do it?

While such cataclysmic thoughts roiled Steve's mind, slowly, over the last couple of hours, an idea began to take form, a way out. It was crazy, like throwing a Hail Mary pass in the last seconds of a football game. Could it work? Who knew? But now his immediate priority was to rescue Maya and her children.

Before leaving the Belgravia bunker, Steve had sent an encrypted message to Maya asking for an urgent meeting at her mother Anna's apartment early the next morning in Moscow. It was the site they'd used for several of their previous meetings. "It's a question of life and death" he wrote, "for you and the family. Be there by 7:00 a.m."

He'd decided to stay again at the Four Seasons. He could have chosen a different hotel, but he figured, as far as Russian security was concerned, they'd pick him up just as quickly as a repeat visitor to Moscow, no matter which hotel he checked into. He attempted to sleep for a couple of hours, but his thoughts were too agitated.

He turned on CNN just in time to catch a report from the UK about the killing of Charlie Doyle. Many Brits were up in arms about the U.S. carrying out a deadly drone strike in England. "Stokes Affront to Our Nation," the *Times* headlined.

Stokes, however, had defended the strike by a series of Tweets: "We are all together in this war against terror! No one can opt out. NO ONE! @PresStokes."

Indeed, one of *The Guardian*'s very perceptive columnists, Robert Slazenger, did some sniffing around and wrote a column entitled, "A whiff of hypocrisy?" The young, goateed Slazenger was now being interviewed on CNN. "It was our MI5 and GCHQ that played the lead roles in locating and tracking Mr. Doyle for the Americans," he said. "Our intelligence services knew full well, or should have known, what the end game would be. The CIA Predator also was operating out of a U.S. airbase in England with full knowledge of local authorities. And so," he concluded with a slightly condescending smile, "the question comes down to this: If it's okay for our great ally – the U.S. – to hunt down and kill terrorists in Afghanistan and Somalia and Yemen without always getting the consent of the local governments, and at great risk of collateral damage to the civilian population then why the dickens can't they do it in the U.K.?"

That should provoke a storm, thought Steve. He took a long, hot shower, put on a shirt and jeans, and left the hotel at 5:00 a.m. Changing taxis three times, he crisscrossed the city before heading for Maya's mother's apartment, alert as always to the patterns of cars and people on the early morning streets. He arrived shortly after 7:00 a.m. and buzzed the apartment from the street. Anna, Maya's mother, answered. "Who is it?" she asked in Russian.

"It's Doug Robb."

"Doug who?"

"The American friend of Maya. You remember?" Without answering, she buzzed him in. He walked up to the third-floor apartment. Anna was waiting by the open door in a light blue housecoat, her gray hair disheveled. She seemed more confused than usual. It was obvious she didn't recognize him. "Who are you?" she began to close the door.

"No, please wait," Steve blocked the door with his foot. "I have a meeting with Maya and the children." He was afraid Anna might do something to wake the neighbors.

"No, I can't let..." she began to say.

Suddenly Maya came clattering up the stairs with the two children behind her. "Mama, it's okay," she said.

"I got here as quickly as possible," Maya said breathlessly, as she opened the door to admit Steve and the children. Though it was Saturday, the children were wearing their khaki school uniforms and backpacks. The young boy, Evgeny smiled shyly at Steve; Sonya eyed him curiously. "The children usually have extra study on Saturday," Maya explained., "I've told them they're not going to be going to school today, but, in case any of the neighbors got curious, I wanted to make it look as if this were a normal day."

She looked up at him with startled blue eyes. He couldn't resist. He took her in his arms. She at first resisted, but she then quickly returned his embrace. Anna and the two children stood there staring at the couple kissing. When Maya finally pulled away, her face was flushed.

"Steve and I are going into the kitchen to talk," she said, trying to recover her composure. The children continued to look at her wide-eyed. "I told you it's a very important day today," Maya said. "Mama and Sonya, get some cookies and milk and take Evgeny into the living room. You can play or watch television. Steve and I have to be alone for a few minutes."

Steve followed Maya into the kitchen and took a seat across from her at the wooden breakfast table. There was a white doily on the table and a bowl of apples and pears. "What has happened?" she said. "You wrote that this is a 'life and death' emergency."

Steve took her hands. "It is," he said.

"I'm sorry about your TV program," she said.

"You heard what happened?" said Steve. "They even wiped us off all the social networks. It was devastating. Stokes probably coordinated that attack with Kozlov."

"He did," she said. "My own unit was involved. We've been developing that tactic for years. There was no way I could warn you."

"But Stokes has gone further," said Steve. "He's demanded that the CIA director give him the names of the Russians who were sources for the hacking investigation."

"And the CIA would obey?" Her eyes were suddenly filled with fear and incredulity. "Give me up just like that?"

"The director has no choice," said Steve. "The president is his boss. In theory, if he had the guts, he could refuse to obey, but he'd be out the next day. They'd simply replace him with someone who would comply with the order."

"But Stokes would give that information directly to Kozlov."

"Exactly," said Steve.

Maya glared furiously at him. "How could I have been so stupid to believe in you and your country," she said bringing her fist down on the table. "And you, of course, can do nothing."

"Not true," Steve reddened. "Why do you think I'm back here? I'm going to get you out of the country. You and the children."

"You've already broken too many promises," she said.

"I am getting you and your kids – our kids – out of here," he repeated.

"And my mother," she added. "I will not leave without her."

"And your mother," said Steve.

Since the Soviet Union ended, Russians no longer needed special exit visas to leave the country, but being an army major with top security clearance was something else. "I can't just buy tickets and leave," said Maya. "I'd be immediately challenged at any border."

"I know the rules," said Steve. "Someone will have to give you a special exit permit."

"How much time do we have?" she asked.

"We're seven hours ahead of Washington," said Steve. "So if the CIA director gets the information about you at 9:00 a.m. Washington time, that's 4:00 p.m. here. It's a Saturday, so assume it takes the director another hour to turn it over to the president and the president to transmit that information to Kozlov. Kozlov then has to put word out to the FSB and all border posts. Add an hour for that, assuming everyone is much more efficient than they actually are, that's 6:00 p.m. here. By that time, you and your family have to have passed through any government checkpoint." He looked at his watch, "It's now 7:30 a.m.," he said.

"That gives us about ten hours," she said.

"As I see it," said Steve. "Our only option is General Borovik."

"Borovik?" Maya paused, "Maybe. He was very close to my father."

"How?"

"They were with the same unit in Afghanistan. They got ambushed by the mujahidin. My father and three others volunteered to stay behind to cover their retreat. The other three were killed. My father was wounded and finally captured and beheaded. Borovik went back that night and found the body. He told me he'd never forget the sight."

"He certainly has the power to return the favor now," said Steve

"But it would be very risky – even for him. How could I ask him to do it?"

""He's an adult. He's survived all his life in this system. If he thinks it's too dangerous to help you, he won't. But, unless you've got some other idea, I think he's your only way out."

She continued staring at Steve.

"Maya, you don't have time to waste. Give him a call. All Borovik can say is 'no.'"

"It's Saturday," she said "He's probably at his dacha. I've got the number. But his line is certainly monitored."

"So you're going to have to call with some kind of excuse that will sound reasonable to anyone listening in."

She paused again, and placed her hand on her forehead. Then she nodded as if to herself, picked up her mobile and keyed in a number. The general answered immediately. She identified herself and put on the speakerphone. "I apologize for calling so early on a Saturday," she said.

"Nonsense," said Borovik brusquely, "I've been up working in the garden for more than an hour."

"I thought you might be at your dacha," she said, nervously twisting the doily in her fingers. "I just dug up an old album of papa with some rather amusing pictures of the two of you together in military school and then in East Berlin with a couple of charming-looking young women. You don't look much more than twenty."

"We weren't," the general chuckled.

"I'd like to give it to you," she said.

Steve applauded silently from the other side of the table.

"I'd be delighted to have it," said Borovik. "These days it's much more pleasant looking back at the past, than contemplating the present and never mind the future."

"I was planning to drive out your way this morning with the children, I could stop by with the album."

"Always a pleasure to see you and your family," said the general. "I have a memorial service for another old friend later this afternoon, but if you come by this morning, we will have a few minutes to talk. You can also try some of Katya's crab apple preserve. So I will see you shortly."

Maya ended the call and placed the mobile back on the table. The doily she'd been twisting was now hopelessly knotted.

"You were brilliant," said Steve.

"But all that does is get us in the front door," said Maya.

It took them almost two hours in Moscow's heavy Saturday morning traffic to cross the city and take the western road. There was little room to spare in her gray four-door Lada. Maya and her mother sat in the front; Steve and the two children squeezed in the back. There was no complaining from the children, however. An excursion to the countryside was always preferable to a morning in school.

Steve recalled his own trip to the general's dacha just a few days before, under very different circumstances: handcuffed and blindfolded and sandwiched between two burly officials. Of course, that would be the real fate awaiting him if Russian intelligence seized him this time around.

For part of the trip, they discussed what Maya should say to the general. That decided, Steve turned his attention to the children. Sonya, playing the shy fourteen-year-old, was reticent when Steve tried to draw her out, but Evgeny was openly fascinated by Steve. "Are you really an American?" he asked.

"I really am," said Steve.

"Where do you live?"

"Near Washington, D.C. You know where that is?"

"Of course, it's where the Capitals are."

The young boy, it turned out was an ice hockey player and an avid fan of the National Hockey League. He peppered Steve with questions about the top teams and star players. Luckily, Steve himself had played hockey as a kid. His Russian grandfather had taught him. He was also a fan of the Washington Capitals and was able to answer the barrage of Evgeny's questions convincingly enough to bond as a fellow expert.

Shortly after ten, they pulled onto the gravel lane in front of the general's two-story wood frame cottage. Borovik was gardening in the front lawn. "So much work at this time of the year," he said, kissing Maya on both cheeks, then her mother and the two children. "You're almost ready for the army," he said to Sonya, who blushed.

Maya glanced at the black mourning band on his sleeve. "My oldest friend," he said, "Sergei Petrov, one of the last honorable military men around," he shook his head. "Passed two days ago. Cancer. He also knew your father well."

Then Borovik saw Steve and scowled. "You are already back? I thought I told you to disappear."

"I had to come back," said Steve.

"What happened to the famous broadcast you were going to do? The one I gave you the information for?"

Maya stepped forward, "Can we talk about this inside?" she said.

"So the visit is not about an old photo album," said Borovik. "Come," he said gesturing towards the front door.

"You kids go play in the garden with Mama," said Maya.

Wearing a large white apron, Borovik's plump wife Ekaterina bustled out of the kitchen to greet Maya, "I am just drying the mushrooms," she said. "You'll take some with you. I am dying to look at the photos you found."

"So am I" said Borovik drily. "Bring us some tea, Katya," he said. "Then give us a few minutes alone. I don't know why, but I have the feeling we have some serious business to discuss." He ushered Maya and Steve into the cozy, wood-paneled living room. A large stone fireplace stood at one end, filled with birch logs, and the polished wooden floor was covered with brightly colored kilims the general had collected during service in the Caucasus. "Sit down," he said gesturing to an old leather-covered sofa. He took an armchair facing them.

"Alright, what has happened?" he looked squarely at Steve.

"Something of a disaster," said Steve.

"I gather that," said Borovik.

"Stokes convinced the owner of the TV network we were working with that it was in his best interests not to transmit the broadcast."

"Your country's become like ours," said the general. He paused while his wife came in with a tray bearing three glasses of tea, some toast, and preserves. She placed it on the table between them. "Thank you, Katya," said Maya. The general said nothing, waiting impatiently for his wife to leave. "So continue," he said to Steve.

Steve nodded. "After we were blocked on TV, we tried to spread the story on the social media, but then our government's cyber unit teamed up with yours."

"I know, I heard about that," Borovik frowned, "Another triumph for my bastard ex-son- in-law."

Steve looked puzzled.

"General Abramovich," said Borovik, taking a sip of tea. "He's the one who talked Kozlov into interfering with your elections in the first place. He also deserted my daughter and her two children."

"I see," said Steve, beginning to feel like he was in the middle of a Russian TV series.

"But, General, I did fulfill my promise not to reveal your name to anyone as a source for some of our information."

The general nodded. "Thank you," he said. "I respect you for that. I thought giving you the information might at least weaken Kozlov, but no." He shrugged. "That shit is stronger than ever."

"We've got a much more urgent problem," said Steve.

The general put down his tea, looked at Steve, and waited.

"Stokes has demanded the names of Russians who gave the CIA information about Kozlov's meddling in the American elections," said Steve. "Stokes's next move will be to turn over those names to Kozlov."

"Why does that concern me?" said the general. "I was certainly against that idiotic hacking program. But I never gave information to the Americans."

"I did," said Maya.

"You spied for the Americans?"

Maya nodded.

The general raised his eyebrows. "You? The daughter of one of our great heroes? You gave information about our military?"

They'd gone too far, Steve suddenly realized. Their plan wasn't working. They were about to be thrown out by the general. Or worse: denounced to the FSB.

"It was partly for Sonya," said Maya. "The Americans got me the medicines; otherwise, my daughter wouldn't be alive today. But I also did it because I was against Kozlov – against what he was doing."

This was the key moment, thought Steve. "General," he said quietly, "You are also against what Kozlov is doing. You also gave me the most sensitive information about his personal holdings. He would certainly call that treason. But you are acting for the good of Russia."

The general paused, then shook his head, and nodded. "Kozlov is the traitor." he said. "He will destroy our country." He looked at Maya. "Your father might not have approved of what you did," he said. "But he's not here. I am."

He looked again squarely at Steve. "How much time do we have?"

"It's all guesswork," said Steve. "But I figure Kozlov will get the information around 5:00 p.m. or so this afternoon. The FSB and border control should have it within an hour after that. You certainly know much better than I how efficiently they work."

"Your estimate's probably right," said Borovik.

"As you know, for Maya to leave Russia she will need some kind of official pass – special permission –

particularly as a military officer trying to get out with all her family."

"Your children also?" said Borovik.

What if the general knew that her son was also my child? thought Steve.

"And my mother," said Maya.

"That could certainly raise eyebrows," said Borovik.

"We developed an idea on the way over here," said Maya. "I have an aunt who emigrated to Mexico twenty years ago – to Cuernavaca. She married a Mexican diplomat who was based in Moscow. Say, I just got word that she has had a stroke, and has only a few days left. I want to take her sister, my mother, and my children with me to bid her farewell. We are the only family she has."

"All very moving," said the general.

"And part of it is true. I do have an aunt in Cuernavaca. The copy of the email to me can be easily arranged. So I am in distress. It is a weekend. All the immigration offices are shut. I come to you as an old friend of the family. And you very kindly write me the necessary pass."

"Won't you need a visa from Mexico?" asked Borovik.

"Not necessary for Russian citizens," said Maya. "As long as you have a Russian passport. And we do. I already have one, and I got ones for the kids and my mother when I took them to Copenhagen last year."

The general looked at Maya, and shook his head, "Such a schemer. Who would have guessed? We should have had you on the army general staff."

"So you'll do it?" said Maya.

The general shrugged. "I will write an official pass. If anyone gets suspicious and calls, I will say that, of course, I wrote it. How was I to know you were a spy? I could never have expected it. I've known you since you were born. Your father was an old friend of mine."

"But," he said grimly, "If something happens. If you are caught, you understand I can do nothing to save you. To your dying day, and that may not be far away, you simply tell them how you came to me with your story about your sick aunt and I fell for it. There is no reason for them not to believe it. Those pricks wouldn't dare come after me as a traitor."

"I don't know how to thank you," Maya brushed her hand over her eyes. "I don't…"

"There's nothing to thank me for," said Borovik, looking very uncomfortable. "I do it for your father. Now make your reservations, so I can write the letter."

After wiping her eyes, Maya called Aeroflot to book tickets for herself and her family to fly to Mexico City that evening. Borovik then went to his basement office and wrote and signed a special authorization for her, her children, and her mother to leave the country temporarily because of "an urgent family emergency."

Maya's eyes were brimming again as the general handed her the document.

Borovik looked at her and Steve; his face grew livid. "This is all outrageous," he pounded the arms of his chair. "After all we have been through, after Stalin and Hitler, after all that, we are still living in such fear. And of what? Of two great thieves: Kozlov and Stokes. It is shameful!" He sank into his chair, breathing heavily.

Steve decided it was time to unveil the audacious plan he'd been evolving since he left London. "General," he said leaning forward, "Perhaps there is a way. It's just a chance, but it could work." The general looked on skeptically as Steve continued with mounting excitement. "We'll need daring and we'll have to improvise as we go, but we could bring it off. Why not? The point is there is a growing dispute between Stokes and Kozlov that we could use to defeat them. It's nothing to do with the Ukraine or Syria. It's over money."

"As befits the two of them," said Borovik. "You're talking about the joint real estate investment they made in Texas six years ago."

"Exactly." Said Steve. "It was part of the information you turned over to me last week, At the time, there were so many major issues, that it got lost in the details."

"A joint investment?" said Maya.

"Stokes and Kozlov each have offshore companies. They decided to combine two of them to form a Panamanian corporation called Quantum," said Steve. "Their idea was to invest in the booming real estate market in Texas. According to documents the general's hackers found, Stokes wanted to keep his connection to Quantum as confidential as possible. So he agreed that formally its administration would be controlled by Kozlov. That's where Stokes made his big mistake.

"Quantum's only purchase was Lakeshore Views. It's a huge residential development on the outskirts of Houston. The original developers ran out of money. So, smelling a big opportunity, Stokes contacted Kozlov and Lakeshore Views became Quantum's first purchase for six hundred million dollars."

"That was in 2014," said Borovik, "that's when I started collecting information on what Kozlov and the oligarchs were up to."

"You did a huge public service," said Steve. "Just before the elections last November, Quantum sold the development for almost a billion dollars. But it was Kozlov, remember, who had administrative control of Quantum. And he distributed only three hundred fifty million to Stokes. He kept six hundred fifty million for himself. According to Quantum's files, Stokes immediately reacted. He demanded an equal share in the profits. Kozlov refused."

"The two deserve each other," said Borovik.

"Kozlov said that Stokes had only put up fifty million in cash. The remainder of Stokes's stake in the company came from a loan to Stokes from a bank that Kozlov controlled. Stokes should consider himself lucky, said Kozlov. After repaying his loan to Kozlov's bank, he was still going to make a hundred million thereby doubling his money. In other words, Stokes had nothing to complain about.

"How did Stokes react to that?" said Maya.

"About as you would think," said Steve. "He completely rejected Kozlov's argument. Stokes is used to robbing others; not being robbed himself. He can't take Kozlov to court because he can't admit that offshore company is his. But his private communications to Kozlov have been increasingly menacing. He's going to get the hundred and fifty million that's due him, whatever it takes.

"So that's where my plan starts," said Steve.

"And where does it go?" said Borovik, still skeptical. It took an hour more of animated discussion before the general finally agreed. "Yes, it could work. In any case, there is no other solution." They reviewed the next steps to be taken; then the general embraced Maya and her children, wished them a safe trip, and shook hands with Steve. "Good luck to us all," he said before they left. "We will certainly need it."

As soon as he returned to the hotel, Steve set his plan in motion. He dispatched an encrypted message to Sarah Levin. Over the next few hours, she was to create the media background for their next move. She was also to come immediately to London.

Later that evening, after receiving a text message from Maya that she had safely passed through Russian border control at Sheremetyevo, Steve boarded his flight to London. As the AirBus climbed from the runway, he sat back in his seat, contemplating his next moves. His scheme was bold, as likely to fail as succeed. But at least he'd saved Maya, her family, and his son.

Unknown to Steve was the fact that, at that very moment, Maya and her mother and two terrified children were in a black van of the FSB heading back in to Moscow. Her Mexico City flight had been delayed for two hours because of engine trouble. Maintenance was a constant problem with the cash-strapped airline. That delay was long enough for the Russian border agents to receive the special alert that had been sent out by the president's office; long enough to discover that Maya and her family had just cleared their post; long enough to board the waiting Aeroflot flight and forcibly remove Maya, her children, and her mother. And charge Maya with treason.

CHAPTER TWENTY-NINE:

London

It was just after 7:00 a.m. in London when Steve arrived back to Heathrow's sprawling Terminal Four. As soon as the plane landed, he checked his cell to see if there was any text message from Maya. Her flight to Mexico City made a stop in London. She would have to remain in the transit area, but had promised to send a text message confirming that, so far at least, everything was okay. Her flight had been scheduled to arrive in London an hour before his, but there was no message from her. According to the incoming flight board in the terminal, the Aeroflot flight from Moscow was running two and a half hours behind schedule. That could mean problems, thought Steve. On the other hand, she had sent a text message the evening before saying that she and her family had passed through the police checkpoint at Sheremetyevo with no trouble. Still, he couldn't rid himself of a nagging fear for her safety.

That angst would only disappear after she'd landed in Mexico City. She was due to arrive there at 7:20 a.m. Mexico time, which meant 1:20 p.m. in London. He had another six hours to wait for her message. But even far from the Kremlin, she and her family would not be totally secure. They might never be safe, as long as Kozlov was in power. He'd had no qualms about ordering his enemies assassinated on the streets of London. Hopefully, if Maya kept a low profile, or completely changed her identity, the Russian president would direct his vengeance elsewhere, but she would always have to be alert, looking over her shoulder. And what of her children?

One thing Steve was sure he wanted to do was recognize Evgeny as his biological son. That would be the first step to the boy's becoming an American citizen. But before that, Steve would have to prove to immigration authorities he was an American citizen himself. In that lengthy bureaucratic process, it was almost certain they would discover he had faked his current identity. He would have no choice but to admit that his suicide was a sham, and that Doug Robb was an imposter. This would put Steve once again in the crosshairs of Stokes's killers.

Which was another reason he had to take down Stokes, and he had to take down Kozlov with him. That was the goal of the audacious plan he'd developed in Moscow. It would require a secure site from which to operate. No place better than the sophisticated reinforced bunker in Pearlstein's Belgravia mansion. As far as Steve knew, Stokes's intelligence services hadn't spotted the bunker when he and Ed Diamond were operating out of it. Charlie Doyle had not been discovered at 51 Belgrave

Place, but when he returned to his apartment in Notting Hill, which had been under surveillance. For the time being, then, the Belgravia mansion was safe. Steve sent an encrypted message to Pearlstein asking if he could continue to use his Belgravia home for another couple of days. "If it takes any more than that, we've failed," he'd written.

"Be my guest," replied Pearlstein. "Best use the place has been put to since it was built."

Mike Rourke and Edith Jones welcomed him back to the white stucco mansion like a long-lost member of the family. "Quick trip, sir," said Edith brightly, as she served Steve scrambled eggs and bacon.

"Less than two days," said Steve, "but it feels like two months. Plenty of coffee, thanks, I'm going to need it."

It was then that that opened an encrypted message from General Borovik and finally learned that Maya and her family had been picked up at Sheremetyevo, because of a freak engine problem.

"Trying to find out where they've been taken," wrote the general, "But, as I warned, I cannot become involved. I have not yet been contacted regarding the special pass. But that should be just a matter of hours. Your plan has to launch soonest."

Steve had just absorbed that message when Sarah Levin arrived. Steve accompanied Mike to the front door, then stood speechless, staring at the male figure in the entrance wearing a black Borsalino hat and carrying a suitcase. "I've come all this way and you're not even going to invite me in?" said Sarah smiling. She removed her hat and coat. Her hair was close-cropped and dyed blond; she was dressed in a bulky blue cashmere sweater, loose slacks, and men's shoes

"The disguise looks good," said Steve. "What's your cover story?"

"On a consulting trip to Edinburgh," she said. "Flew there from the States, then took the train from there to London with this gear on. I'm certain no one's spotted me."

Steve knew he was running a risk by bringing in another member of Deep Strike, but he had no choice: he needed her here for this. Besides, as long as Stokes's killers were searching for the team, 51 Belgravia was as safe as any other spot and probably safer.

"We stay here until this operation is finished," said Steve. "No one goes out." It was the same instruction he thought grimly, that he'd given a few days earlier – before Charlie was killed. "Now let me show you where we'll be working."

"Like being back in Langley." said Sarah, as they stepped out of the elevator into the bunker and Steve gave her a tour of the sophisticated facilities.

"We're going to need it," Steve said.

"Your plan is for real?" she said.

"Absolutely. It's going to work."

"And if it doesn't?"

"We don't want to go there. Your network is ready?"

"Already up and running."

After getting the encrypted message the day before from Steve in Moscow, it had taken Sarah just a few hours to establish her own fake news network. She created a new Washington news blog called "Stokes Watch," for which a stable of hungry, hawkeyed reporters from

"The Foggy Bottom News Service" would keep stories coming. To give them substance, Sarah cut and pasted scores of reports that Stokes Watch and the FBNS had supposedly already published since Stokes took office.

Before leaving the U.S, she had already begun uploading her new sites with their first breathless reports.

Heads up from Stokes Watch:
Stokes labels Kozlov "a hundred and fifty-million-dollar chiseler."

To: all media
Urgent

According to a bulletin from the usually reliable Foggy Bottom News Service, at a fundraising event in Pittsburgh yesterday evening, President Stokes, when asked for his latest views on Russian president Kozlov, replied, "You mean that hundred and fifty-million-dollar chiseler?" His comment was picked up by a microphone the president apparently didn't realize was turned on. When queried about that statement, the president denied having made it, though it was clearly heard by hundreds of people in the room. The president's press spokesman also played down the reported quote, calling it "another example of fake news."
Ben Silver

Heads up from Stokes Watch
Stokes "not at all unhappy" that his 'chiseler' charge
against Kozlov has leaked

To: all media
Urgent

The capital is still buzzing over the statement first reported by the Foggy Bottom News Service earlier today. The PBNS scoop claimed that the U.S. president accused his Russian counterpart of being "a hundred and fifty-million-dollar chiseler." PBNS now reports that a confidential source very close to the president says that "Stokes is not at all unhappy" that his strong feelings were made public. "Perhaps that will bring some action from Kozlov," the president is quoted as saying, adding "I would like nothing better for our former warm friendship to resume." When queried, the White House denied knowing anything about the dispute.
Ben Silver

Heads up from Stokes Watch
Stokes veiled threat against Kozlov if "the chiseler doesn't stop chiseling."

To: all media
Urgent

The Foggy Bottom News Service now claims White House insiders confirm the mounting anger of the American president towards Russian President Kozlov. Though the President Stokes apparently refuses to specify what the source

of the dispute is, according to those same insiders, he now maintains he is ready to take action himself "if the Russian chiseler doesn't stop chiseling."
Ben Silver

* * *

Trending on Twitter

North Korea threatens missile test.
Stokes to Kozlov: $150 million chiseler!

* * *

REUTERS

White House denies mounting reports of friction between President Stokes and President Kozlov.

* * *

CNN

Reports currently circulating on Facebook and Twitter of rising tensions between the American and Russian presidents are "totally false" says the Stokes White House. "We are still trying to get at the source of these lies," says White House spokesman Crawford.

* * *

Heads up from Stokes Watch
Stokes threatens unspecified action against Kozlov within "hours, not days."

To: all Media
Urgent

According to their usually reliable White House sources, the Foggy Bottom News Service now reports that President Stokes is confiding to his family and advisers that he is "fed up" with waiting for "chiseler Kozlov" to act. "Either he comes across now, or I take action myself. And I am talking about hours, not days." FBNS reporters have still not been able to ascertain what the issue is between the two heads of state. The White House press office continues to deny there is any problem at all.

* * *

MCCLATCHY

Our reporters unable to find any truth to the sudden claims of bad relations between Presidents Stokes and Kozlov. Fake news – or not??

* * *

Russian Television

According to a statement just issued by Russian President Kozlov, he is totally puzzled by the views being attributed lately to U.S. President Stokes. "If he really feels this way, President

Kozlov said, President Stokes has no grounds for such insulting views. Perhaps he just had a bad night," he said jokingly.

* * *

Trending on Twitter

Stokes-Kozlov: food fight or much worse?
N. Korea launches new ICBM

* * *

"Terrific stuff" said Steve, as he scrolled through the stories Sarah had put out and their impact as they spread worldwide. "It's amazing the way they're being picked up everywhere."

"Including the Kremlin." Sarah beamed. "Instead of throwing away my life with the agency, I should have been a press baron."

* * *

Action Memo:
Urgent, Urgent.

From: Jean Swanson
To: list`

Re: Sarah Levin/Steve Penn/ Fake Kozlov news
Sarah Levin is again on the move. After eliminating Charlie Doyle, we decided not to move against Levin since she remained our best chance of tracking any further terrorist actions planned by Penn.

Levin left JFK last night on flight to Edinburgh, supposedly as part of an IA consultancy contract. We immediately alerted British counterparts. MI5 agents at Edinburgh Airport, didn't spot her. Nor did an immediate search of CCTV footage in the arrival area.

Now suspect she has radically changed appearance and that Edinburgh was not her final destination. Much more likely to be London, the locus of Penn's last aborted operation. British counterparts will continue to monitor Edinburgh area but have also extended surveillance to London. But cannot count on facial recognition to pick her up. Forwarding further data on Levin's basic eye/nose measurements, plus manner of walking for possible gait recognition.

OSGH and MI5 also reviewing surveillance data on Charlie Doyle. Attempting to trace his movements back from when he arrived at his apartment, to determine where he actually came from, i.e., where Penn and Ed Diamond prepared their treasonous report. A laborious process, analyzing millions of CCTV images. But may be worth it. It's conceivable they still may be using that location."

At 11:30 a.m. in the bunker at 51 Belgrave Place. Sarah downloaded the encrypted data dump Ed had been expecting from General Borovik.

"If this doesn't do it, God help us all," wrote the general in an accompanying message. "Let the operation begin."

CHAPTER THIRTY:

Sochi

At noon at his vacation home in Sochi, the renowned Russian violinist Alexander Vasiliev had just begun the second movement of Tchaikovsky's Violin Concerto, which he was due to perform next weekend in Paris, when he received an urgent email from Vasily Kozlov: *"Sasha, for business transaction of exceptional importance, transfer soonest US$150 million from Quantum's account with Mid Atlantic to account 107865 at the Banco del Pueblo in Panama City. Extremely tied up. Take care of this immediately. Kotzy"*

Vasiliev was one of the oldest, most trusted friends of the Russian president. The two of them had grown up together in Leningrad and then gone their separate ways but never lost touch. One of the unlikely things linking them as children was the similarity between Alexander's family name – Vasiliev, and Kozlov's first name – Vasily.

When it came time for Kozlov to set up Pyotr1, the offshore holding company for his increasingly vast resources, his lawyers drew up papers naming Alexander Vasiliev as the owner. For his troubles, the violinist would receive twenty million dollars a year, a four thousand square foot condominium in Moscow's Sparrow Hills, and a lavish retreat overlooking the Black Sea in Sochi. In return, he was to act as the punctilious front man for Pyotr1, directing the banking operations of the offshore company and its holdings, like Quantum, and implementing the often complicated of instructions he received from Kozlov.

One such order was the peremptory email he had just received that morning. Vasiliev was used to the vast sums involved. The violinist could also be assured it was really the Russian president issuing the orders, since his instructions invariably began and ended with "Sasha" and "Kotzy," the nicknames they used for each other in the playgrounds of Leningrad when they were six years old.

Unknown to Sasha and Kotzy, however, was the fact that the military hackers on General Borovik's staff, ordered to comb the files of Pyotr1, had discovered the surprisingly naive method that Kozlov used to communicate with Vasiliev.

They chalked such carelessness up to arrogance on the part of the Russian president; his certitude that no one would dare reveal the secret of Pyotr1. They were wrong. And though hacking into the president's server would have been an extremely difficult, perhaps impossible, task, breaking into Vasiliev's communications was relatively simple – particularly with the information provided by General Borovik's hackers.

Thus, Steve and Sarah had no difficulty drafting the email in Russian that Vasiliev received that day in Sochi, which appeared to come directly from Kozlov. Used to executing such commands, Sasha immediately emailed a transfer order to Raul Cepeda, the manager of the Mid Atlantic Bank in the British Virgin Islands.

Dressed in an impeccable white linen suit, Cepeda had just arrived at his office in Road Town, the capital of the BVI. His wife was away on a three-day shopping trip with their daughter to Miami, enabling him to spend a worry-free night with his Cuban mistress. Cepeda was a man of immense discretion, who handled the accounts of several of Russia's wealthiest oligarchs. He was also used to dealing with princely sums.

Before carrying out such instructions, however, he would need confirmation – particularly verbal confirmation – to ascertain that the email was legitimate and not some amateurish attempt to rip off Pyotr1. Back in Sochi, Vasiliev immediately answered Cepeda's call. *"Buenos días,* Raul, *como está?"* Cepeda instantly recognized the violinist's distinctive nasal tones. They had spent several agreeable evenings together over the years in Panama and elsewhere dealing with the nuts-and-bolts of Pyotr1 and its various holdings. Of course, Cepeda didn't really believe that the violinist was the actual owner of all that wealth, but that wasn't his business.

"Just checking, as always," said Cepeda. "Can you confirm today's order?"

"One hundred and fifty million to account 107865 at the Banco del Estado," replied Vasiliev.

"Thanks, how's your weather?"

"Nothing like yours, but I can still go swimming. And Raul, make sure this goes through immediately."

"*A sus órdenes,*" said Cepeda.

Three minutes after Cepeda ended the call, one hundred and fifty million dollars were transferred from the account of Pyotr1 to account 107865 at the Banco del Estado in Panama City. It was 9:30 a.m. in the British Virgin Islands, 1:30 p.m. in London.

Actually, that numbered account in Panama City had just been set up three hours earlier by Steve through a tax lawyer in Panama. The fee for such rapid action was huge. But so was the payoff. As soon as the one hundred and fifty million dollars were received in the first account, Steve immediately ordered it transferred to a second numbered account he'd set up at the Banco del Sur across the street. As soon as the second transfer was completed he sent an encrypted message to Steve in London. Steve then gave Sarah the go-ahead with a second message to Alexander Vasiliev.

The violinist was in the middle of a call with his agent in New York planning a concert tour in the United States for the following summer, when an incoming beep indicated the arrival of the second pressing email of the day from the Russian president. *"Sasha, transfer immediately an additional one hundred million dollars from Quantum's account with Mid Atlantic to account 107865 at Banco del Pueblo. Still extremely tied up. Take care of this immediately. Katzy"*

Saying he had an urgent email he had to deal with, Sasha told his New York agent he would call him right back and prepared to send the second instruction to Raul Cepeda in the British Virgin Islands. It was then he noticed that Kozlov had signed as "Katzy" not "Kotzy." Strange, since the Russian president was usually extremely meticulous about such matters. Wasn't it also somewhat strange that Kozlov was sending two separate transfers rather than one to the same account within a couple of hours? Of course, it was possible that he had two separate deals in the works with the same individual. But wasn't it also possible that some shyster, seeing he had gotten away with the first fraudulent transfer, decided to push for more?

He realized his suspicions were probably absurd and Kozlov had made it evident he was extremely tied up with urgent affairs of state. Just the same, Alexander Vasiliev was being compensated very generously to watch over his old friend's burgeoning wealth. At the risk of incurring a tongue-lashing, he decided to check with Kozlov on the president's personal mobile.

Which is just what Steve Penn was hoping he would do.

The Russian president answered immediately. He was breathing heavily. "Sorry to disturb, you, Kotzy" said Sasha, "I know you are very busy."

"What is it?" asked Kozlov. "I am working out with my judo instructor."

"I just want to confirm the two transfer instructions you sent," said Sasha, now a note of concern in his voice.

"Transfer instructions? What are you talking about?"

Sasha's note of concern turned to fear, "The email you sent me an hour ago."

"What email?"

"For an urgent transfer of one hundred and fifty million U.S. dollars from Pyotr1." Vasiliev's fears had been right. They'd been had.

"That's bullshit," barked Kozlov. "A transfer to where?"

"To a numbered account at the Banco del Pueblo in Panama."

"To who?"

"I have no idea. I said it was numbered."

"You dickhead! And the second order?"

"For $100 million to the same numbered account."

"And your donkey's ass put them both through?"

"No, thank God." Sasha's voice was quavering. "Only one, Kotzy. Only one. I suspected there might be a problem."

"You suspected! You motherfucker. How long ago did you request the first transfer?"

"About an hour." He mumbled. He didn't add that he'd told Cepeda to make the transfer immediately.

"What was the fucking account number?"

"107865."

There was a pause. "It must be Stokes, that shithead!" Kozlov exploded. There was a crash, and the line went dead.

A minute later, Sasha's phone rang.

"What happened?"

"I threw my fucking phone at the wall," said Kozlov. "I would have thrown you if you'd been here," said the president. His fiery tone had turned to ice. Sasha recognized the flat, metallic pitch as the voice Kozlov always took when crossed and when he contemplated vengeance.

"I'll call immediately to cancel the transfer," said Vasiliev, petrified. Kozlov would naturally suspect him of being part of the scam.

"Do it."

Two minutes later, the violinist called the president back. "The transfer went through more than an hour ago. No way to recall it."

"Of course there isn't, you prick," said Kozlov.

The president's judo trainer stared open-mouthed at Kozlov as the president ended the call, then turned and ordered the trainer out of the office. Kozlov went next door to his private bathroom to take a shower. He breathed deeply. He had to think for a few minutes, stay calm, carefully plan his next moves. He would deal with Sasha later to find out if he was involved with Stokes or not. The violinist was his oldest friend. He had trusted him implicitly. But these days – who knew when money was concerned? Who knew what unscrupulous men would do?

Kozlov had contacted Stokes a few hours ago. He was concerned by the flurry of news reports citing Stokes's vague references to money he said he was owed by the Russian president. Stokes had told Kozlov to ignore the stories. "Fake news, Vasily, all fake news, believe me. Believe me. Everything's good."

"And the hundred fifty million you still claim I owe you?" said Kozlov, "That's fake news too?"

"Vasily, that's a business disagreement between you and me. We are going to have a beautiful relationship, beautiful. But as far as the hundred fifty million is concerned, I am right and you're wrong," Stokes chuckled, "but, like I said, that's business. Look, I'm a great businessman – the best. I am going to get that money back one day. But the other stuff – like I said, fake news."

Stokes was lying now, Kozlov knew it. The transfer that went through totaled one hundred and fifty million dollars, exactly the amount Stokes claimed he was owed. The second order was just Stokes seeing if he could get away with more. Kozlov had been robbed in broad daylight. Everyone said Stokes was a crook, and this was the proof.

He immediately called Major Sergei Mikhailov, the official in charge of cyber security for the presidential office. Without going into details of the fake emails that had been sent to Vasiliev, Kozlov demanded an immediate investigation. "This is an outrage. I want to know how the hell some criminal was able to send false messages that appeared to have been sent by me, the president of Russia. Get me the answer--now!"

Half an hour later, the major called back. "They didn't hack your line, Mr. President. I can swear to that. They hacked Alexander Vasiliev's. "There is no real security on his line. He's not part of the presidential office. Your own security is excellent."

"But who the fuck did it?" said Kozlov.

"I can't be certain, but the hack bore the digital fingerprints of the U.S. cyber command."

Those fingerprints had been purposely left by Sarah when she originally hacked into Vasiliev's mobile. Kozlov, however, had no way of knowing that. Instead, he was trying to comprehend why the U.S. military would hack the phone of Sasha unless they'd been ordered to do so by the American president. Kozlov couldn't believe things had progressed to the point where the American president would be able to use military hackers to steal one hundred and fifty million dollars from the Russian president. Perhaps the hacker was from the U.S. military, but worked in some freelance capacity for Stokes. But who knew? Nobody could figure out what was going on in Stokes's America these days.

* * *

At the same time, in London, Steve received another encrypted message from General Borovik: *"Everything on track. Source in Kozlov's office reports that the president erupted in fury after a personal phone call about an hour ago.*

"Also, I have confirmation that Maya Chertkova is in the Lubyanka, likely facing a charge of treason. Believe her children and mother are also being held, but they are safe for the time being. I was questioned by the FSB on the special exit pass issued to Maya & family. The officer seemed to accept my defense: "What else was I supposed to do for an old family friend?" But we will see.

"Depending on how the next phase of your plan goes, I may have to disappear shortly."

* * *

Meanwhile in the Kremlin, President Kozlov had decided how he would take his revenge on Stokes. He fired off a smoldering message to the American president. *"Your brazen thievery is an outrage. Our business dealings are at an end. You already owe our banks more than one billion dollars. I am ordering those loans immediately cancelled, on grounds that they were based on fraud.*

"Either you repay the loans immediately or we will begin proceedings in U.S. and international courts to seize your assets."

President Stokes was completing a game of tennis on the south lawn of the White House when he received the message. He was stunned. Was this some bad joke? "I have no idea what you are talking about," he immediately texted back.

"Talking about the $150 million you ordered your military hackers to steal from my company and transfer to your Panamanian account."

"Are you out of your mind?"

"Just look in your account."

"What account?

"107865, Banco del Pueblo, Panama."

"Not mine!"

"Bullshit! That's your bank. That is the exact sum you claim I owe. The digital fingerprints on the hack is your military."

"Believe me, I know nothing about it."

"You are lying."

"Cancelling Russian loans would destroy me," texted Stokes. *"You can't do that."*

"Just watch."

Panicked, Stokes lashed out on Twitter. Since he didn't want to reveal the existence of his offshore holdings and his huge indebtedness to the Russians, he kept his message vague, but still threatening: *"Russia playing dirty games again. U.S. will react with more tough sanctions against Chiseler Kozlov unless he immediately ceases provocations. DIRTYBUSINESS! @PresStokes."*

President Kozlov Tweeted back in kind: *"American president is thief and liar. Russian banks immediately cancelling all outstanding loans to Stokes. GOOD RIDDANCE. @VKozlov"*

And so it went:

"Klepto Kozlov must immediately cease & desist & reverse actions. Otherwise…!!! WATCHOUT @PresStokes"

"Stokes as usual issuing empty threats. Owes Russ banks more than 1 billion. A truly bankrupt president. SHAMEFUL @VKozlov"

Heads up from Stokes Watch
Stokes continues vague but violent threatens against Kozlov.

To: all Media
Urgent

The mounting hostility that the Foggy Bottom News Service reported on earlier today between the American and Russian presidents has now broken out into an open and very ugly Twitter war between the two leaders. The White House press spokesman says the American president has no idea what the issue is. But our usually reliable White House insiders tell us it is all about President Stokes appropriating $150 million from an offshore company controlled by Kozlov. They say it is a bitter business dispute between the two leaders.

True to his Texan heritage, President Stokes seems to be approaching this like a show-down between two gun slingers. The fear is that this whole affair could spiral out of control.

* * *

Meanwhile, claiming to be worried by the vitriolic exchanges being hurled between the leaders of the world's largest nuclear powers, General Borovik quietly consulted with other top Russian military commanders. They were also aghast at the sudden unexplained escalation of tensions with the U.S.

There was some question among the officers about whether President Kozlov was still in full control of his mental faculties. There was also some very preliminary talk that the Russian military might have to act on its own. The Russian generals decided to put out confidential feelers to their American military counterparts. "Of course, we would never challenge or disobey President Kozlov," General Borovik told the Russian officers, "but we must keep a close eye on this very dangerous situation. We can't let it get out of control."

"If Russian aggression continues, cannot say what the outcome will be. No cards are off the table. DANGER!! @ PresStokes"

It was after that last Tweet from Stokes, that Russian President Kozlov decided to up the ante. He would present his case directly to the American public. "If they knew what was going on," he told an aide, "they would be as outraged as myself."

Ignoring the pleas for caution from some of his staff, Kozlov ordered the Russian cyber command to enact a sophisticated maneuver they'd been perfecting for years: taking over control of America's major TV and cable networks, as well as other key broadcasting facilities around the globe.

Thirty minutes later, having changed into a dark black suit and blue tie, the Russian president went live from his Kremlin office. In calm, measured tones, he denounced "the newest American plot against Russia." An interpreter gave a running English translation:

"We have tried to begin a new era in our relations. But the thievery and lying of the American president make that impossible. He is now threatening more sanctions to impoverish our country. Instead, it is he who will be impoverished. He will be destroyed by our decision to cancel all outstanding Russian loans to his businesses. America, your bankrupt president will now be truly bankrupt. It is time for the American people to choose a new leader, an honest leader we can work with to bring peace and prosperity to the world."

* * *

At the same time in London, after days of frustration, Captain Jean Swanson was triumphant. The sophisticated analysts of Britain's GCHQ surveillance had finally come up with the solution.

She immediately called George Ramos, who headed the S-Team, the White House's clandestine action unit. Ramos was watching dumbfounded on his office monitor as Russian president Kozlov continued his violent diatribe against President Stokes.

"This is Ramos," he said impatiently. "What is it Swanson?"

"The Brits have located Penn's operation," she said.

"Jesus, it's about time. The White House is going wild. Are you sure you've got the location?"

"Certain," said Swanson. "By analyzing CCTV coverage, GCHQ were able to retrace the movements of Charlie Doyle last Friday to a mansion in West London, 51 Belgrave Place. I'm uploading a live picture of it to you right now."

"That's two days ago," snapped Ramos. "How are you sure that's where Penn is operating now?"

"We've checked the past forty-eight hours of CCTV images covering the main entrance of the house. At 7:16 a.m. this morning, a person arrived by taxi and entered the building. He was carrying a suitcase. Here's the image. He doesn't have the physical appearance of Penn, but the basic eye-nose measurements are identical."

"What about gait measurements?"

"They didn't match Penn's. But it's not that difficult to fake if you know what you're doing."

"Go on."

"At 8:30 a.m. another individual arrived, dressed like a man, but with the height of Sarah Levin. Here's that image. GCHQ can't be dead certain but her gait also seems to match Levin's. Eye-nose measurements also the same."

"What about electronic surveillance?" asked Ramos.

"So far we're unable to determine what if any communications are emanating from the site. It appears to be totally shielded, like it's the goddamned Russian

Embassy or something. We've also checked ownership. The house belongs to Jake Pearlstein."

"The startup billionaire?" said Ramos.

"The same."

"Jesus H. Christ! So what are you suggesting?"

Here at last was the opportunity to shine, thought Jean, to show her superiors what she was made of. "This is the way I see it, sir," she said. "Even if we can convince MI5 or the police to raid the place, it could lead to lengthy questioning and interrogations. There's no way of knowing what could result."

"So?"

"So, I say that we terminate the targets as quickly as possible. I've also got a good idea how we can handle any PR problems regarding collateral damage."

"Look, Swanson. Things are in an uproar around here. Kozlov's still laying into Stokes on the tube. We haven't been able to regain control of the networks. Stokes is going absolutely wild. Things may be falling apart at the seams." He's panicking, thought Jean with disgust as Ramos rushed on, his voice quavering. "The Republican leaders are peeing in their pants. We've got reports that there even may be a military coup in the making. At this point, Belgrave Place is just a sideshow for us."

"So what do I do?" said Jean.

"I gotta go," said Ramos. "It's your call."

CHAPTER THIRTY-ONE:

Washington, D.C.

In the Oval Office, President Stokes, switched channels on his TV monitors with mounting fury. They were all carrying Vasily Kozlov's rant. Livid, Stokes buzzed his National Security Advisor, John Bradbury. "What the fuck is going on?" asked Stokes. "All our stations broadcasting lies from a foreign leader attacking me, the president of the United States! Outrageous!"

"Mr. President, I've just had word. The Russians have hacked our main cable and TV networks.

"Hijacked American broadcasters?"

"We've been working on the same thing ourselves, sir. But only in case of a major conflict."

"It's an act of war! Get me the chairman of the Joint Chiefs. And get Kozlov off our air."

"Sir, the only thing we can do is order all networks to cease broadcasting, to go black."

"Do it," barked Stokes.

"It will take a few minutes."

"Goddamnit, just do it"

Meanwhile Stokes was unable to tear his eyes from the images of Kozlov on all six of the monitors facing him:

"I will now reveal to the American public the true duplicity of your leader," said Kozlov. "Six months before your elections, Walter Stokes asked me to journey to Iceland for a secret meeting to discuss possible measures we might take together. As I have always been interested in improving relations with your country, I agreed."

As he continued, Kozlov was briefly distracted by his military aide who slid a note onto his desk. Irritated by the interruption, the Russian president glanced away from the teleprompter to read the scrawled message: "Strongly advise you not proceed any further. General Staff extremely upset by what they see as 'another dangerous provocation of the U.S.'"

Kozlov shook his head vigorously. There was no way he was going to stop; not until he had destroyed Stokes. The generals would pay for their treasonous views. He looked back straight into the lens. "As I was saying, President Stokes and I met in very great secrecy at our Russian ambassador's residence in Reykjavik. We spoke for three hours, with only our interpreters present. It was there that Stokes promised me a new era in Russian-American relations."

In the Oval Office, President Stokes was striding furiously around the room, screaming into the speakerphone, "How the fuck can American TV still be broadcasting such Russian crap!"

"Sir, it will be just another couple of minutes, it's just not that easy to do."

In the Kremlin, Kozlov continued:

"I went to meet the American president out of a desire to improve the chances for peace in the world, I soon found your President Stokes had a much different goal in mind. He made it clear he expected to profit personally from any rapprochement between our two countries. You Americans should not be fooled. Your president is not out to benefit America but only himself. Look. This was five months before the U.S. election."

Kozlov was abruptly distracted again. His military aide was standing beside the TV camera vigorously shaking his head. He held up another scribbled message, "Situation critical. Chiefs of General Staff furious." Let them be furious, thought Kozlov. I appointed those pricks myself to power. I will deal with them after this broadcast. He looked at the broadcast director and nodded forcefully for him to play the waiting tape.

The screen was filled by a video of Walter Stokes and Vasily Kozlov with their interpreters sitting across from each other in a teak-paneled library. The scene had been captured by two hidden Russian cameras. "Russian Ambassador's Residence – —Reykjavik, July 8," read the caption underneath. The meeting concluded, the two men rose and shook hands. Stokes grinned broadly and clapped Kozlov on the shoulders. "Vasily," he said, "this is a marvelous deal. It's going to make both of us very, very rich, You don't know how much I'm looking forward to showing you around my new spread in Texas. We've got a great relationship ahead of us. You can bet on it!"

In the Oval Office, watching the broadcast with Cliff Dayton, Stokes stared in disbelief at the monitors. But all he could do was Tweet.

"All lies, all lies what u hearing from crazy Kozlov. U.S. television has been hijacked. all lies, ALL LIES. @PresStokes

"That is not me. Was never in Iceland. Never. Just actors. Fakefakefake @PresStokes

"Don't believe any of this. Klepto Kozlov hallucinating. LIES LIES!@PresStokes

"Following that meeting," continued the Russian president, "our security services informed me that President Stokes employed the services of three local prostitutes in the most lascivious manner. We have tape of that as well as similar shameful erotic excesses of the man who has become your president. We are making those tapes available on Wiki Leaks."

"Klepto Kozlov" is lying, folks. Tape is a fraud! Not true! Believe me. All the tapes are frauds. Don't believe a word! DISGUSTING! @PresStokes"

"What can you Americans do about this?" Kozlov looked gravely at the camera, "It is not for me to interfere in your…"

Suddenly the monitors in the Oval Office were filled with visual static and went black for a couple of seconds. When the programming resumed, it was the normally scheduled broadcasts.

There again on CNN was Wolf Blitzer: "We are back after an incredibly successful Russian takeover of America's major broadcasts. This has been an amazing fifteen minutes. We are putting together a panel of experts to discuss what this all means. Meanwhile…"

In his Kremlin office, Kozlov turned from the camera, a grim smile on his lips. He had destroyed Stokes. Now to deal with the generals.

In the Oval Office, despite Cliff Dayton's attempts to restrain him, Stokes was still venting his rage.

By attacking America's President, Klepto Kozlov is attacking our beautiful country itself. We will not stand for it KOZLOV BEWARE!@PresStokes

KleptoKozlov don't forget who is world's strongest military power. Don't screw with us. USA.USA!@PresStokes

In Corridor Nine of the E Ring of the Pentagon, in the offices of the Joint Chiefs of Staff, Army Colonel Arnold Lawson, tasked with monitoring social media, forwarded the latest flurry of presidential Tweets to Admiral Len Coop, chairman of the Joint Chiefs.

"Shit," said Coop. He shot off a message to the other four Chiefs: "Looks like what we were concerned about is actually happening. Meet in the Tank in five minutes. Bring only yourselves." Coop then ordered Colonel Lawson to set up an encrypted call with General Artyom Borovik in the Kremlin.

And the Tweets continued.

Either Klepto Kozlov retracts lies & undoes thievery of his hackers, or I take action. No weapon is off the table!@ PresStokes

Stokes also called the White House bureau of Fox News. "Got an extremely important statement to make about those fucking Russians and our national security, possibly even nuclear war. Who knows? Tell your people to get their asses over here immediately," he ordered.

There was a slight hesitation at the other end. "Yes, Mr. President. It may take us a few minutes, sir."

"I said immediately," said Stokes hanging up.

Meanwhile, in the Kremlin, as the TV technicians were removing their equipment, Vasily Kozlov summoned his military aide. "I want to know who were those sons of whore generals trying to stop that broadcast. I want their names now."

The aide, however, was white-faced, staring at the office door. Standing there in full dress uniforms were General Artyom Borovik, with four of the five top officers of the General Staff.

"The officers you are looking for are here," said Borovik, striding into the office.

Kozlov froze, then snarled, "You wouldn't dare." He lunged toward his desk drawer.

"Don't make another move," said Borovik.

Behind him was a squad of Russian troops from the Spetsnaz, the equivalent of the US special forces. Three of them leveled their weapons at Kozlov.

"You are under arrest," said Borovik.

"Traitors! You will never get away with this," roared Kozlov.

"I think we will," said Borovik. "Particularly after we release the information about how you and your friends have been robbing this country blind over the past twenty years."

"All lies," said Kozlov, with less assurance.

"You can either choose to come voluntarily with us," said Borovik, "and face trial in a few weeks. Or…"

"Or what?" said Kozlov, only now beginning to comprehend what was happening.

"We cut your phones and leave you alone in this office for a few minutes with whatever it was you were trying to get from your desk drawer."

On the other side of the world, in the Oval Office, the red-faced American president continued his furious Twitter offensive, with no idea what was happening to his Russian counterpart.

Back off Klepto Kozlov or missiles could fly! USA-USA!@PresStokes

In a frenzied daze, Stokes hit a key to begin another Tweet. Nothing happened. He pounded the key again. Still nothing. A notice came up: "Your Twitter account is no longer active. Contact Twitter.com/admin."

Back in the bunker in London, Steve Penn kept waiting, monitoring CNN and the BBC for any sign that the next phase of his plan had kicked in. Now that he had set Stokes and Kozlov at each other's throats, it would be disastrous if the Republicans still lacked the guts to oust an obviously dangerous and deranged Republican president. But it was the military that acted first.

A "BREAKING NEWS" alert, suddenly appeared on CNN. It was CNN Pentagon correspondent Jim Dreyfuss. "Wolf, I've just been informed that all commanders of U.S. nuclear forces have been instructed by Admiral Len Coop, the chairman of the Joint Chiefs, to execute no orders from the president unless those orders are first confirmed by the chairman himself. We are…"

The reporter paused for a moment to listen to a message in his earpiece. "Excuse me Wolf, but things are breaking real fast here. The chairman has also just ordered all U.S. military units on full alert. No troop movements to occur without specific authorization of the chairman. General officers known to be sympathetic to Stokes are being relieved of their commands. Chairman Coop has also apparently been in touch with his Russian counterparts to ensure that calm is maintained on both sides. That's all at this point, Wolf, but obviously this is a very fast moving situation."

Steve immediately put in an encrypted call to Senator Bill Gurd in the Rayburn Building.

"Jesus," said Steve, "It sounds like a military coup."

"At least a partial one," said Gurd. "I just spoke with the chairman of the Joint Chiefs. He put in a conference call to me and the other leadership. Gave us an ultimatum. Either we act and get rid of Stokes, and at least preserve the façade of civilian government or the military will do it themselves."

"So what's stopping you?" said Steve.

"Most of the leadership *is* ready to act," said Gurd. "But a few are still holding out. The White House is threatening to release some pretty strong stuff the Russians hacked from the Republican National Committee prior to the elections."

"Blackmail? This late in the game?"

"Exactly,"

"Including you?"

The Senator paused. "I think I made that clear when we first met. But it's not going to work, not any longer. It's my relationship with one of my legislative assistants. She's—she's only twenty-one—and black. I may one day be able to work things out with my wife, but politically, it will probably destroy me. In any case, no turning back.

Gotta go. I'm meeting with the leadership in a couple of minutes."

Two miles away, in the Eisenhower office building, Cliff Dayton and Jorge Ramos, who ran the secret S-Team, were calling sources, attempting to determine what exactly was going on in the Pentagon. They were interrupted when three officers walked in, one colonel and two captains.

"Who the hell are you?" Dayton barked.

"Colonel Tom Dean, U.S. Army Military Police. As of this moment, your office is shut down. My men will also impound all your records. Any attempt by you or anyone on your staff to destroy files will be considered a criminal act. You and Mr. Ramos are under arrest."

"Under arrest for what?" said Dayton drawing himself up.

"A number of suspected crimes," said the Colonel, "We could start with conspiracy to murder two former CIA officers: Brian Hunt and Charles Doyle."

"Really," sneered Dayton, "And under what authority are you acting?"

"The Joint Chiefs."

"That's bullshit, they can't do that." Dayton picked up the phone to call the Oval Office. There was no dial tone.

Back in London, Steve called Ed Diamond at *Focus* to relay the latest information he had from Senator Gurd. Five minutes later, Diamond called back. "Steve, I've checked with a couple of my own sources. This is definitely the wildest situation the U.S. has ever known. The military is ready to move. Congress still doesn't have the votes to act."

"That's what Gurd told me," said Steve.

"Stokes is screaming military takeover," said Diamond. "But he's unable to get anyone to broadcast his statement. His Twitter account has also gone dead."

"So why don't you finally air the report we did. If you put it out, there's no way Congress could still hold back."

"Exactly what we're planning," said Ed. "The asshole who ordered us not to broadcast the report is now saying to put it out immediately as a special. We're doing a quick, new open and close. It'll be on in an hour."

"But have you heard what's just happened in Moscow?" said Ed.

"What?"

"The reports are still very sketchy, but it looks like Kozlov is out. Also some kind of military coup."

"What happened to Kozlov?" said Steve.

"No one knows. There's talk of shooting in parts of Moscow. Everything still very vague."

Steve's mind was whirling. If there was chaos in Moscow, what was happening to Maya and her family? Could she have been executed as some last act of vengeance by Kozlov and his thugs? And what had happened to the kids, to his son? He repeatedly attempted to reach General Borovik, but was unable to get through. The line was constantly tied up.

Nearby in London, in the working space she'd been given at MI5's headquarters at 12 Milbank overlooking the Thames, an increasingly agitated Jean Swanson was also watching live reports of events in Washington, when she received a call. It was her boss, Jorge Ramos.

"Captain Swanson, our operation has been shut down." Again, his usually firm voice was quavering.

"Shut down?"

"As of five minutes ago. It's over. Done."

"It can't be," said Swanson.

"It is. You are to stand down immediately, end all operations."

"On whose orders?"

"On mine. On Dayton's. On the Pentagon's."

"But I'm ready to act. You said the mission was mine."

"Yeah, well, forget the mission. It's too late."

"How do I just forget the mission?"

"Another thing. You never heard this from me. But destroy all records of everything you've done for the S Team. Everything. Something else…"

"What?"

"Don't be in any hurry to come back to this country. You might think of going somewhere far away where no one knows you and stay there for many years."

"What the shit? It's my country."

"You heard me."

"Fuck you, Ramos."

She hung up.

CHAPTER THIRTY-TWO:

London

It was seven-thirty in the morning in London. Golden hues of the early morning sun already illuminated the stucco façade of 51 Belgrave Place. Inside, Steve and Sarah were having breakfast, switching back and forth between the BBC and CNN as they attempted to ascertain what the hell was happening in Moscow and Washington.

Mike Rourke had been dispatched to the newsstand in Sloane Square to pick up the morning papers. Steve had been up since five, attempting to learn something about the chaos still roiling Russia. There definitely had been a military coup led by General Borovik. But a small number of commanders, and no one knew how many, had refused to go along with the army leaders. There were still reports of fighting in some areas of Moscow and elsewhere in Russia. There was also a rumor that President Kozlov was dead.

Steve, however, was still unable to get through to Borovik. Obviously if the general had led the coup, he had better things to do with his time right now than to answer calls about Maya. All Steve could do was keep trying.

It was only 2:30 a.m. in Washington, but according to the BBC, the coming day also promised extraordinary changes in the U.S. "It looks as if the civilian politicians have chosen the route of impeachment," said an exhausted Jane Barrett, the BBC's Washington correspondent. "The House is planning to conduct a trial in the morning. If the majority votes to impeach President Stokes, then he will immediately be put on trial in the Senate. If two-thirds of the senators find him guilty, he's out."

"What's he going to be charged with?" said James Steele, the BBC anchor.

"No one knows yet." Jane Barrett raised her eyebrows and shrugged. "According to the U.S. Constitution, a president can only be impeached for 'treason, bribery and other high crimes and misdemeanors.' However, that can mean just about anything," she said. "And in this case the American military leaders have laid it on the line. They want President Stokes out. They're still offering the civilians a chance to do it. But they want impeachment to be handled immediately; the entire procedure to be carried out in just one day."

"Doesn't sound very realistic," said the anchor.

"Maybe not, but the word from the Joint Chiefs is it's not just the unemployed coal miners in West Virginia who are fed up with what has been going on in Washington."

"Do you have any further information on President Stokes?" asked Steele. "Will he actually try to defend himself against impeachment?"

"No one seems to know at this point," said Barrett. "In fact, one rumor making the rounds is that the president has suffered a severe mental breakdown."

Steele gave a tight smile. "That would be interesting news to those who claimed all along that Stokes was borderline psychotic."

Meanwhile, in the basement security office at 51 Belgrave Place, Mike Rourke was checking the previous twenty-four hours of images from the surveillance cameras positioned around the house. He stopped the monitor, then rewound it, moved ahead to another frame, and saved that image, comparing it with three other frames. He repeated the process two more times, an increasingly concerned look on his face. Finally, he called Steve on the intercom and asked him to come down and take a look.

"What is it?" said Steve, looking over Mike's shoulder at the large monitor.

"See this image on camera four, yesterday at 2:54 p.m.?

"That woman, yeah."

"She turns up again at different times on four of the other cameras. "Yesterday at 5:18 p.m., 6:20 p.m., 9:27 p.m. Then again, just after midnight. She is definitely casing this place."

"Can you go tighter on her?" asked Steve.

"I'll bring up the contrast too."

"The one at 5:18 is the clearest," said Steve.

"I'll zoom in a bit more," said Mike. "Hey, not at all bad looking. Except there is something here on the right side of her face. It looks like a bad scar."

"Could have been a burn," said Steve. "I've seen that face before, but no idea where." He was usually pretty good at recognizing people, part of his training. But he just couldn't place her.

"Funniest thing," said Sarah, who'd come down with Steve. "I've also seen her before."

"But you don't know where?" asked Steve

"Nope."

"Hard to know what she could be up to," said Mike.

"Maybe nothing," said Steve. "I mean Stokes is already on the way out. I'd imagine his people are either locked up or on the run."

"I'll still keep an eye peeled," said Mike. He went over to the wall and opened a steel cabinet. "Also, just to be safe, I've got a small cache here. He handed Steve a Glock 17 with some ammunition clips. "And a Glock 42 for you, Miss Levin. I assume you know how to use this."

She examined the weapon carefully, expertly inserted a clip.

"Must have to do with your skill on the cello," said Steve.

"And I've got my Beretta," said Mike. "Along with a permit. Unfortunately, we've got no permits for your weapons, but no point now in worrying about details."

"Another thing," said Mike as they returned to the ground floor, "I don't like having that long stretch of open sidewalk in front of the house. Be right back."

Two white construction company vans were just parking in front of the Malaysian Cultural Centre next door, where a larger basement was being excavated. Mike strolled over to the two drivers. "Hi guys, mind parking your vans in front of our place this morning?" They looked at him a bit strangely. Most normal people didn't want the parking area in front of their homes to be tied up. "There's fifty pounds apiece if you'll do me that favor," said Mike.

"No worries, mate," said the shorter driver.

Still puzzled, the drivers returned to their vans and parked them, one behind the other, at the curb in front of 51 Belgrave Place.

"Thanks," said Mike, handing them each a fifty-pound note. "Enjoy."

Smiling with satisfaction, he returned to the house, poked his head in the kitchen where Steve and the others were continuing to watch the latest news, and said, "Think I'll go back downstairs now and keep an eye on the outside cameras."

Forty-five minutes later, Jean Swanson drove past Victoria Station and headed for Knightsbridge. She was driving a black Toyota. The trunk and floor of the back seat were filled with several plastic-wrapped parcels – more than twenty of them. They contained two hundred pounds of powerful HMX explosive. She had requested it the previous day from a high-ranking MI5 officer, with whom she had once worked in Afghanistan. She had convinced him she was on a secret antiterrorist mission for the White House which, indeed, she had once been. By the time someone in Washington finally notified MI5 that Jean's office had been disbanded and her mission cancelled, it would be too late.

She had carefully rehearsed the route yesterday afternoon—turning on to Cadogan Place, past the Jumeira Hotel, and straight on to West Halkin Street, then slowly clockwise around Belgrave Square. The early morning traffic was light. She knew precisely where she had to position the car for the blast to be most effective: directly before the front door, as close to the curb as possible.

Shit! Two construction vans had taken the space. She had seen them yesterday, but parked next door. They had moved. Why? Hold it – there was a large gap between the two of them. Almost three yards. All she had to do was back her car into that space. That would still place the trunk almost against the curb. Definitely would do the job. Then she'd set the timer, get out of the car, walk up the street—calmly—don't run--and two minutes later – BOOM.

In the basement, Mike continued to monitor the outside cameras. As usual, there were few people on the street. There was the regular morning parade of Mercedes, BMWs, Bentleys, and Jags carrying the bankers and brokers to work in the City. Mike's attention was drawn to a black Toyota, moving a bit more leisurely than the others. It continued approaching, slowly, as if the driver was trying to figure something out. Then it stopped a bit beyond the front door of their mansion, and began backing towards the curb.

What the hell were they up to? There wasn't room for the Toyota to parallel park there. But that was obviously not what the driver had in mind. Instead, whomever it was planned to back in between the two vans bringing the Toyota's trunk right to the curb. That would leave the front of the Toyota protruding illegally into the street. But that obviously didn't bother the driver. Mike zoomed in with the camera: It was that woman again, the one with the scar.

He jabbed the intercom to the kitchen. "Someone trying to park right in front. Looks like scar face!" He grabbed his Beretta and raced for the stairs. Seizing their own revolvers, Steve and Sarah were already out the front door.

Outside, Jean continued to back the car carefully between the two trucks. It was a tight fit, but she could make it. There was the screeching sound of metal on metal. Took some paint off the Toyota, she thought grimly, but no one's worried about resale value. She pulled out again, readjusted the angle slightly, and started backing in once more. Right, that'll be perfect. She was so intent on her efforts that she didn't see the people racing out of the house towards her. Steve was in front, yelling. "Get that goddamned car out of here."

"Fuck you," she screamed back through the open window. "I'll park anywhere I want."

Steve was in the street now. He continued approaching her on the driver's side. "You don't have a parking permit," he screamed again, "Get out!"

This guy was not going to ruin her plan, she thought. Only one way to deal with the asshole. She grabbed the Sig Sauer from the seat beside her, and brandished it at him. "Come one step closer," she said, "And you're dead meat."

Steve froze, staring back at her. That red scar. He suddenly remembered where he had seen her: at the back of the church when Brian Hunt was buried. She continued pointing her gun at him as she backed towards the curb. Suddenly Steve had his Glock out and leveled at her.

"Up yours," she said and pulled the trigger, just as the car abruptly jerked backwards.

Steve fired at the same instant; then toppled to the ground. He was sitting on the street, staring at the car. The driver raised her pistol again. Steve waited for the impact. He heard a shot from behind him. The driver slumped against the wheel, but her foot was apparently still on the accelerator. The Toyota jerked backwards again until it banged to an abrupt halt against the curb. Gripping his bleeding right shoulder with his left hand, Steve turned towards Sarah. "Thanks. I thought that was it," he said.

Jean was bent over the wheel. It was funny she thought, she'd been hit twice, once in the shoulder, the second time in the chest. She knew it was the chest because she could see the blood pumping out. But she hadn't felt that second shot. If she could just move her hand enough to push the timer. Then she would have two minutes herself. Out the door and up the street and she'd be away.

Concentrating her efforts, she watched her hand move toward the gray timer button, as if it were someone else's hand. Slowly, slowly, and then, yes, she pushed it. Now open the door. But she couldn't move. All she wanted was for her arm to reach out and her hand to open the door, but nothing obeyed. It's the weirdest sensation, she thought.

Aiming his own revolver at the open car window, Mike raced by Steve and Sarah and then peered down at the driver crumpled in the front seat. It looked like her chest had exploded. It was drenched in blood. Her eyes were open. No time to check if she was dead. She clutched a small gray metal box in her hand. "Everyone out of here," Mike screamed. He turned and raced back to put his arm under Steve and, aided by Sarah, helped him stumble back to the house and into the elevator.

They had just entered the bunker, and the elevator door was still open, when there was a deafening explosion and a huge rush of air. A giant hand seized Steve and hurled him across the room, crashing against the far wall. The pain in his shoulder was excruciating. Everything went black.

When he came to, his shoulder hurt like hell. But that was all. He didn't know how long he was unconscious, probably just a few minutes. The walls had held. The ceiling was still intact. Mike called out from the other side of the room. Sarah and Edith answered. Everyone seemed to be okay. But there was no way to get out. After a few minutes, there were sirens and searchlights probing the darkness. Then another long wait as rescuers tried to figure out how to get in. Steve was finally carried in a stretcher, past scurrying police and emergency workers, and into an ambulance. The TV cameras were already there.

In the ambulance, a doctor put a preliminary dressing on the wound in Steve's shoulder. Amazingly, except for the bullet wound and a couple of bruised ribs, he was fine. Sarah had also survived with a few scratches. As had Mike and Edith.

The plainclothes police captain who questioned Steve at the Royal Brompton Hospital marveled that they had all come through with relatively minor injuries. "I don't know how much explosive there was in that car," he said. "Brought down your entire house -- all five bloody stories. Buildings across the square were damaged. Three people killed, ten others seriously injured. We're still digging them out. But it looks like your basement was built to withstand World War III."

"What about the person driving the Toyota with the explosives?" asked Steve.

'Nothing much to say," said the captain. "Possibly a female. Really not enough left to tell for sure. Our lab people are trying to scrape up whatever DNA they can find." The captain paused and examined Steve closely, "Not some way involved with the Middle East, are you?"

"Why do you ask?"

"An hour before the explosion, two Internet sites related to ISIS posted a statement claiming credit for the blast," said the captain. "They said it was directed against the 'American Capitalist Jake Pearlstein and the international Jewish conspiracy.'"

"I'll give you a different lead," said Steve.

At 2:30 p.m. in London, the doctor at the Royal Brompton Hospital agreed to discharge Steve after X-raying his shoulder. "Damn lucky nothing vital was hit," he said." Just don't overdo things, and get the dressing changed in a couple of days."

Sarah and Mike, who had been waiting, decided to go off and have a beer. Steve went to the Sloane Street Hotel and checked in. Once again, he tried reaching General Borovik in Moscow. This time, however, the general's assistant answered the phone. Steve explained who he was and left a Skype and mobile number, with little hope of actually getting a call back.

He turned on his TV. CNN was broadcasting from the U.S. Congress, where the House was just beginning to debate impeachment proceedings. White House Correspondent Ira Rosen was reporting to anchorman Wolf Blitzer. "Wolf, we've just heard that President Stokes is refusing to defend himself before congress. He says the charges are all lies and fake news. He says he wants to take his case directly to the people. So far, however, the president has been blocked from direct access to any media, including Facebook and Twitter. The word we have from the Pentagon is that restriction is going to continue at least until impeachment has been voted by the Senate, probably by this evening."

"Thanks, Ira," said Blitzer, "This is probably the most perilous moment in U.S. political history – certainly since the Civil War. In the end, everything is going to depend on whoever is elected to take Stokes's place. That is, assuming it is possible to organize new elections. According to latest polls, the number of Americans supporting President Stokes has plummeted to only twenty-one percent. But that still represents tens of millions of people, and a lot of them are dead set against this congressional action. Don't forget, there are also more than three hundred million guns in this country. There have already been violent protests in a number of American cities, and unrest is growing.

"For more on that, we're taking you to Milwaukee…"

Steve's iPhone signaled a FaceTime call. "Sorry, but I've been a bit busy," said a grim-faced General Borovik. "I have to congratulate you on your operation's success."

"Yours too," said Steve. All he wanted to know was about Maya and the children, but the general had other concerns. "The situation in your country remains very messy," said Borovik. "Frankly, we are very nervous about it. It would be nice if some solution could be found to deal with Stokes. In our country, we had a stroke of luck. It has not yet been made public, but Kozlov decided to take his own life. It would be nice if a neat ending like that would happen to Stokes."

"I'm not so sure," said Steve. "That would make him something of a martyr. The conspiracy theories would go on and on."

"That will happen no matter how Stokes leaves," said Borovik. "Kozlov will also be seem as a martyr, but…."

"General, please," Steve interrupted. "I have to know how is Maya?"

"She is fine."

"Where is she?"

"Right here," The general, panned his iPhone to three chairs across from him where Maya was sitting with her two children. She was white-faced. There were dark circles under her eyes.

"Hello Steve," she attempted a wan smile.

"Are you OK? What did they do to you?"

Her voice was shaking. "It was horrible. I can't talk about it now. Not in front of the kids." She buried her face in her hands.

Sonya put her arms around her mother. Thousands of miles away, Steve looked on helplessly.

"Hi, kids!" he said, his throat tight. Sonya looked towards him and smiled timidly. Evgeny raised his hand as if to wave.

"When are you coming to see us again?" asked the boy.

"Yes, when are you coming?" said Maya, wiping her eyes. "Your son is waiting. So are we all."

"I'll be on the next flight to Moscow," Steve said. Had she already told her son that Steve was his father? This was not the time to ask.

Russia he knew wouldn't be their home. And America? There were a lot of other countries out there. Who knew where they would wind up? But they would be together as a family.

Steve felt his eyes welling. He couldn't believe it: When had he last cried?

Meanwhile, on the TV, CNN anchor Wolf Blitzer continued to monitor what looked like a growing crisis, as he debriefed Pentagon correspondent Josh Bonin. "Wolf, our sources here tell us that a major dispute has broken out within the Joint Chiefs of Staff and other key military leaders. It's apparently between those insisting the military should continue to prod civilian leaders, but remain behind the scenes. Others, however, are now arguing that in the face of the mounting civilian unrest, the military has no choice but to openly take power –

at least until the situation has cleared – for one or two years and perhaps more."

"In other words, Josh, It's not at all clear what we're heading into."

"You could certainly say that, Wolf. Absolutely."

The End

Author's Note

Dear Reader,

I hope you enjoyed reading *Deep Strike* as much as I enjoyed writing it. Support from readers like yourself is crucial for any author to succeed, particularly in this E-book era.

If you enjoyed this book, please consider writing a review at amazon.com and if you are inclined, follow me on twitter at @barrylando or @PresStokes to continue the fun.

Also, if you think the book is worth the read, please like the Deep Strike Facebook page. https://www.facebook.com/barrylando1/

The reviews are important and your support is greatly appreciated.

Thank you,
Barry Lando

About the Author

After working as a correspondent for *Time-Life* in South America, Barry Lando spent twenty-five years as an award-winning investigative producer with CBS "60 Minutes."

The author of numerous articles on international affairs, he produced a documentary about Saddam Hussein that has been shown around the world.

He has also written a nonfiction book on Iraq, *Web of Deceit: The History of Western Complicity in Iraq, from Churchill to Kennedy to George W. Bush*. That was followed by his first novel, *The Watchman's File*, about the attempts of an American investigative reporter to uncover Israel's most closely-guarded secret. (It is not the bomb.)

Originally from Vancouver Canada, Lando is a graduate of both Harvard and Columbia University. He is married, has three children, and currently lives in London, England.

You can follow his writing and other projects at http://barrymlando.com

Acknowledgements

I owe a huge debt to the many people who read the manuscript in all or in part: Neil Bulstrode, Charles De Groot, Liza Fleissig, Marilyn Harris, Jeffery Hertzfeld, Adam Horowitz, Dana Isaacson, Lloyd Jassin, Dominique Lando, Edward Lando, Elisabeth Lando, Jeffery Lando, Chris Roberts, Timothy and Marie Louise Ryback, Victoria Skurnick, Judy Sternlight, Dave Turecamo, and Johnson Wu.

Their advice, perception, and enthusiasm were invaluable.

I am particularly grateful to the time and insights provided by my publisher, Michael Fabiano.

Other Books

If you liked this book, you might check out another novel by Barry Lando.

Ed Diamond, reporter for "Focus", America's preeminent TV news show, is summoned urgently to Israel by an old friend, Dov Ben-Ami, formerly a top official of Israel's Mossad.

But before they can meet, a terrorist bomb blows Dov apart. Determined to discover why the Israeli was killed, Diamond embarks on the most astonishing investigation he's ever undertaken.

From the Dead Sea to the Old City of Jerusalem, to Tel Aviv and Paris, Washington and New York, he unravels an on-going mystery that began with the nefarious links between America's greatest corporations and Hitler's Third Reich. In the end, Ed attempts to thwart a deadly terrorist attack targeting Manhattan.

He's pitted against one of the U.S.'s most powerful families and a fanatical group of right-wing Israelis, ready to kill to protect a World War II intelligence coup that is still Israel's most potent weapon and most closely guarded secret, "The Watchman's File."

Available at Amazon.com

KCM Publishing
a division of KCM Digital Media, LLC